THE SLOW WAY BACK

THE SLOW WAY BACK

a novel

Judy Goldman

WILLIAM MORROW AND COMPANY, INC. NEW YORK

This book is a work of fiction. No character represents a real person.

Portions of this novel first appeared, in different form, in the following journals: *The Southern Review, The Kenyon Review, The Ohio Review, Quarterly West, Poem.*

In the following anthologies: *Her Face in the Mirror: Jewish Women on Mothers and Daughters* (Beacon Press); *Claiming the Spirit Within, A Sourcebook of Women's Poetry* (Beacon Press); *Ladies, Start Your Engines: Women Writers on Cars and the Road* (Faber and Faber); *Life on the Line: Selections on Words and Healing* (Negative Capability Press); *No Hiding Places: Uncovering the Legacy of Charlotte-Area Writers* (Down Home Press); *Anthology of Magazine Verse* and *Yearbook of American Poetry* (Monitor Book Company).

In the author's poetry collections: *Wanting to Know the End* (Silverfish Review Press, 1993, 1994); *Holding Back Winter* (St. Andrews Press, 1987).

In the following newspaper: *Creative Loafing.*

Excerpts have also been read by the author on WFAE-FM, Charlotte's National Public Radio affiliate, and WUNC-FM, Chapel Hill's National Public Radio affiliate.

Lines from the poem "Aria," by Paul Morris, originally published in *The Bloomsbury Review*, appear by permission from the poet.

It is the policy of William Morrow and Company, Inc., and its imprints and affiliates, recognizing the importance of preserving what has been written, to print the books we publish on acid-free paper, and we exert our best efforts to that end.

Library of Congress Cataloging-in-Publication Data

Goldman, Judy.
The slow way back : a novel / Judy Goldman.
p. cm.
ISBN 0-688-16598-2 (alk. paper)
I. Title.
PS3557.03688S58 1999
813'.54—DC21

99-25487
CIP

Printed in the United States of America

First Edition

3 4 5 6 7 8 9 10

BOOK DESIGN BY CHERYL L. CIPRIANI

www.williammorrow.com

For Henry, Laurie, and Mike—my first and most loyal readers,
my first and most loyal everything.
And for Bob and Brooke—new readers in the family,
new sources of joy.

Acknowledgments

For the gift of memories, which I used in inventing a book of fiction, I thank my sister, Brenda Meltsner, and my aunt, Emma Lavisky Bukatman. For urging me on, I thank my brother, Donald Kurtz. Special gratitude to Fred Leebron, whose extraordinarily generous nature I rely on time and time again. Thank you to the people who plumped me up when I needed plumping and counterbalanced with good, solid criticism: my writers' group (Mary Hunter Daly, Lucinda Grey, Susan Ludvigson, Dannye Romine Powell, Julie Suk), Kathryn Rhett, Nanci Kincaid, and Peggy Payne. Much appreciation to Baila Pransky, whose knowledge of Yiddish introduced me to my grandmother and gave my book its backbone, and to the people I met in Denmark, South Carolina, who provided historical background. For early, and continuous, boosting—Debbie Rubin, Judy Pera, Ruth Cohen, Bobbie Campbell, Ann Haskell, Laurie Johnston, Clarissa Porter. For medical information, Dr. John Glover. For my poetry students who gathered around my dining room table every week for years, I thank you for giving back more than you received. To my agent, Jennifer Rudolph Walsh, deep appreciation for your faith and hard work. An appreciative nod to Jessica Baumgardner, Katherine Beitner, Sharyn Rosenblum, and Marly Rusoff at Morrow and Claire Tisne at the Virginia Barber Literary Agency for answering a first-time novelist's endless questions. And, most important, Claire Wachtel, my editor at Morrow: You have been a gracious guide, with your meticulous scrutiny and sound judgment.

THE SLOW WAY BACK

Chapter 1

It was the only time in her entire life her mother ever slapped her—just one quick crack, a motion almost graceful in its economy. Of course, her mother had always been dramatic and unpredictable. Down one day, up the next. Moody. But never moody to Thea, her favorite.

Thea was ten and had been playing jacks on the hardwood floor in her parents' bedroom upstairs. It was one of those Sunday evenings in August, after dinner, when the air's so muggy you know it could turn sour any minute. Her younger sister, Mickey, was playing catch, as usual, with their father in the backyard. Thea could hear him calling out, "Aim for my glove!" and "Great throw!" and "Okay now . . . watch the ball!" Her mother was in the kitchen baking, using her new heart-shaped cookie cutter.

There were four jacks left. Thea tossed the rubber ball up in the air but when she tried to scoop the last silvery pieces, she hit the ball accidentally with the side of her hand and it veered under the bed, like a smooth rock skipping water. She lifted the dust ruffle. All she saw was a large cardboard box, a lady's dress box with *J. E. Steadman's, Where Your Dollars Have Cents* printed in old-fashioned green lettering across the lid. She had to angle her shoulders and bird-legs to inch under the bed and pull the box out.

The lid was mashed in on one side so she lifted it with both hands to keep it from falling apart. Inside was a cream wedding dress with long skinny sleeves stuffed with tissue paper. It looked like the person who'd worn it had taken it off so quickly she'd left her arms in it. There was also a small headpiece with a veil and a pair of shoes lying on their sides. The neck of the dress was trimmed in cream fur. The matching shoes had sharp-pointed toes and spike heels, as if they could be aimed at something.

Thea threw off her striped shirt and shorts. Her cotton underpants slipped down, by mistake, along with her shorts. She looked around to make sure nobody had come in and quickly pulled her pants back up, over her naked rear. She undid the covered buttons down the front of the dress, lifted it above her head and let it fall over her shoulders. The silky fabric felt slippery against her chest. The fur tickled her neck. She looked down at the hem of the dress, pooling around her bare feet like milk, then buttoned the buttons and dropped the shoes on the floor, stepping into them. They almost fit. Holding the headpiece, she clomped across the room to the full-length mirror on the back of the door.

She tried the headpiece one way, then decided it must go the other way. Walking slowly to keep her balance, she went back to the box and gathered up the hairpins loose in the bottom, then to the mirror again where she pinned the headpiece in place and unfolded the veil down over her small, round face. She thought she looked glamorous, like a movie star—a movie star bride on the cover of *Photoplay*. She smiled and gave a little wave of her fingers to an imaginary audience, pretending this was a moment they'd remember the rest of their lives.

That's when her mother opened the door to the room. Thea was still smiling and waving, but her mother was standing as close as Thea's reflection had been one second before. She was wearing bright orange toreador pants and a matching halter top. There was a smear of dough on her cheek in front of her ear. Her mouth was clamped together, eyes narrow.

"What do you think you're doing?" she said through her teeth.

Thea couldn't tell how she meant that so she asked a question back. "Is this your—"

"Is that my what? My wedding dress? Is that what you want to know?" Her mother never screamed but she was suddenly screaming now. "Where'd you find that?"

Thea stumbled back and tried to answer. "Well, I—"

"Well you what?" This didn't sound at all like her. Not the words. Not the voice.

"I just found it under—"

"You went through my room, didn't you? That's what you've been doing up here all night! Going through my things! What right do you have to—" She grabbed the edge of the door and heaved it against the wall. Thea had never seen her do anything like that. It was as if she'd been saving something up for a long time and finally let it go. The doorknob left a cupped place in the pale yellow paint. Thea took another step back. Her mother was sobbing as if she were strangling. Her arms were flailing like she could come out of her body, her hands flopping around like fish.

Then one hand locked into place and blistered Thea's cheek.

For an instant, she was deafened. Her mother's mouth was open and moving, and her face was wet and clenched like someone half-lost, but Thea couldn't hear a word she was saying. Noise had turned into the sound a fan makes waving in front of your face, a cool wind blowing over a hot surface. Thea reeled, falling backward. Her mother caught her before she hit the floor.

Thea was trembling. The right side of her head ached. Her mother was holding her tight, crying, kissing her face through the veil, then holding her cheek to Thea's cheek, then kissing her again. "I'm sorry, darling! I'm so, so sorry!" her mother kept saying.

The air around them began to shimmer. The walls turned wavy and started dissolving. Her mother picked her up and carried her through the thin, watery membrane that now covered everything, across the landing, into the room with the ragged robin wallpaper, the room she and her sister shared. Surprisingly, Mickey was already there, in the twin bed next to hers, a hand buried in her hair; she always twirled that one strand of hair just before she fell asleep. The cream dress, veil, and shoes somehow vanished as though they'd never existed, and Thea now had on blue-checked shorty pajamas, like her sister's. Her mother turned back the covers on the bed while Thea lay down. Then she pulled the parrot-colored quilt over her daughter, folding the sheet back and smoothing the hem flat with the palm of her hand. All Thea could feel next to her was the cool cotton of the sheets.

Her mother sat down on the side of the bed and leaned close enough to touch her face with her lips and listen to her breathe her shivery breaths. Thea could smell her mother's perfume. Then she trailed her finger around and around Thea's cheek, lightly, tenderly, as though she could erase the ugly mark she'd made.

. . .

All Thea had ever heard about her parents' wedding was that her mother had hives so bad she went from her bed to the ceremony. There wasn't a single photograph, she said, because she didn't want anybody to remember how splotchy and swollen her face was.

After the night of the slap, Thea would slip in questions—with great caution, of course—in a thin, toneless voice so it appeared that she had hardly asked.

Her mother could be standing on a wooden stepladder with a bucket of sudsy ammonia water, taking apart the chandelier over the dining room table, one prismed crystal at a time, holding each like an expensive earring, dipping it in the bucket until it caught the lime or violet light from the window. Thea would be sitting in the upholstered armchair at her mother's place, fingering the tiny flowers threaded into the fabric, listening to her mother tell about this or that. If the conversation had anything at all to do with a wedding, with somebody being sick, any subject that could be considered even vaguely related, Thea would ask under her breath, "And what *about* your wedding? *Why* did you have hives?"

Her mother could be sweeping a broom through a dark

corner high in the tool shed, rooting out the ashy fragments of a wasp nest, and Thea would be sitting on the brick step leading outside, her body turned toward the cinder driveway, head twisted all the way around so that she could look at her mother. Thea would scratch a mosquito bite on her leg and quietly ask, "Was it that you were *upset* about something?"

She asked because she knew it was up to her to get the true story; she could never depend on her sister to inquire about anything. Mickey was eleven months younger and eleven thousand times luckier than Thea. Mickey had it so easy, she didn't *have* to be curious. Everything was in place for her. She was adored by their father, the only reliable source of attention in the family. Thea was adored by their mother, their not so reliable mother. Mickey and her father. Thea and her mother. Two separate teams. With the strength clearly on the other side.

When Thea asked her endless questions, her mother would just shoo her away—those small, skittish fingers flicking air—and say something like, "Let's not worry about that, darling. No need to worry. No, no!" or "The past is past, and anyway, I wouldn't know where to begin. I would have no idea!" As though none of this had ever been the taboo subject it was that summer night when Thea was ten. As though, if she ever did decide to tell, it might take her a lifetime to find the right words.

"But, but— " Thea would push, thinking if she could just get her talking, the story would come and there'd be a long, neat chain of sensible answers, each part fastening onto the next.

But her mother would eventually turn away from her, humming.

After a while, Thea stopped asking. And began instead to have headaches.

. . .

She was fifty-four now. Her last radio program of the week was done, and she was driving home from the station, thinking about one of the callers—a young man from a small town in Georgia who'd dreamed his fiancée turned their wedding into a Tex-Mex event, with tacos and mariachi bands and piñatas. They were getting married soon and he was feeling jittery. He said he and his fiancée were both children of divorced parents, and his question for Thea was how they could possibly make their marriage last.

Thea pulled in the driveway, next to the handkerchief-sized rose bed in the corner of the yard. On her way to the porch, she stopped to pinch off a spent bloom. Deadheading, she thought. That's what you call getting rid of faded flowers to encourage further blooming. The caller's question popped into her head again, which made her think of her own engagement, when her sister had engineered a "talk" with her about Reid's not being Jewish.

"There are enough problems in a marriage when people have the *same* backgrounds," Mickey—already married at that point—had said, jabbing the space between them with her strong, square hands. "I'm telling you, you're doing the wrong thing. Jewish guys are *known* to make better husbands anyway. And have you thought about how you're going to raise your children? If you ask me, you're looking for trouble." She'd shaken her head for emphasis, her straight brown hair not moving an inch.

"But, Mickey," Thea had pleaded, drawing back, looking

up at her sister, having a sense for a moment of just how big she was, "I really *want* you to *like* him. Can't you just do that for me?"

Not much had changed since then. Mickey was still bigger, still had those strong hands—strong everything, for that matter. And she was still finding fault with Thea. Thea was still trying to win her over.

Thea reached in the mail basket hanging on the wall of the screened porch just inside the front door. At the top were bills from the dentist and Duke Power, a notice for Reid about an English teachers' conference, and one of those flyers with shadowy blue photographs of missing children, two girls so ordinary-looking you'd swear you just saw them in the drugstore or on the escalator at Belk's. In the bottom of the basket lay a letter—a packet, actually, it was so thick—from her mother's sister, Florence.

Thea pulled her reading glasses from her pocketbook. She liked the dark metal frames because they gave her face definition, which is what her washed-out blue eyes and light, no-color hair, brows, and lashes needed. She went into the kitchen, opened the flower-printed café curtains wide to let in the last light before sunset, and sat down at the breakfast table to empty the packet.

Old letters spilled out, all postmarked Denmark, South Carolina! Letters from her grandmother to her grandmother's sister in Lebanon, Pennsylvania. One was mailed December 28, 1937, six days before Thea's parents' wedding, another on January 6, 1938, three days after the wedding. Thea's elbows stuck to the rings of orange juice left on the table from breakfast. Her heart raced. Paper-clipped to one was a note from her aunt Florence saying that a distant cousin had found the letters in an old trunk in his attic and had mailed them to her. She wanted them to go to Thea since she was the one who used to ask all the questions about family.

Odd that each envelope was addressed by a different person. The letter written right before the wedding was addressed by Thea's mother. No mistaking that exuberant, flowery handwriting, with all the flags and streamers, the peaks of the capital M, the swoop under the rs in Mrs. One address was definitely Aunt Florence's handwriting, similar to Thea's mother's, only more controlled, held in.

Thea tucked the letters under her arm, took a glass from the pine cabinet next to the refrigerator, and filled it with ice and Coca-Cola. Because she was hurrying, she poured too much. The dark liquid purred and the cap of foam started rising. She squeezed her arm to her side to tighten her hold on the letters and plunked one finger across the rim of the glass. It was an old trick of her sister's. Something about your skin, Mickey used to say with that all-knowing air of hers, lets the foam go right up to the top but keeps it from rolling over the side.

Their mother had loved Coke. Even when she was depressed, sleeping long hours, not eating, she'd always say yes to a Coke. It was one thing Thea could count on. Once, after a bad bout, her mother wrote a letter to the president of Coca-Cola. *Dear Mr. President, Thank you for making your marvelous, life-saving product!* she'd written. She believed in that drink the way other people believed in aspirin.

Thea took a long, slow sip and walked carefully out to the screened porch. She sat down in the wicker rocker, held up one envelope. The two-cent George Washington stamp was the color of a sweet cherry. She pulled out the letter. The paper felt feathery; it was almost transparent. She unfolded it, gingerly—

The writing! No vowels or consonants. No English letters at all. Just splintered pen scratches, tiny curled and angled characters spread in choppy lines across the page, from the right-hand margin to the left. It looked like an intricate design on a rug. So foreign-looking it could be Arabic or Sanskrit. Or Yiddish.

The entire letter was written in Yiddish! Her grandmother must not have been able to write in English. No wonder other people had to address the letters. But could she *speak* English? Surely she could. Living in Denmark, South Carolina, how could she get along if she didn't? Within seconds, Thea went from being intrigued, to feeling indifferent—*This outdated language has nothing to do with me*—to being curious—*This could be what I've been looking for*—to a strong, unsettling yearning. Hurriedly, she took out the second letter, then another and another, running her fingers over the words as though she could *feel* their meaning.

Outside, the starlings that flew into the older neighborhoods every fall wheeled down, hundreds of them, dropping like a curtain. She picked up the heftiest letter, the one written after the wedding, and unfolded the pages. A corsage, the size of her palm, fell in her lap, like a fat insect. She jumped and instinctively brushed her skirt with both hands, almost knocking the corsage to the floor. It was a single rose that had kept its color, a deep shade of pink, flattened but intact, in a nest of olive-green fern that was shedding needles in her lap as small as eyelashes. This had to be the corsage her grandmother wore to her mother's wedding! And she'd sent it to her sister. It made the wedding seem so normal. A corsage for the mother of the bride—what could be more normal than that? Even her grandmother sending the corsage to her sister was normal. At least in this family, where sisters mattered more than anything. Thea realized she was holding her breath. She picked up the powdery flower so lightly her fingers barely touched it.

She knew from photographs that her grandmother was petite, with a pinched-in waist and those wise eyes the women of that generation always had. Thea pictured her mother—also small, but wiry and intense—pinning the flower on her grandmother. Thea's mother would make a big point of holding the dress out and sliding her hand between fabric and skin so she could push the pin through the shoulder of the dress. Then she'd stand back and narrow those bright eyes to see if it were straight, cocking her head to one side and the other. "Okey-dokey!" she'd say. It would take two or three tries before she'd finally get it right, but she'd stay with it as though that corsage and that shoulder were the most important things on earth. Unless, of course, something else caught her attention. Then she'd be off, tending to that as though *it* were the most important thing—

"Hello-o-o," Reid called from inside. "I'm home!"

Thea could hear him hang his keys on the brass hook inside the back door and drop his book bag beside the kitchen cabinet on the linoleum. She always knew exactly where he was and what he was doing even when she wasn't in the room. She used to find that comforting, the way she could depend on him to do the same thing day after day—the certainty of the jingle of keys, a book bag hitting the floor. He'd be loosening his knit tie now, his index finger unhurriedly pulling the knot from side to side. Reid might be rushed but you would never actually *see* him rush.

He ambled out to the porch.

"Hey, what's all this?" He was tall and broad—wide-shouldered and barrel-chested, Thea's mother used to say.

Thea's father was wide-shouldered and barrel-chested, too, but Reid had heavy-lidded eyes, bushy eyebrows, and generous features, which gave his face a softness, a quality Thea's father's face did not have, except, of course, when he was looking at Thea's mother. Or Mickey.

"Just wait'll you see! These were written by Mother's mother in the 1930s. They just came—in the mail—eight of them!—Aunt Florence sent them, out of the clear blue, and they're written in Yiddish, every one of them, and there's this corsage—"

"Now wait a minute," he said, dragging a chair over and propping his feet up on the ottoman, then slowly rolling his shirtsleeves to the elbow and pulling his tie the rest of the way off. "First of all, we need some light. It's dark out here." He folded the tie into his shirt pocket and switched on the wrought-iron floor lamp Thea's mother had used for a sunlamp. When Thea brought it home, she told Reid how she and her mother and her sister would lie under the lamp on beach towels on her parents' bedroom floor in the winter "getting a glow," as her mother put it, another one of her basic beliefs for good health. "Okay. Now. Tell me about the letters. And slow down. Who wrote them? And where'd you get them?"

The starlings in the yard lifted, chattering like people calling out to each other. Thea read her aunt's letter aloud, but because of the birds, she had to read slightly louder than normal. She heard her voice take on her aunt's staccato cadence.

"Well," he said. "How 'bout that."

"And can you believe I have my grandmother's corsage?" she said. "That it traveled from Denmark to Lebanon to Columbia to Charlotte? And look at the letters! This one *has* to be describing Mother's wedding, and look how long it is. Seven pages! And the writing's so small. Here's everything. Don't you just know it?"

He took a sheet from her and held it up to the light. "This Yiddish is amazing. Do you think your grandmother could *speak* English?"

"I have no idea. I never knew her. She died the day after I was born. All I ever heard is the one thing Mother said about her, that she was 'an absolute saint.' "

"Now your grandmother and her sister came over to this country together, right?"

"When they were maybe twenty years old. From Eastern Europe."

"Jews always come from Eastern Europe! Never Poland. Or Romania. Just Eastern Europe. Like it's one big country."

"True . . ." Thea took off her glasses and touched an ice cube in her Coke, then pressed her finger to her eyelid. A pain was gathering behind her eye.

"It fascinates me how your grandparents ended up in Denmark, South Carolina."

"It fascinates *me* how these letters ended up here, in Charlotte. Now I just have to find somebody to translate them."

"But who?" Reid took his tie out, refolded it—a little too meticulously, Thea thought—and put it back in his pocket. Why did he have to be *so neat?*

"I'll figure something out," she said. "I don't have to worry about that now."

"How about your sister? Maybe she knows somebody in Charleston."

"No, I think I'll try to find somebody here." Turning the

letters over to her sister was the last thing she wanted to do. Anyway, just because Mickey happened to teach tennis at a Jewish Community Center didn't mean she knew people—

"Don't you think it'll be tricky, finding somebody who can read Yiddish?" he said. "We're not exactly talking about Spanish. Or French."

"Don't you think *I* know that?" Now why did she have to say that?

"How about calling the synagogue? Wouldn't a rabbi know what to do? Or maybe you could put a notice in that magazine that goes to all the Jews in North Carolina."

"Maybe." She didn't want to hear any more of his suggestions. He could get too involved, try to be too helpful. Receiving these letters had overturned something inside her and she was feeling headachy, tired, annoyed. She rubbed her cheek, opening her mouth to stretch the muscle in her jaw. "I'm thinking of a woman I read about in the paper. Fein-something. She might be the one to do it. The article was about a Yiddish Institute that meets every summer. In the mountains, I think. And she's part of it. A Yiddish Institute in North Carolina!" She forced a laugh. "That's one for the books!"

She thought of the Yiddish expressions her father had used, with their knuckle-hard stutter of consonants that sounded like people clearing their throats. In some Jewish families, it was a language parents relied on when they didn't want their children to understand what was being said, as if they were talking in pig Latin. But her family didn't need a foreign language to help them keep things hidden. Thea's father used Yiddish to make a sentence clearer or more vivid, as though it were some kind of special-occasion puncuation, like a semicolon. Thea had never heard her mother speak any Yiddish.

Reid got up and stretched, arching his back and bracing it with his hands. Then he walked around behind the rocker and massaged Thea's neck, his hand moving down between her shoulders to the small of her back. She let her glasses slide off her lap onto the floor and rolled her head to one side, folding her arms lightly over her breasts, her grandmother's words pressed in that close space.

"It's pretty unbelievable that you have those letters," he said, bending down to kiss the top of her head and pick up her glasses.

Thea thought about Mickey and how she'd said Jewish men made better husbands. Who could be sweeter than Reid? Thea had a theory about marriage anyway, that people usually got what they were looking for. But because they were trying to offset what they grew up with, they usually got what they wanted in spades, and then they wished for something else, usually less of what they had. Like the caller the week before who'd said that her mother and father had been millworkers, resigned to live their marginal lives. They'd lived in a mill-owned house, bought everything they owned at the mill store. The woman ended up marrying a man so determined to succeed, she and her children never saw him.

In Reid, Thea had a husband she could depend on. In a way that she could never depend on her mother. Or her father. Reid's caring could revive her, keep her going, like cool water washing over her. But sometimes it could be too much, like wet, heavy clothes pulling her under.

Before their wedding he was the one who thought they should engrave something sentimental inside their rings.

They'd sat on a bench outside the jewelry store at the shopping center trying to decide what to engrave. At first he'd joked, imitating Jerry Lewis in that movie where he read a long, endless inscription in a wedding band as the sun behind him set and the screen turned dark. Reid had slowly rotated an imaginary ring in his fingers, grinning, droning on and on, "And to my beloved on the most important day of our lives, I pledge my undying devotion, looking toward years and years of happiness together, with children and grandchildren and . . ."

But then he turned serious. He'd just read *The Great Gatsby* and quoted a phrase from the last page of the book. He said he liked the idea of using a line from one of the greatest endings to mark what he considered a great beginning.

They'd gone in the store, picked out brushed gold bands, and told the man behind the counter what they wanted.

"*Greatest of human dreams*, eh?" the man mumbled, bearing down with his pencil on the pad, making sure they saw him cross the t's with hard, stubborn lines. "It'll *be* the greatest of human dreams if we can fit all those words inside these rings. How come people are always asking for more than they can get?"

Chapter 2

A bright, clear Saturday, one week after the letters arrived, Thea, Reid, Mickey, and Joel were at the Metrolina Flea Market. Mickey and Joel had driven up for the weekend. It was not a bad trip from Charleston to Charlotte, a little more than three hours, but unless there was a specific reason for a visit, Thea and Mickey hadn't been making the trip to see each other lately. Thea was pleased when Mickey called to say she and Joel wanted to come. This would give Thea a chance to tell her about the letters. She'd almost brought it up at breakfast that morning. Maybe she'd tell her while they were looking around the flea market.

Just inside the largest building, in the first booth, Reid

was buying a St. Louis Browns pennant and Joel was flipping through a box of South Carolina picture postcards from the 1940s, pulling out all the ones of Charleston.

Mickey and Thea wandered over to the next booth, where Mickey stopped to look at an old kitchen spoon with a green wooden handle. Then she maneuvered sideways, edging herself between a leaded glass window leaning against a chest of drawers and a warped tobacco sign, heading straight toward a small oak table in the back corner, as though she'd known all along this one piece of furniture would be waiting there for her.

"Look at this, Thea. It's ideal! Just what I need for the guest room," she said, running her hand over the varnished wood, then grasping the top and rocking it to see if it was steady.

"Do you have a tape measure?" Mickey asked the man in the vinyl recliner, his slippered feet propped up, a barbecue sandwich in one hand, Dr. Pepper in the other. He slowly placed the can on the floor, wrapped the sandwich back in tinfoil, wiped his mouth with a paper towel, and pushed himself up.

"Don't need one," he said to the tobacco sign.

"Well, I'd like to see how tall—"

"Let me teach you a trick," he said, sidling up to the table, frontways. "All you need to know is what your inseam is."

"My inseam?" Mickey asked, stepping forward. Thea stayed where she was, behind her sister.

"I can get you a yardstick, but all it'll say is this here table is twenty-six inches high." Thea was trying not to focus on the man's crotch, which was now resting on the edge of the table. "My insteam is twenty-eight inches. The table is two inches shorter. Now let's get you a yardstick since that's what you want and we'll see how close I am."

He twisted his tousled body around and pulled a yardstick from behind a glass fishbowl the shape of an elephant and almost the size of one. A tambourine fell to the concrete floor. It made such a loud, brassy noise, everyone around them hushed, as if an announcement were forthcoming. He held the yardstick up to the table. Twenty-six inches. Exactly.

"I'll take it," Mickey said.

"Don't you want to look around?" Thea whispered. There were tables in almost every booth. "This is the first building we've been in. What if you find something better?"

The noise picked up around them.

"I won't," Mickey said, not bothering to whisper. "This is the one I want. I'm going to paint it white. Look at the shape, the curves, the spool legs. It's perfect. I'm not like you, you know. You go back and forth on every decision. 'On the other hand' ought to be your epitaph!" She poked Thea's arm good-naturedly, as though she'd just cracked one of her funny jokes. Then she turned toward the man. He was still holding the yardstick to the table, waiting for them to acknowledge how accurate he'd been.

"How much is it?" Mickey asked.

"I can tell you one thing, you don't want to paint it," he said. "Look at the wood. Took me a whole week to refinish this baby. Even planed it."

Mickey wasn't listening. She was bending down, looking under the table. "How much did you say?" she asked.

"Sixty-five bucks," he answered. Thea expected him to say sixty if one of them would say how right he'd been about his inseam. Fifty-five if they'd promise not to paint it.

"Okay. You got a deal." Mickey reached in her purse for her checkbook.

"Thanks," Thea said to the man. "We'll remember that trick. About inseams." She'd wait to tell Mickey about the letters. Maybe later. There really wasn't any hurry.

Mickey wrote the check for sixty-five dollars, handwriting solid and sure. She ripped it out, handed it over, then hoisted the table above her head.

. . .

Not easy to see the number half-hidden by azaleas—101 Plum Nearly Lane. When Helen Feinman had told Thea the address, she'd said that years before, the street had been "plum out of the city and nearly out of the county." Now it was just another suburban neighborhood, where a lot of Jewish people lived. Thea didn't know anyone who lived there. She and Reid lived in the Elizabeth neighborhood, close to downtown. No Jews there that she knew of. Other than herself. It had been funny hearing Helen Feinman give that very Southern explanation of the street name with her thick accent, which was Russian, or maybe Eastern European. Most people in Charlotte would probably call it a Jewish accent.

Monday, after the flea market weekend, Thea had gone through the old newspapers stacked on the floor next to her side of the bed and found the article about the Yiddish Institute and Helen Feinman. Luckily, there was only one Feinman in the telephone book. When Thea called to ask her about the letters, she could tell Helen was interested in translating them—in the possibility, anyway; she wasn't making any promises. "You know, there are many different versions of Yiddish," she'd said in her slightly formal, but warm voice. "Lithuanian Yiddish, Russian Yiddish, Polish Yiddish. And each has its own variations. I don't know whether I'll be able to read your grandmother's Yiddish. We'll have to see. Come tomorrow morning and let's take a look."

Thea turned off the motor in Helen's driveway. Her hands were shaking. When she pulled the keys out of the ignition, they clanged against the whistle and pocketknife she kept on her key chain for emergencies. This was ridiculous. Why would she be nervous? First of all, she didn't even know if Helen could do the translation. She should be putting all her energy into hoping Helen would say yes. Into hoping she'd finally get a straight perspective on her family. Even if the letters didn't tell everything, at least she would get to know her grandmother and what she was like, maybe hear what her grandmother thought of her grandfather and if she complained about his gambling and the family having to move so many times. Still, there was emotion in the air. Almost like pollen. It stung her eyes and caught in her throat.

Helen Feinman's house was a brick split-level on a street lined with brick split-levels that fed into other streets lined with brick split-levels. A *mezuzah* hung slanted on the wood trim of the door. Thea rang the bell and took a step back to wait for the door to open. She looked down at her shoes, black loafers. She'd gone back and forth about what to wear and had decided to keep it casual and simple. Black jeans, long-sleeved white knit shirt, black tweed vest, and the funny little gold pea-pod pin Reid had given her for her birthday last year.

"Come in, dear! I'm Helen. And I'm so glad you're here!" She sounded like she was singing. She was a friendly looking, well-put-together woman, in her late sixties or early seventies, with such perfect posture that Thea found herself standing up straighter.

Helen took her arm and led her into the living room. "I've been looking forward to seeing these letters from your grandmother. By the way, I've heard you on the radio. I'm so impressed having you in my home!" More singing. "Now tell me this, who are you married to? And have I seen you in temple? During the High Holy Days? You're a member of sisterhood?"

This was just the kind of conversation Thea hated. Like the Chinese woman at the dry cleaners who'd figured out somehow that Thea was Jewish and asked her, out of the blue: *Do you know Mrs. Shapiro?* As though Jews everywhere were connected and all did the same things.

"Reid McKee is my husband," Thea answered. "He teaches out at the university."

"My daughter teaches there! Political science."

"What's your daughter's name?" She looked at Helen's face. Her skin was silk, almost no wrinkles.

"Lila. Lila Stern. Married to Robert Stern. They live two streets over from me. Aren't I fortunate to have her back in Charlotte? Since you counsel people on the radio, you'll be happy to know I'm very careful not to meddle! She's our only child. I'm surprised you don't know her. The Jewish community is not *that* big! Oh, maybe your husband knows her at school. What does he teach?" Helen was pointing her toward the sofa.

"English. And one writing workshop."

"Writing! He must be very intelligent . . . and interesting. Speaking of writing, I've been thinking about your letters since you called . . ."

The living room was beige and white, and the oversize sofa had down cushions Thea let herself sink into as though she'd run the whole way. The soles of her shoes barely grazed the shag carpet. On the wall opposite the sofa was a Chagall print with people flying through the air, their feet like tiny propellers. Mosaic tile knickknacks from Israel were arranged on the coffee table. Menorahs lined the mantel, their brass fingers pointing.

Helen sat down beside her.

"You are so nice to take a look at these," Thea said. She pulled the tissue-thin letters from the rubber band and handed them over, one by one, to keep her hands busy. "Here they are." Her hands felt abnormally large, her arms long, her feet so unwieldy she had to consciously keep them from flapping.

"No need to wait! Let's see," Helen sang, as she opened an envelope and started scanning the first page. "Hmm. This is going to be complicated. I'm not so sure about being able to do this."

Thea didn't answer. She wanted her to concentrate.

"This is a challenge! Your grandmother mixes her Yiddish with English expressions and writes them all phonetically, which makes it very, very difficult to read." Helen laughed a short aria and fingered a thin gold chain at her throat.

Then it was a while before she said anything. She didn't glance up. Her gray hair was parted down the middle. Even when she was bent over reading, the shoulder pads of her dress stayed horizontal.

"Oh dear, I'm not sure about this at all," she finally said, and turned to the second page.

Thea waited.

"Oh yes." Another laugh.

Another wait.

Thea allowed herself a quick glance at the page.

"Now I see . . . mm-hmm . . ." Helen crooned. The mm-hmm sounded like a good sign. "Now I see what she is doing. Isn't this delightful?" She read on. "Mollie and Mike? Who are they?"

"They're my parents!"

"And are they still living, dear?"

"No, they're not."

"Your grandmother talks a good bit about them. See, here's something about Mollie and Mike." Helen lowered the page and ran her finger in an S curve down it. "And here's something. And here. Now what, or who, is Easy? Is this a person?"

"That's my grandfather. My mother's father. His initials were E.C.—for Ervin Charles—but everyone called him Easy. Easy Bogen was his name."

"Easy. What an unusual name!"

Thea remembered the names her father called him. Scoundrel, rascal, charlatan. Her father thought her grandfather was the most selfish person in the world, the type who was always taking his own pulse to see how he felt about whatever was going on, never stopping to consider anybody else's feelings. Her grandfather used to take the bus to Rock Hill to visit them, but if they were the least bit late picking him up at the Greyhound station, he would call a taxi to take him to the Elk's Club, the only place in town that allowed gambling. He'd play poker into the night while Thea's mother sat by the phone at home, waiting for him to call, smoking one cigarette after another. There'd be a place still set for him at the dinner table and the kettle would be left steaming on the burner.

"What was your grandfather like? *Was* he easy?" Thea liked that Helen was so interested.

"My grandmother died a few months after these letters were written, some kind of kidney disease. Cancer, I think." Thea tucked one leg up under her. She'd already slipped off a loafer. "My grandfather outlived her. He moved to Miami Beach after she died. Every week, I remember, he'd send my mother a postcard—with palm trees on the front, a beach scene, or whatever residential hotel he happened to be living in at the time—you know those hand-tinted picture postcards the colors of sherbet?"

"Sure. I probably still have some myself, from various relatives!"

"Well, there was one long period of time when my mother didn't hear a word from him. She tried to get in touch with him but her letters kept coming back and his phone had been disconnected. Finally, after I don't know how many months, he sent a postcard: *Sorry I haven't written. I've been busy getting married. Love, Papa.* That's how she found out about her father's second marriage."

"Oh dear, he must not have been easy at all. He sounds colorful though."

Thea wondered what it had been like for her mother, growing up with a "colorful" father. Did anyone wonder what it had been like for Thea, growing up with a colorful *mother*?

"I didn't know my grandfather very well. I remember he wore an elk's tooth on a chain hanging from his vest pocket. Sometimes he'd let me wear it." She decided not to tell about the Elk's Club and the gambling. "No, he wasn't easy. He'd pace from the front hall in our house through the den to the living room and back again, his hands clasped behind his back." She also wasn't going to mention the small farts as he paced. "And oh, I definitely remember the smell of his cigars! He walked fast and his leather shoes squeaked, like little mice. And he teased me about being quiet and shy. He called me *Flimely*—"

"Yes, yes, that's Yiddish for slight," Helen said, nodding, one eyebrow raised. "*Flimely* is someone so fragile, they could"—she twiddled her fingers upward through the air, her voice going up the ladder of scales—"slip away! How long ago did your grandfather die?"

"Well, it's funny. That's probably my strongest memory of him, the night he died. I was thirteen. My father was in New York on a buying trip for the store—"

"Oh? What kind of store?"

"He owned the Smart Shoppe in Rock Hill. Women's clothing."

"Ready-to-wear. Mm-hmm."

"Well, anyway, the night I was talking about, my younger sister was spending the night out with a friend." Mickey was always gone when something bad happened with their mother. "It was in the summer and—isn't it funny how you remember certain things?—I know it was a Thursday because that's the night my mother always watched her program on television, *You Bet Your Life*. She never missed it. Do you remember that show?"

"Of course I do. Groucho Marx!"

Thea shifted her eyebrows up and down and tapped her index finger against her thumb like she was flicking ashes.

"He was ruthless, wasn't he? But funny!" Helen said,

laughing at the Groucho imitation. Or maybe at her word, ruthless.

Thea thought of her mother's laugh, rattly and rough-edged from years of smoking, and how she would throw her head back and laugh every time Groucho cracked a joke—especially when a contestant said the secret word and the duck dropped down.

"My mother and I were watching her program and about halfway through, the phone rang." Her mother had leaned forward, chin resting in her hand, which meant she wanted Thea to get the phone because she didn't want to miss anything. Thea always read her mother's gestures like a weather map so she could be prepared for whatever might come next. "It was my aunt."

For a second, Thea could see her mother putting the phone to her ear. Her arms would be suntanned and her fingernails polished red. She'd be concentrating, intense, but beautiful, her gray hair curly from a permanent wave, as they called it then, her eyes brown as coffee, the tiny half-wrinkle above her left eyebrow. Thea could almost hear the floor fan shuddering, turning its face from her to her mother.

"Suddenly, my mother's expression changed. And she was saying, 'Oh! Oh!' " Thea didn't know why she was going into so much detail. She couldn't even remember Helen's original question or if she'd answered it. "After she hung up, she walked into the living room, to the window. I followed her. She didn't turn on a single light. The two of us just stood in the dark, in front of the window, looking out."

Thea stopped there, before the part about her mother whispering over and over that she didn't have a mother or a father, before the part about her staying in bed the next day, days after that, not speaking a word other than the whispering, *Now I don't have a mother or a father, now I don't have a mother or a father*. Before the part about her not getting out of bed to go to her own father's funeral.

"Oh my," Helen was saying, "that is a difficult memory . . ." She looked off for a few seconds, toward the Chagall print, with its houses turned upside down, then at Thea. "By the way, dear, I can't help but notice your fair skin and blond hair. You have lovely coloring."

"Thanks, but my hair looks awful today. The humidity makes it so limp. Actually, there's plenty of gray mixed in with the blond but it all ends up looking like the same color." She stirred her curly hair with the tips of her fingers, trying to fluff it. "I think a great aunt in my family had this coloring, I'm not sure." She didn't like her looks. She didn't have much of a chin. And she thought she was *too* fair, with that thin-skinned complexion. Her face was nondescript, the color rinsed out of it.

Helen was studying the letter again. "Yes, your grandmother is definitely concerned about her husband, Easy . . . and she's concerned about business."

She folded that letter back in the envelope and pulled out another.

"Now," she said. "This one appears to be describing a wedding dinner. Silver dishes. Candlesticks . . . four of them on the table—"

"That's my mother's wedding! That's the letter I'm dying to—" How could Thea ever have been the least bit nervous? This was exactly what she wanted. She wished she could grab the letter and read it herself.

"This is very interesting. Two P.S.'s. The second one seems to be—well, a bit intriguing." Helen's voice was suddenly unmusical. "Now I wonder what *this* implies."

She read on silently. Thea tried to read the expression that passed over her face.

"What does it say?" Thea asked.

"I'm not entirely sure." Helen's left eyelid flickered.

"Can you just read me the words?"

"I don't quite understand this part. Perhaps it's not good for me to read any of it aloud until I can analyze—"

"I don't mind waiting—"

"I believe we'd better hold this for a later time, dear."

"Is it something—"

"I need to examine your grandmother's style of writing. I wouldn't want to make a mistake. After all, these are Bella's words and she deserves my best effort." She fit the sheets back into the envelope and slipped it under the others in her lap, out of sight. "But, yes . . ." Her voice rose. "I'll be delighted to do it. I can't guarantee that I'll be fast, but as I finish each one, I'll mail you the translation." She patted Thea's hand. "How's that?"

"That's fine, great. I really appreciate what you're doing." It wasn't fine *or* great. Why wouldn't she just go ahead and try to read the thing? Right then. But Helen had already pulled herself up from the sofa and left the stack of letters on the coffee table. They looked like a sandwich that'd been carelessly assembled, slices of bread and filling stuck this way and that. "Of course, I'd like to pay you—"

"Oh no, I wouldn't dream of that. It's my pleasure. Reading Yiddish is so nostalgic for me. It takes me back to the town where I grew up . . . Bialystok . . . where I was born. Yiddish was the language everyone spoke . . . Of course, that was a long time ago. Come, dear, I'd like to show you something I've been working on. Of all things, at my age, I'm taking a sculpture class! From a wonderful artist, a Jewish woman who moved here from California. She lives next door to my daughter, in fact. You might be interested in a piece I just completed. Here, in the dining room . . ."

A monogrammed towel with raveled edges was spread across the table and on it was a female head and shoulders. The wet, gray clay had been rubbed so smooth the contours glistened. A Star of David was sculpted into the strands of hair.

"That's so nice. Really nice," Thea said, realizing she had a sudden sense of sadness. She didn't know whether it was a letdown from not getting to hear the letters or from being with someone who obviously derived so much pleasure from her Jewishness, someone who naturally assumed Thea felt the same way. There was a settledness, a contentment, about Helen. No ambivalence. She knew where she belonged.

Thea thanked her a second time. Then she was outside, walking backward toward her car, waving good-bye and smiling an unnatural smile, one a sculptor might pinch in hurriedly as an afterthought.

. . .

At the radio station that afternoon, the news director was cueing her through the glass—four minutes left in the program. Tim looked like the geology professor she and Reid had had in college, their one class together. Tim was a narrow, sweaty man with spindly arms and legs. His medium-blue pants were too short, as though he'd just had a growth spurt. A good three inches of black sock showed.

"This is Thea McKee," she said, lifting her hair off her neck, letting it drop back down, loose and flat. She adjusted the headphones. "We have time for one more caller. Hello, Jennifer, you're on the air."

"I'm probably too young to be calling. See, I'm only sixteen —"

"Oh no, Jennifer." Let's get to the point. "It doesn't matter whether you're sixteen or sixty. What would you like to talk about?"

"Well, my mother is *my* big problem! See, she wants me to go to church with her every Sunday *and* she wants me to go to Young Life meetings *and* she wants me to read my Bible every night. She's real religious and it kills her I'm not just like her. Any holiday that comes along, we're in church. The whole time around Christmas, we go to church more than other people go to stores! I don't even know if there *is* a God, but I can tell you one thing: If there is, I want to find out by myself, without somebody cramming Him down my throat."

"You must be feeling a lot of frustration."

"Wouldn't *you* get mad and want to do the opposite if somebody was telling you what to do every minute? I'm not three years old, you know! Boy, I can't wait to go to college!"

"How's the communication between you and your mother in areas other than religion?"

"Communication? Ha! My mother communicates, all right. By talking. She doesn't listen at all."

"You know, Jennifer, it sounds like what you're doing is trying out different values and beliefs so you can define yourself. When you're older, you may end up thinking and believing just like your mother. Or you may think and believe very differently from her." Let that register. "I also wonder if you're dealing with separation. First, you pull away from your mother, emotionally, by looking at life through your own lens. Then you'll be able to pull away physically, when you leave for college. The process is normal, but it can create strong feelings on both sides. You don't like her rules and criticisms, and she doesn't like your disobedience and rebellion."

"You're right about me not liking her rules!"

"You do have a choice here though. Either you can get angry . . . constantly. Or you can choose your battles. By that I mean give in on the little things and try—I'm saying *try*—to discuss the important ones."

Silence.

"One other thought, is there a family member? Your father? An aunt? Or a teacher? Somebody you could go to for support, who might be able to help you figure out how to approach your mother in a way she can hear you?"

"Maybe. I've got a pretty cool English teacher. I could try her."

"Well, good luck, Jennifer." Tim was cueing her. Wrap it up. "I do hope you and your mother can find a way to communicate. We're running out of time so we're going to have to stop for now." She hit the switch. "I want to thank all of our callers for joining us today. We'll be back tomorrow . . ."

Tim gave a thumbs-up and disappeared out the door. She finished the program, took off her headphones, and held them in her lap. It would take more than the last minutes of a radio call-in show to deal with the subject of religion, she thought. More like a lifetime.

Chapter 3

That night she was looking all over the kitchen for the pesto recipe she'd cut out of the food section of the paper. It wasn't under her *The more you worry, the longer God lets you live* refrigerator magnet Mickey had sent saying Thea would probably live forever. That held a recipe, but it was for Mickey's delicious soy sauce marinade. Maybe she'd put it in *Food Thrills from Rock Hill,* at the bottom of the pile of cookbooks next to the phone. Everything was such a mess in this kitchen. She needed to get organized. When she pulled the cookbook out, the others toppled onto the floor. She'd get to them later. Duff Hearn, a friend of Thea's mother, had sent *Food Thrills* when she and Reid got married. Written inside the front cover was *Thea, do try my corn dressing on page 50! Fondly, Duff.*

She automatically flipped through the hors d'oeuvres section to her mother's "Chicken Liver pâté." Wasn't that her family's story right there? Good old Jewish chopped liver—a pound of chicken livers, hard-boiled eggs, minced onion, rendered chicken fat—turns into pâté in the Episcopal Church of Our Savior cookbook. Her mother's added instructions were printed at the bottom of the recipe: *May be used for sandwiches or for a salad—absolutely marvelous either way!* Dead giveaway, Mother, Thea thought. That's okay for chopped liver, but when is pâté ever used for sandwiches or salad?

Thea's mother had done everything she could to fit in. While other mothers baked a pie or one recipe of cupcakes for the school bake sale, she would bake dozens of cakes, all elaborately decorated. She'd fill her car with them, each safe and protected in one of the old hat boxes she'd saved for years. "Less is more" never would have been her motto. If someone she knew was in the hospital, she'd send a little gift or bouquet of flowers every day until that person was well again. At Christmas, she delivered poinsettias to everyone in town, one huge cardboard box full for "people who helped you," meaning the man who ran the elevator in the bank, checkout girls in the grocery store, the couple who sold tomatoes on the bypass. She wrote letters in response to Christmas cards and thank-you notes in response to thank-you notes. This last habit really annoyed Mickey. "You're so . . . you're so . . ." she'd mumble under her breath, trying to land on the right word. Their mother would ignore Mickey's comments. Ignore Mickey, in fact, most of the time.

But Thea didn't mind their mother's extravagance where other people were concerned. Because of her efforts, the whole family had been accepted in Rock Hill. They belonged. They were insiders. Not like the eleven other Jewish families, who kept to themselves and were definitely outsiders. Thea's mother had pushed her husband to be on the board of the bank, to be one of the founders of the country club. Thea and Mickey had been debutantes—no Jewish or Catholic girls before or after them had ever been asked. And Mickey had been ranked in the state in tennis. Well, that really didn't have anything to do with acceptance. Or with their mother. It was a result of all the attention their father paid to Mickey.

Thea twisted the neck of the Cuisinart to start it whirring and dropped in two peeled cloves of garlic. She probably remembered enough of the pesto recipe. Garlic, basil, cheese, nuts, oil. After the garlic slivers spun and spit, she turned off the machine to stuff the plastic bowl with the last basil leaves of the season from the pot on the porch. Then she ground them into confetti, the seedy scent filling the kitchen, and tossed in grated Parmesan and pine nuts. Her father used to bring home pine nuts from his buying trips to New York, only then they were called Indian nuts. She and Mickey would spend hours cracking open the tiny, ivory-colored nuts with their teeth, saving the meat until they each had a mound they could scoop up and pop in their mouths. She remembered the time Bullet Jackson—his real name was Ben but everyone called him Bullet because he could run so fast—came over from next door. Thea and Mickey had both cracked a pile of nuts. "Isn't that the doorbell I hear, Thea?" Bullet asked, tilting his big head and crooking his elbow in the direction of the front hall. She hopped up to see who it was. Nobody. She came back in the room just as Bullet was funneling all of her Indian nuts into his mouth. Mickey grabbed him by the shirt. "Tell her you're sorry," she demanded. "That's okay, Mickey," Thea said, not wanting to bear the brunt of her sister's bravado later. "Just let him go. I'll crack some more." Bullet, still chewing, didn't say a word. Nobody was going to get the best of him, not even Mickey, who was every bit as tough as he was and still holding him by the shirt. All of a sudden, she balled up her fist and hit him smack in the jaw. His mouth flew open and instead of an apology, out came the nuts. He pulled himself loose and ran out of the house. Mickey drew the side of her hand through the middle of her shelled nuts like a wedge and pushed one half over to her speechless sister.

. . .

With the machine still humming, Thea poured in the olive oil. Reid's key turned in the lock. She scraped the pastelike pesto into a bowl of cooked pasta. The back door opened. He hung his keys on the hook, dropped his book bag, and walked over to kiss her on the forehead. The faint smell of aftershave was still on his cheeks from that morning. He always smelled so clean. When they were first married, she loved to hold his arm to her face because the soft, light hair held the sweet scent of soap all day.

"Hi," she said. "You look tired."

"I am tired. Tired of standing in the front of a classroom looking at a bunch of college freshmen whose main interest is how wasted they got the night before. Plus, I've got a breakfast meeting with the dean at seven A.M. tomorrow. Not the face I want to be seeing first thing in the morning. What's been going on around here?"

"Well, my program went okay, and the man came to fix the dryer—"

"Yeah? I want to hear all that, but first, did Al call? He's just about to buy a house and wants me to help him move."

"Al, the poet at school? Isn't he always just about to buy a house? Why doesn't he just get a mover?" Another annoying thing about Reid. Too generous. He practically gave himself away. "Well, anyway, he didn't call. But the dryer's fixed, something about a wire shorting out. It works pretty well now. Not perfect, but good enough." She pulled forks from the drawer, took two paper napkins from the basket, and left them in a jumble on the counter.

"So your program went okay? And the dryer's working? How much?"

"The bill's over there. Fifty-nine dollars."

"Not bad," he said, starting toward the bill, stuffed under the radio at the end of the counter. "Oh, I have to tell you what happened in the workshop this afternoon. There's this student who's always jumping in and telling everybody how to fix their short stories. Anyway, today we're doing her story and everybody is being complimentary—she *is* a good writer—and she's smiling and happy and agreeble, but then somebody says that her ending doesn't sound believable. Well, she goes crazy! 'What do you mean, my ending doesn't sound believable?' she says. 'That's the way it really happened!' She goes on and on, blasting everyone, telling them they don't know anything about writing, all kinds of insults. Then she gathers up her books and stomps out of the room!"

"Oh, my gosh. No wonder you look tired."

"It does get old. And that business of saying that something is good because it actually happened makes me exhausted!"

"Maybe you should make a list of 'don'ts' and give them out the first day."

"Maybe I should. Hey, I almost forgot the most important thing—how'd your meeting with Helen Feinman go this morning? What'd she say about the letters?"

"She seemed very excited about the whole idea." Thea went back to blending the pesto into the noodles.

"She was able to make them out? Here, let me have that spatula. This calls for some muscle." He smoothed away the hard clumps of sauce, making sure each pasta spiral was coated.

"I don't think it's going to be easy for her, but she said she thought she'd be able to do it. She's going to send them to me, one at a time, as she finishes them."

"It'll be like you're Celia, receiving letters from Bella! You'll finally get to know your grandmother. That business of her being a saint is one hell of a reputation!" He raised the spatula and licked it clean.

"Come on, let's eat," Thea said, taking the spatula from him and dropping it in the sink. "Everything's ready. Want to sit at the table or watch the news in the den?"

"Wait a minute. That's it? We talk about it for two minutes and the conversation's over?"

"I don't know, I feel so muddled about the whole thing. I want to read the letters—I'm *dying* to read them—but on the other hand, you know how knowing can sometimes be more of a burden than not knowing? Helen reacted very, very strangely to something she saw in one of the letters—"

"You're probably jumping to conclusions."

"If you'd seen the expression on her face . . . What got me was that she refused to tell me what she saw."

"Refused?"

"Think how long I've wondered what my mother was

keeping from us. What if the letters tell everything and it turns out to be something that really hurts?"

"Like what I saw on television the other night. Was it *60 Minutes* or the news? Anyway, one of those. They were talking about how Huntington's disease is passed down, genetically, and strikes some people and not others, even within a single family. Doctors can now tell which people will eventually get it, but there's no way they can prevent it from happening. They just can predict who'll end up with it."

"Uh-huh." How had they ended up on Huntington's disease? Why were men always reporting facts instead of just talking?

"Which leads to the big question: Should a person be informed that one day he's going to have a full-blown case of this horrible disease? Would he want to live under that shadow?" He put his hand on her arm. "Are you wondering if you really want to know what's in the letters, when there's nothing you can do to change what you find?"

Thea turned away and cupped her hands to her cheeks. She was getting one of her headaches and the pain was radiating along the right side of her face, the way it always did, becoming more and more severe. Her right eye was beginning to tear.

"Let's see what Peter Jennings has to tell us about the world," he said, taking a plate from the cupboard and spooning a big helping of pasta on it. He poured a glass of iced tea, took a fork and napkin, and went in the den. She heard the tight click of the remote control, then a smooth, confident voice telling about an entire family who'd been found alive under the rubble of their house in Mexico, two days after an earthquake.

. . .

Two weeks later, she still hadn't told her sister about the letters. She'd unload the dishwasher first, then call her.

She lifted out the silverware holder and set it on the counter. Mickey used to invent competitions between the forks, spoons, and knives. She'd give minute-by-minute commentary, like a throaty announcer at a horse race, as she took the silverware from the dishwasher and dropped it into the divider in the drawer: ". . . and the forks are ahead, ladies and gentlemen, but the little spoons are catching up, knives are lagging far behind, big spoons are gaining, but wait!—little spoons are now in the lead . . ."

Thea finished the silverware and put the plates and cereal bowls in the overhead cabinet. The glasses could wait. She went to the phone hanging on the wall between the oven and desk, tucked the receiver into her shoulder, and dialed the number. While it rang, she pushed her cuticles back with her fingernail, jabbing until she could see moons.

"Hello." Mickey's deep voice, the inflections just like their father's. When they were growing up, Thea thought her sister deliberately tried to sound like him, talking low on purpose.

"Mickey, hi, it's me."

"Thea! How're you doing?"

"Great. Great. How's everybody there?"

"Humming along. No complaints."

"What's that noise?"

"Oh, sorry. I thought I could kill two birds with one stone. I was washing my new eggbeater when you called."

"Your eggbeater?"

"Have I told you what I started collecting?"

"Eggbeaters?"

"Not eggbeaters! Antique kitchen utensils with painted-green wooden handles. Remember how I kept noticing them when we were at the flea market? Well, I bought two big spoons and a rolling pin a while back. In this great antique store on King Street. And then today I found an eggbeater. In perfect condition, which is pretty rare."

How in the world had she thought to collect antique kitchen utensils with painted-green wooden handles? All their lives, Mickey had come up with original ideas. All their lives, Thea had wished she'd thought of them first.

"How're the girls?" she asked, jabbing at her cuticles again, the way you keep picking at a scab, even though it hurts.

"Fine. They were over here for dinner last night, in fact. Belle says she's had it with her boss at the sight-seeing tour place—but then, she has a history of not getting along with bosses. This is only the umpteenth time she's changed jobs, right? She *was* funny last night, though, telling us things she says to the tourists, like pointing out some 1950's split-level and telling them it's the oldest house in Charleston! But I'm ready for her to get serious and settle on a real career. She's too old to be moving around like this. And it bothers me she hasn't met anybody. Ann, too."

"I know, but it'll happen when it's right. Everyone's timing is different." Thea felt a strong connection with Mickey's girls, especially Belle, whom she'd held minutes after she was born. Mickey had called when she went into labor and Thea had immediately driven to the hospital in Charleston, through one of the worst snowstorms the Carolinas had ever had. That was thirty-one years ago. "How's Ann liking the J.C.C.?"

"Oh, you know Ann. She likes being busy. And she's

great with the little ones. Still taking her art classes at the College of Charleston." Ann was twenty-six and had just started teaching tennis with Mickey. She was also working toward her degree. She'd dropped out of college after her sophomore year, played regional tennis tours for four years, then had gone back to school two years ago.

"She's pretty close to finishing, right?"

"I don't ask any questions!"

"Well, let me tell you why I called. You can't imagine what's been going on."

"What?" Maybe that wasn't such a good way to begin. It sounded like she was getting ready to tell Mickey something really bad.

"Tuesday—no, I guess it was Monday—anyway, one day this week—" Not exactly the truth. "Aunt Florence sent me eight letters written by our grandmother to Aunt Celia—*Tante* Celia, Mother would say—back in the thirties. And listen, they're all written in Yiddish!"

"In Yiddish? I love that!"

"Well, I had to find somebody who could translate them. I figured the woman would just read me the letters right then and there, and I'd call you and tell you what was in them, but it turns out she's going to translate them one at a time and mail them to me."

"You just got them in the mail and you've already taken them to somebody? Why didn't you call me? We have a group of elderly people who meet every Wednesday at the J.C.C., called the Chai Group, and I could've gotten one of them to do the translating."

"I know. I thought of you right away, in fact. I even told Reid I was going to send them to you, but he suggested this woman here, thinking it might be faster." Now why couldn't she be straight with her sister?

"Well, I guess that makes sense. Can you send me copies?"

"Unfortunately, I left the letters with the woman who's going to translate them. I should've made copies before I went to her house, but you know how those things just evolve. Before I knew it, I'd left them with her. Helen Feinman, that's her name. I wish I'd thought." Another fib. Thea wanted to be the first to see the translations.

"I wonder what they'll say—"

"Oh, something I almost forgot: In one of the letters, the letter that was written right after Mother's wedding, there was a corsage!"

"From the wedding? That seems kind of bizarre to me, our grandmother sending *her* memento from *her own daughter's wedding* to her sister! Pretty weird, don't you think?"

"I guess."

"Funny, the only thing I've ever heard about our grandmother is she was an absolute saint. Isn't that all you've heard?"

"She must've been a wonderful woman."

"That's crazy though. Nobody can be a saint."

"Still," Thea said doubtfully.

"It's so typical of Mother, the way she'd exaggerate everything. Of course, you believed everything she said, didn't you?" Mickey's big laugh.

"But actually, I didn't. Remember, I tried to get the true story—"

"Who could forget you and your detective questions? Did you ever think maybe you accepted the things you should've been questioning and questioned the things you should've been accepting?" Mickey, the little sister, using her big-sister tone. Was it her height, her physical strength that gave her the right?

"Well." Thea walked over to the dishwasher, pulling the telephone cord tight around the corner of the cabinet. She took out the glasses, one by one, and put them away, dripping water across the floor. Reid would've blotted the bottoms with a dish towel before he took the glasses out. "The only time I asked questions was when things didn't make sense to me."

"But a *lot* of things didn't make sense to you! You know, it's possible some of your suspicions weren't really based on reality."

"What do you mean, not based on reality? But wait, how did we get on this subject?" Thea sat down at the desk, the cord limp around her feet. "I just wanted to tell you about the letters—"

"Okay, let's talk about the letters." A pause. "Look, I'm sure there'll be plenty of interesting details in them."

"That's exactly what I'm thinking—"

"A lot to learn there."

"For sure, Mickey. I totally agree with you."

"They'll probably be very charming and maybe even have some historical value . . . The J.C.C. here, I'm sure, would be very interested—"

"Of course they would."

"But besides that, I doubt—"

"You doubt what?"

"I guess I'm just not looking for psychological clues in everything that comes along," Mickey said, "like you are. How Jews ended up in small towns down South *is* fascinating to me. The whole thing about two sisters leaving home, coming to a new country, living in New York, meeting their husbands, uprooting themselves all over again to move to these remote little towns—one in the low country of South Carolina, the other in the Amish country in Pennsylvania—probably the first time in their lives they weren't surrounded by Jews."

"First time in their lives they weren't living near each other."

"But the Jewish part—" Mickey added.

"The Jewish part." Here we go.

"Thea, you know how I feel about this attitude you have about being Jewish—"

"Mickey!"

"Listen, here's what I'm thinking about those letters. Why dredge up the past? They're from such a long time ago and there are only eight of them anyway." Mickey stopped talking for a second. "The truth is, I'm not so sure we should get into all that. They could open up a lot of stuff we don't need to be worrying about. Why can't we just leave them alone? Let sleeping dogs lie."

"Leave them alone? What are you talking about? You mean don't get the letters translated?"

"I mean don't get them translated."

"Why in the world would we leave them alone?" Thea wished her voice hadn't cracked at that exact moment.

"Now don't go getting emotional. Sometimes, it's not good to put our nose where it doesn't belong. And you know how you like to examine every little detail of what someone really meant when they said this or what they really meant when they said that. There are things we need to just shrug off. Let's face it, Thea, you're a delver."

"A delver?"

"Yeah, you know, you like to delve into things. And then you start to psychologize. And worry." Mickey was probably nodding that square-shaped face of hers to emphasize every word. "You and I are very different, that's all. We always have been."

You and I are very different. In other words, why can't you be ______ (fill in the blank: strong, practical, clear-headed, plain-talking) like me? Thea knew what Mickey really meant, deep down, was not that Thea was different from her. She meant that Thea was *less* than her, that she had some lack. Thea wished she didn't care so much what her younger sister thought of her. Wasn't it normally the younger sister wanting the older one's approval? Why was everything in this family so mixed up?

And what about that other comment? They'd grown up in the same house, with the same parents. How had her sister slipped so seamlessly into her very Jewish life?

Mickey had married Joel Laster after her first year at Sarah Lawrence in a big wedding in the synagogue in Charleston, where the Lasters had lived for three generations. Mickey and Joel were a striking bride and groom; in fact, they still were striking—tall, dark-haired, straight-backed as posts. He was the type of husband who gazed adoringly at his wife. Whatever pleased her, pleased him. He'd gone into the family business, a shoe store in the historical district that expanded over the years to the size of a city block. They were both very involved in the Jewish community.

Thea was a different story.

When she got married (two years after Mickey), she joined the synagogue in Charlotte, which is what she thought she was supposed to do: You get married and settle into your religion, the message she'd gotten from her father. On Rosh Hashanah or Yom Kippur, she'd find a seat near the back of the temple and after five minutes, check her watch, trying to decide when it was reasonable to leave. Surely, she'd thought, this was not the feeling a person should have. She wanted to like it. She didn't understand why she didn't. She'd study the elderly men in their fringed shawls on the *bima* reading from the Torah, the way they swayed to the rhythm of their chanting, and she wished she had their passion, their uncomplicated acceptance of their religion. But all she felt was impatience. And guilt. Because she knew that just one lukewarm Jew automatically let down generations of Jews. She also felt annoyed. Because even if she did stop going to services, she could never get rid of her Jewishness. It wasn't something you could switch from, like going from Methodist to Presbyterian. It stuck to you. All your life. If you were born Jewish, you had to stay Jewish.

It wasn't long before she'd stopped going to synagogue.

. . .

"Think about what I'm saying." Mickey's voice was soft now, kind. "I care about you, and I know you'd be better off—heck, I have a feeling we'd both be better off—if we forget about those letters. Sometimes we have to concentrate on the present and not dwell on the past."

"Okay, okay, I'll think about it."

"Good. Now, before we hang up, I want you to be on the lookout for a package from me in the mail. I can't wait to hear how you like it. I know it's going to arrive way before your birthday, but I couldn't wait. Meanwhile, I can't believe you're going to be fifty-five!"

This was the way it went. They could be intimate, then

distant, then intimate all over again in the span of a few minutes. Like two birds, flying close, releasing, then flying wing to wing again.

"I can't either. But since you think I believed everything Mother said, I'll remind you how she told us when she turned fifty that the fifties were the best years of a woman's life. That's why I'm excited to be in the middle of them."

"First of all, Thea, the fifties were not so wonderful for Mother. And second, no matter how old you get . . ." Mickey's voice was deeper even than usual. ". . . no matter how many years it's been since Mother died, you're still tied to her. You haven't changed a bit." She punched out each word of that last sentence like a telegraph. "Makes me think of when Mother and Daddy took us to New York. In junior high. Remember?"

"Oh, I remember."

"I'm talking about when we were leaving the Broadway theater after we saw *South Pacific*."

"I know. When Daddy spotted Ed Sullivan in the audience and you rushed over and got his autograph before anybody else recognized him."

"Well, I just moved quickly," Mickey corrected. "And everybody else did, too. But it took you forever to get over there. And then it was too late."

Neither of them needed to to be reminded how the story ended: Their mother had taken Thea by the hand and marched her through the throng right up to Ed Sullivan himself. She'd explained to him, with dramatic hand gestures and facial expressions to match, that her other daughter had gotten his autograph but this one, her "precious Thea," had been pushed to the back of the crowd and was . . . "autographless." Ed Sullivan asked Thea how to spell her name, how old she was, where she was from. Then he scribbled his autograph on the scrap of paper she held out to him, and he bent down until he was eye to eye with her. "Young lady," he said, "if these Yankees up here give you any trouble, you just let me know."

Thea had been dazed. The rest of the evening she kept repeating, over and over, "He said that to me. Just me. 'Young lady, if these Yankees up here give you any trouble, you just let me know.' He said that to me. 'Young lady, if—' "

"We all *know* what he said to you," Mickey had finally yelled. "Now *cut it out*!"

. . .

"Oh yes," Mickey added just before they said good-bye and hung up, "Mother took care of you. And you let her. You were tied to her like a puppy on a leash. Still are."

. . .

Thea hated that Mickey was right. It had been nineteen years since their mother died and Thea was still tied to her. Every time Thea cut through Laurel Avenue on her way from Providence Road to Randolph Road, every time she drove past the grape-colored brick cluster of buildings—the condominiums her parents had been thinking of moving to—the years surrounding her mother's death became as clear and defined as the strands of balconies that traversed the buildings.

It had started the night they were on the phone, when her mother, fifty-four then, said she was considering selling the house in Rock Hill and moving to Charlotte, closer to Thea and Reid.

"Your father and I might just buy that *condonimium* . . ."

she said. "I mean, that *condo—nimi—um . . .*" Every time she tried to say it, the syllables came out jumbled. It was the first time Thea had ever known her mother to have this kind of trouble with words. She'd had plenty of experience with her mother becoming depressed and not saying anything, with her mother intentionally not telling what Thea wanted to know, but *stumbling* over words was something altogether different.

It got worse. Her speech grew more hesitant and she began forgetting entire words. Soon she began forgetting other things, too. One day she couldn't find her way home from downtown. She'd ended up at Rock Hill Feed & Supply, all the way out on the edge of town. She had no idea where she was. Mr. Childers, the owner, had one of his men drive her home. When Thea's father saw the old red truck bouncing up the driveway with Mollie inside, a bewildered expression on her face, the hem of her sundress caught in the door, flapping, he knew it was time to find out what was wrong. Dr. Buddin sent her to a specialist in Charlotte.

A week after the appointment, Mickey called Thea. "I'm meeting Daddy at Shoney's in the Rock Hill Mall tomorrow at three. Do you want to come? He says he has some news about Mother."

"I can be there, sure," Thea answered.

When she walked into Shoney's, her father was sitting in a booth near the back, a glass of iced tea on the table. He still had the appearance of a football player, husky and knotted, though it had been a lifetime since he was a high school star back in LaGrange, Georgia. He looked over the top of his glasses and smiled his lopsided smile. She smiled back, then realized he was looking past her. She turned around. Mickey was behind her, then in front of her, sliding in beside him, next to his good ear. If Mickey had sat any closer, she'd have been on the other side of him. Thea sat across from them.

"Girls," he said, clamping his arms over his chest and glancing sideways at Mickey, whose arms were clamped over her chest, "I'll get right to the point. The neurologist says it's Alzheimer's disease."

Thea looked straight down at the table. Alzheimer's. Suddenly, the restaurant felt hugely empty. She looked at her father and sister, now turned completely toward each other. They had the same face, the same thick, straight hair. Her father's hair, now gray, had been brown like Mickey's. Even their eyes, small and dark as seeds, were alike. And the shading beneath their eyes, their finely shaped heads, the boxy jawlines, which made them look as if they were gritting their teeth, and they both did grind their teeth, in fact, in their sleep. Her father and sister were a match. Always had been. She could've been back home in Rock Hill, sitting on the front steps, watching him teach Mickey how to throw a ball like a boy so she'd have a good tennis serve. All those Sundays—her mother in the kitchen baking or in the bedroom sleeping (depending on her mood, up or down), the ball hitting her father's glove, then Mickey's glove, the sound like a door hitting a wall, or a slap.

The waitress refilled his glass.

"You ladies want to see a menu?" she asked, separating mascaraed eyelashes with her little finger.

"Just water, no ice," Mickey said.

Thea nodded. "Me, too."

The waitress wandered off.

"Alzheimer's?" Mickey said to their father. "That's terrible! I've read about it, how in the early stages people undergo big personality changes. We have to prepare ourselves for that. Mother'll become really mean, even violent. That's what I've read."

"Actually," Thea said, trying to hold herself together, "you can't— well, the truth is, each case can be different. What you're saying may not happen with her at all." Why did Mickey always assume the worst about their mother?

Their father heaped two spoons of sugar in his tea, stirred it, tasted it, half-frowned, put in more sugar. Tasted it again. Still not sweet enough. Another spoon of sugar. He stirred more vigorously this time, his spoon clinking against the sides of the glass. The noise was too loud in the empty restaurant. He took a sip. It was finally the way he wanted.

"I'm going to take Mother to the Mayo Clinic and see what *they* have to say," he said. "These people in Charlotte may not even have the right diagnosis. I'm not buying it yet."

. . .

The night her parents returned from Mayo, Thea and Reid picked them up at the airport and drove them to Rock Hill. The men watched TV in the den while Thea sat on the bench of her mother's dressing table and watched her undress. Her skin was gray, like her hair, as though everything were turning to smoke. She pulled off her top, then the pants of the tan polyester suit Mike had brought home from the store for her before the trip. Elastic waist, no buttons or zippers, easy to put on and take off without anyone's help. If she were her old self, she would never wear anything this plain and ordinary.

She turned so Thea would unhook her bra. Then she slipped off her panties, faced her daughter, and just stood there—her breasts loose, nipples pointing down, the girlish waist, soft curve of her stomach, her body spare and compact. For Thea, seeing her mother naked was a shock, not because it was a female body other than her own, not because she hadn't seen her mother nude in years, and not because that aging body gave Thea a preview of what she would one day look like. The shock was in seeing how little room her mother actually took up, yet she still managed to be such a presence.

She flipped her nightgown over and over in her hands until she found the neck, then let it drift down over her head. Electricity from the nylon made her hair sizzle and look wild and strange. Normally, she would've known to push it back into place.

"When the doctor told me I had Alzhei—Al—that disease . . ." she said, her voice quavering, "I asked him how in the world I was going to tell Florence, and how I was going to tell my two daughters. Especially you, Thea. Especially you, darling." Her standard order of importance, no matter what the situation: her own sister, then Thea, then Mickey. She had never tried to hide it. The husband would fall in just after the second daughter.

Thea smoothed down her mother's hair and held out her robe. Obediently, she slid her arms into the sleeves. Thea buttoned the pearl buttons down the front and stuffed the lining of each pocket back where it belonged, inside.

. . .

Her mother's speech grew more and more uncertain. She became extremely forgetful and Scotch-taped notes everywhere, reminding herself to put out her cigarette, water the plants, turn off the burner on the stove.

Eight months after she'd been to Mayo, she had a fall. Thea had gone to Rock Hill for the day, and while they were out shopping, her mother tripped over one of those narrow concrete ridges that mark the end of a parking space. Her hip was broken—a bad break—and had to be operated on.

After the shock of the fall and surgery, her mental condition worsened drastically. With each day she became less and less of a person. She ended up going straight from the hospital in Rock Hill to a nursing home in Charlotte. By the time they moved her into her room at Roswell Towers, she no longer recognized anyone. She stared a blank stare and couldn't talk at all. The only sound she made was a low, animal-like moan full of wanting.

After all those years of alternating between breezy, restless chatter and flat silences, she was finally, truly, unable to speak. She went from not wanting to say certain things to not being able to say anything at all. She spent the last two years of her life in the nursing home.

Thea had a theory about hard times: When you begin complaining about what God has dealt you, He sends along something else, as if to say, "Oh, you think that's bad? I'll show you what bad is."

One month after they put her mother in the nursing home, her father was diagnosed with colon cancer and had surgery. Six months later, the malignancy was in his lungs, his bones, his brain.

During that time, he lived with Reid and Thea for several weeks, then with Mickey and Joel, moving back and forth between their houses. When a tumor popped up in a new place in his body, he called it "another hot spot." That was it. No complaining. It was as if he lowered his head, dug in his heels, and bore down. Whatever came next—the intense pain when he was standing or sitting, the exaggerated droop of his mouth, then the whole right side of his face, fistfuls of hair left on his pillow, loss of bladder control—he accepted as something he simply had to deal with, the same way he'd accepted a slow Christmas season in the store or a shipment of blouses arriving later than promised.

"If you're going to do business, you have to do it in today's market," he would say.

When he stayed with Reid and Thea, he was like the giant in a fairy tale, a silent figure casting a broad shadow through the rooms of their house. Some nights, he remained at the kitchen table after Reid went into the den to grade papers. He'd sit there, quiet, while Thea cleaned up after dinner. Once or twice, she heard a sudden intake of breath as if he were about to say something, something that might require a lot of words and energy. She knew time was running out and she wanted him to say that she mattered to him, as much as her sister mattered to him. And she wanted him to say yes, there was a secret in the family and he was going to be the one to tell her. She would dry her hands and move toward him to hear, but he'd shake his head, vaguely, as though he were answering no to what she'd been wanting for years.

. . .

One winter afternoon, when it was too cold and damp to take her mother outside in the wheelchair, Thea rolled her down the hall to the activities room, where there was an old upright piano. Thea sat at the piano and pulled her mother close enough for her knees to lightly touch the legs of the lyre-backed chair. Thea lifted the cover and began playing the bottom half of a duet she and Mickey had played in a recital years before. As her fingers arched above the keys—wrist low, fingers rounded, as her piano teacher had drilled into her—the entire piece came back to her and she found herself swaying and pumping the pedal, her whole body moving with the music, fast, then slow, the notes loud, then soft. It didn't matter that there was no top half; she didn't need her sister's part at all, even though she'd had the melody.

Thea glanced at her mother. In that instant, she had a look that would have to be called bright. She appeared surprised, pleasantly surprised. She raised her eyebrows, looked right at Thea, and smiled a big, natural smile, as if she were about to say, "Oh, I remember that piece!"

Thea couldn't believe she was responding.

Maybe she's coming back, Thea thought. Maybe the music is bringing her back.

Thea looked around the room. Red hymnals were stacked on an aluminum table in the corner. A darkened picture of somebody's uncomfortable ancestor was hanging too high on the wall. Plastic chairs were arranged in rows with gaps left for wheelchairs, like missing teeth.

They were all alone, nobody else there. This was her chance.

She'd reached the end of the piece so she started at the beginning again, and while her fingers moved over the keys, she put her face near her mother's and asked as clearly as she could, "What is it I don't know about you? Tell me. Tell me about your wedding. Tell me about you and Daddy. Tell me something. Anything. Whatever it is I don't know."

Her mother looked as if she were about to speak. Her back straightened and she tilted her chin in her daughter's direction. Her bowlike lips parted.

Thea held a chord.

But then her mother fastened her lips to one side and her face began closing up again. If this were years ago, she would've started humming. Instead, she was sliding back down in the chair, completely silent, her bones collapsing into one another.

"Wait," Thea said, hitting the keys harder, her thin fingers straining, "don't go, I'm sorry, I'll just play, I won't ask any more questions."

But her mother kept sliding until she was slumped over the arm of the wheelchair, on the other side, as far from Thea as she could get. She stared at the piano leg, her lower lip hanging loose. Thea played the final chord of the piece to see if she'd react. She let it go. No reaction.

Her mother did not respond in any way—to her or to anyone else—ever again.

. . .

While her father was staying in Charlotte, before his cancer got too bad, he spent every day at the nursing home, sitting in a chair pulled beside his wife's bed. He rubbed her arms, brushed her hair, held her hand. Sometimes he'd prudishly lift an edge of the sheet with the tips of his fingers to check her legs to make sure the aides were keeping them soft with lotion. He dabbed Vaseline on her lips. He bought her expensive nightgowns and bed jackets, made appointments for a "wash and set" every Friday in the beauty parlor down in the basement so "she'd look nice for the weekend," as if everything was as it had been and they were going to a movie at the Pix or taking a trip. He was doing what he'd been doing their whole married life: caring for his Mollie. But she just lay there, her jaw slack, eyes open but not seeing. Every now and then, she made that white sound.

One afternoon Thea sat in a vinyl chair in the corner of the room watching them. Her father was polishing her mother's fingernails a glassy pink. Her small hands were fidgety, but he held one, then the other, in his thick hand and carefully dabbed the tiny brush over each nail, taking time to wipe away stray polish on her skin with the side of his finger. "September Song" was playing on the radio he'd brought from home. Tears began to fall down Thea's cheeks. She tried to catch them with her sleeve, but they were coming too fast.

It had never occurred to her that her mother would one day actually die. For as long as she could remember, her mother had been swinging back and forth between living life more fully than anyone else—those sunny, frantic, up times—and coming as close to dying as she could without crossing over—the depresssions. Her real death was something Thea had never been able to imagine.

But she did die, and a month later Thea's father died. And because Mickey and Thea spent so much time during that period at the funeral home, it took years to erase from her mind the grim-faced man in the dark suit and starched white shirt, the "family representative," who, no matter what question she asked, answered, *We're only here to serve you.*

Chapter 4

Almost a week after the phone call with Mickey, the package she'd mentioned still hadn't come. But there, in the basket on the porch, was a book Thea had ordered, the usual pieces of mail, and a letter from Helen Feinman.

After the conversation with her sister, Thea had considered calling Helen and telling her not to bother with the translations. After all, it was what Mickey had told her to do. And Mickey had sounded so sure it was the best thing. In the end, though, Thea made a decision by not deciding. She could always tell Mickey she was *going* to call Helen, but before she could get around to it, the first letter arrived.

She pitched the new book on her night table—*How to Do*

Every Single Thing Right, Tips for People Who Want to Be Informed and Fully in Control of Their Lives—and stretched out on top of the comforter. It had been a long day. Errands all morning—Little Hardware to pick up the ingredients for her homemade rose fertilizer, grocery store, dry cleaners, baking a birthday cake for the morning news woman at the station—and doing the show that afternoon, along with a couple of promos.

On Memo from Helen Feinman paper, Helen had written: "The family saga is unfolding. I am becoming familiar with your grandmother Bella's writing style and her transitions to English. I asked an Eastern European friend of mine who is a swift reader of Yiddish to glance at some of the difficult to decipher words and she was of great help. Now, I can better vouch for the authenticity of the translation. I hope you don't mind that I have added a little punctuation here and there for your reading ease."

She ended her note with, "As publishers are heard to say . . . Watch for Chapter II, The Bella Bogen Story!"

Folded inside Helen's note was the original letter from Bella to her sister, written on faded blue stationery with a rendering of a hotel at the top of the page above these words: *Jefferson Hotel, Columbia, South Carolina. A Radio in Every Room.* Folded inside the original letter was Helen's translation.

The salutation made Thea's breath catch.

Dear devoted sister Celia leben—Yiddish for *life*, as in *you are my life*.

In her family, a sister was as important as—a self.

Thea's eyes danced over the translation, unable to focus. She nudged off her left shoe with the toe of her right foot, then caught the heel of the other shoe on the edge of the mattress and let it drop.

December 28, 1937

Dear devoted sister Celia leben:

I am letting you know that I with my family are, thank God, well. I hope to hear the same from you.

I find myself now in Columbia, writing this letter in the hotel. My dear Easy and I are here since Sunday. It is a lovely place and quite big. Our room is on the fifth floor. It is something to be so high up. Easy says we are closer to heaven! Tomorrow, Wednesday, we think to go home. We brought Mollkeleh (Mollie) here to shop for the wedding, to arrange. And everything will be fine, with goodness, hopefully.

I already have my dress, a pretty black dress with light colored lace trim, a long dress. Also a hat from thick straw that is worn here. Surely the same is worn where you are. In black with a fancy pin from J. E. Steadman's. It cost me almost four dollars but Easy says it looks so well on me it is worth the price. Also the good black kid gloves that you bought for me. I have become all dolled up. Sorry you cannot see to give your opinion. I wonder often what would you, my dear Celianke, think about this, what would you, my dear Celianke, think about that. I know that you would not hesitate to give your opinion.

Mollkeleh also has her entire outfit, complete with everything. Even the license from the courthouse. Lastly, purchased the wedding ring. Her beloved Mike came Sunday and was with her shopping Monday. Both purchased everything. They also bought the wedding ring. It needed to be made smaller. I have not as yet seen it.

Mollie is very pleased with all of the plans. She is thrilled with the wedding ring. With diamonds yet.

I hope that by tomorrow our trip will be finished and we will travel back to Denmark. I will have enough to attend to these few days. We have had to take care of much in a short time. Other families have longer to handle such things. But with us all is rushed. No need to speak of that now.

Await next week when I will write a long letter to you with everything detailed, everything you should want to know . . .

I must end because I am very, very tired, am going to bed to sleep. Easy is already sleeping good. He fell asleep with the radio on. He must be tired because he normally would listen very late to the music and the talking, which we find interesting.

Mollie is staying with her friends who live here but first she took a nice bath in our hotel room with much hot water. This was calming for her.

She says her heart tells her that Tante Celia will make a surprise trip and will come to her wedding, thus thinks Mollkeleh. I myself cannot think that my daughter will be marrying and my own sister will not be here to see such an event. There is no way for you to come south? There is still time for you to purchase a train ticket. I would only want to do the same for you. Such a shame for sisters not to share each other's naches, our joy.

I and my entire family send regards, very heartfelt. We will drink to everyone's health who will not come from the family to Mollie's wedding.

Your sister, Bella

Was it possible Thea was wrong and there wasn't any secret at all? The letter was charming, as Mickey had predicted it would be. Their grandmother sounded like a delightful person. Plus, everyone seemed excited about the wedding—all the shopping, the clothes, the ring. Of course, there was that one comment about having to rush to handle everything. But maybe her mother and father had been so in love they didn't want to wait. Or maybe it was the war. No, that was four years away. *No need to speak of that now.* Of course. There were always subjects the women in her family didn't want to talk about.

She'd told Aunt Florence she'd mail copies of the translations as she received them, but she wanted to ask her a few things, so she rolled over to Reid's side of the bed, pulled the phone to the pillow, and dialed the number she knew by heart.

"Hello?" Her aunt's voice had the same raspiness Thea's mother's voice had.

"Aunt Florence, it's me. I've got the first letter from your mother—it's been translated—and I'm dying for you to hear it."

"Well, I'm ready! I just walked in this minute from shopping. I have to tell you, I finally found shoes to go with that mauve cocktail dress I bought the last time I was in Charlotte. You know the dress, don't you? From Belk's? With the fitted sequin top. Well, the shoes are peau de soie and the exact same color as the dress. Perfect for the temple dance. I took back the other shoes I'd gotten. Did I tell you I had a date for services last Friday night?"

"A date?"

"This one is really after me. But when we were walking up the steps to the temple, he took my arm and he was so old and decrepit I couldn't tell who was holding on to who!" Florence used to be a homey, housedress type of person. Now, at eighty-eight, she was fashionable, fancy, interested in men.

"I guess that was the end of him!"

"I sure don't want that! But, about the letters, I was just this morning thinking about them. Go ahead. I want to hear."

Thea read the letter. When she reached the end, her aunt didn't say anything. Was she crying or was she just letting the words sink in? Had Mickey told her she didn't think the letters should be translated?

Finally, Thea broke the silence with a question. "Do you remember this period of time before Mother's wedding? The shopping and all? Why was everything so rushed?"

"Of course I remember all the excitement before her wedding." Florence sounded teary, maybe not teary exactly, but there was something in her voice. "You wouldn't believe the goings on. When *I* got married, they couldn't give me much of a wedding because Papa wasn't doing so good in the store. You know my wedding was after your mother's. Well, it wasn't that Papa wasn't doing so good in the store. The truth is, he took the profits from the store and got on a train to New York. I guess he was going on a buying trip. Anyway, he got in a poker game *on the train* and lost all his money. So, your uncle Jack and I had a small ceremony in Columbia, in Rabbi Kline's living room, and all we had was cake and coffee afterward. The only people there were Mama and Papa, Uncle Jack's parents, and of course, your mother and father."

"Aunt Florence, I hate hearing that. You must've felt so bad." Thea flipped the bottom corner of the comforter over her feet. "But what did your mother not want to talk about in the letter?"

"You know I'm not one to complain, but I've always said your uncle Jack and I never had the right start from the beginning. Not like your parents had. Because straight from the honeymoon we moved in with Mama and Papa. In that little wooden house in Denmark, South Carolina. You know Denmark, don't you? Down the road from Norway and Sweden. Those three little towns right together."

"Is there really a Norway and Sweden?"

"Oh yes, look at a map. They're there. Finland, too!

They're all really just crossroads. Denmark is the main town. Used to be called Graham's Turn Out."

"The town was called that?"

"Something to do with the railroad. Where the trains turned around, I think, going from Charleston to Augusta. The name was changed to Denmark, after some man whose last name was Denmark, who came down with the railroad. Three trains intersected there, the Atlantic Coastline, the Seaboard, and Southern Railway."

"I never knew all that. But what about the subject my grandmother didn't want to talk about?"

"Your mother was never interested in history, that's why you don't know these facts about Denmark. Anyway, let me get back to your uncle Jack and what a hard time he was having making it on his salary at the jewelry store. I used to say that, with us, the romance ended overnight. Mama and I would sit on one side of the room and talk about the cost of eggs, and Papa and your uncle Jack would sit on the other side of the room talking about the cost of running a business. It just wasn't the way newlyweds should begin a life together. But your mother. Now, that was a different story. Oh, was it a different story! When Mollie married Mike, there was such a big fuss made. Mama and Papa went all out. The clothes! The shopping! The wedding gown! The flowers! The food! You wouldn't believe it. And Mike rented rooms in somebody's house, like a little apartment, I mean, for them to live in in Newberry. I remember their kitchen. It had everything. And everything matched. Blue and gray. Including the curtains Mama made for them."

Oh, what a familiar tune this was, how her sister always got more than she did. While Thea's mother was alive, Thea never heard a word about any rivalry between them. Had her mother resented Florence? Thea had no idea. All she'd ever heard from her mother was how close they were. But after her mother died, her aunt would slip in one story after another, each based on the same theme: jealousy.

"You know, Thea, your mother loved pretty things, luxurious things. She used to give Mama *silk stockings* for a present. I'd always give practical things. Your mother knew good and well Mama wouldn't wear silk stockings but she gave them to her anyway. And sure enough, your mother would end up with them."

And here was the refrain: Thea's mother's selfishness.

"Did I ever tell you about when your mother and I were still living at home in Denmark but we were grown and both working? When Mama made me take your mother shopping? Maybe I was making a *little* more than your mother. But not that much more. All I was making was ten dollars a week. They thought that was a lot of money, so I had to buy your mother clothes."

"Oh, Aunt Florence."

"Now what am I telling you all this for, talking and talking like a *meshuggeneh*! Let's hang up. It's already six o'clock and Evelyn is picking me up in five minutes to get a bite for supper. Just between you and me, I worry about her. Why wouldn't my daughter find a man? You tell me. Gorgeous figure. Smart. I'll tell you why. She works all the time. What kind of job is that for a girl? Stockbroker! She's had at least five or six proposals though. I could name the names. Oh, here she is, ringing my bell. Bye, dear. We'll talk more later."

After Thea's parents had died, she and Mickey were clearing the last things from the house before turning it over to the realtor. When they got to their mother's closet, they called Florence to ask if she would like any of the clothes.

Florence wanted only the shoes, even though Mollie had worn a six and a half and she wore a seven. Thea never forgot the picture: Her aunt, sitting on the bench in front of the dressing table, squeezing her feet into black patent leather pumps as shiny as oil, red sandals, white sandals, pale silk sling-backs—all a half-size too small—determined to wear them at last.

. . .

"So, thanks for calling, Ralph. I wish you and your brother-in-law good luck in your new restaurant. It *is* possible for family members to work together. Just keep your expectations of each other—and of what you can accomplish in the business—reasonable. And let me hear how it's going."

Friday. Last show of the week.

"Hello, Marsha. Welcome to the program."

"Am I on the air?"

"Sure. Go ahead."

"Well, I just had a baby. Six months ago. And I've decided to go back to college." The caller's voice was husky. She was probably a smoker. "My sister doesn't have any children and she told me she would be glad to take care of my baby a few hours a day while I'm in class. It's really nice of her to say she'll do this. My mother's always wanted my sister and me to be close. She loves it when we help each other out. The problem is my sister has a rottweiler. The dog is very hyper and aggressive and sometimes he gets a little weird around the baby. I keep an eye on him when we're at her house, but God only knows what happens when I'm not there. My sister would never be as careful as me because she doesn't believe her dog would do anything. She thinks I'm just being nervous and overprotective. What do you think?"

"It sounds as though you have realistic concerns about the welfare of your child. Does she have a fenced-in area she could put the dog in while your baby is at her house?"

"God, no, she would never pen him in. She treats him like a child. The only time that dog goes outside is when she takes him herself."

This was easy. Very easy. "Is it possible for you to make other arrangements? We've all heard stories of large dogs attacking children. Can you thank your sister for her offer, but explain that her dog *does* make you nervous? In other words, can you go ahead and take responsibility for your protective feelings?"

"But what'll I tell my mother? I know she'll be upset if I turn down my sister's offer. She's always telling us sisters should get along."

"You don't have to make your sister wrong. It's just that she trusts her dog more than you do." Thea swiveled her chair away from the soundproof window separating her control room from the next, where Tim, the news director, looked as if he was getting ready to cue her. "Mothers usually do want their daughters to be close. *I* grew up with a mother who not only talked about how close she was with her sister but how close *her* mother was with *her* sister."

"Oh God, yes. My mother and her three sisters are super-close."

"It's pretty common in families, the myth that sisters should be as tight as braided strands of hair. The reality is that sisters are often resentful of each other, jealous of each other's beauty, brains, goodness, or strength. Rivalries and tension can co-exist for sisters like matching dresses, twin beds, or differing versions of the same memory. Think about it. Parents bring home a newborn baby and tell the older child they'll still love her as much as they always have; it's just that there'll be two children now, instead of one. It feels the same to that child as it would to a wife if her husband brought home another woman and insisted he would still love the first wife just as much, only now there'd be two women to share his love."

"That's so true! I never thought of it that way," the caller said.

"Bound to be trouble, right? But what's passed down from generation to generation is the fabrication that in this family things are different. Mothers are probably saying all over the world this very minute, in this family sisters help each other, they love and cherish each other." Thea caught a glimpse of Tim gesturing wildly. "Maybe our mothers want their daughters to achieve what they were unable to achieve themselves. So, sisters become hopelessly entangled with each other. And we spend our entire lives trying to figure out a way to break free. If we ever do manage to separate from that mirror image called sister, we can then decide for ourselves, on our own, that we love our sisters after all. At that point, we can fashion our own version of sisterhood."

"Well, uh, thanks for all that." The caller sounded worn out. "I'll think about what you said. I'll just hang up now."

"Thank you, Marsha, for calling. You raised an interesting question. And thank all of you for listening. We're out of time now but we'll be back at the same time Monday, on this station . . ."

. . .

Tim stuck his head in her control room and motioned with his thumb toward the door. "I'm outta here. Going to Georgia for the weekend."

"Where in Georgia are you going?"

"That Bavarian-themed tourist town. Catch you later." He'd actually used a multisyllable word! But who would want to go to a Bavarian-themed tourist town in Georgia? He was so jumpy—so *not* a talker—she knew nothing about him.

"You're going where?"

"Helen. Helen, Georgia. That's where I'm going. By the way, you got a little carried away with that last caller, don't you think? Let's try to stay focused and keep the program moving. Seemed like you just went off on something. We could've gotten in another caller."

"Maybe, but—"

He was already down the hall. She gathered her papers and tried to catch up with him.

"Just remember," she called after him, "sometimes I have to bring in different things to get a point across." The back of his head was flat; his mother must've left him lying on his back in the crib too long. He scuttled ahead, stopping in the station manager's office and pulling the door shut behind him. When she shook her head at the closed door, she realized she was getting one of her headaches. It hurt to move her head. She dropped her papers at the front desk and didn't say good-bye to the receptionist, who was busy filing her fingernails anyway.

Thea opened the private back door to the parking lot. The air was nippy and felt good on her face, but her body was cold. She blew on her hands and rubbed them together, then rolled down the sleeves of her cotton shirt. She wished she'd worn a blazer. A man in a sportcoat and a woman wearing a sweater were coming out of the building next door. How had they known it would be this cool? She wished the people who gave the weather wouldn't just tell what the temperature was going to be, but would say, *It'll be fifty degrees, you need a turtleneck and a sweater—or, sixty-three degrees, wear a long-sleeved blouse or cotton top but not necessarily a sweater.* Or did sixty-three degrees mean a sweater? She could never translate temperature numbers into clothes.

She walked toward her car, head down, wishing she could do everything in life twice. She didn't know why she always did things wrong the first time. The second time, that's when she finally caught on. She was constantly having to revise what she'd said or done. Why hadn't she told the appliance man the dryer still wasn't working right? Why had she told him what a great job he'd done? Why did she always end up planting flowers and bushes in the wrong place the first time around? The sun-loving peony she'd set in the shade, the tiny violas hidden behind the tall, stalky clump of Siberian irises. Everything ought to be on wheels.

Why *had* she gone on and on with that last caller?

Tim's dented van was beside her Honda. She started the engine and backed out of the parking space. Quickly, she turned right, out of the lot, shooting into the closest lane of traffic. She should've waited for the next driver to go by. A teenaged boy in one of those sleek, white, chromeless cars that looks like a ski boot was suddenly on her bumper. He was leaning hard on his horn. When she looked in the rear-view mirror, he gave her the finger, not just once, but over and over, thrusting his hand toward her again and again, as though he could imprint the gesture on the back of her neck. She flipped her mirror up.

The car radio blared. "Golden oldies from the eighties," the D.J. said. Oldies from the *eighties*? A song came on, one of those relentless songs that keeps pushing. She switched it off. Her head was killing her, the whole right side of her face—around the orbit of her eye, up and down her jaw, to her ear.

Back to the woman who'd called about the dog. Back to what Thea had told her, how sisters have to break free and decide for themselves, without their mother's influence, that they love each other—or don't. How sometimes they can't begin to do this until after their parents are gone.

That cold, bare-boned afternoon in the Hebrew Cemetery, in a run-down, industrial area on the outskirts of Charlotte, when she and Mickey buried their father, a month after they'd buried their mother—they'd stood there, the heels of their shoes sinking into the soggy earth, the torn black ribbons of mourning pinned to their coats. As the rabbi chanted the Mourner's Kaddish, Thea and Mickey had moved closer to each other. Their shoulders touched and they reached for the other's hand as they watched the first shovels of dirt land on their father's casket, the sound like heavy, heavy rain. Inches away was their mother's grave, where new grass was already beginning to grow.

. . .

Thea turned into her driveway and saw a package propped against the screened door. She hoped it was from her sister.

"Hello!" Herm Proctor, from next door, called out. He was on his knees weeding the bed that separated their houses, unraveling crabgrass from the ivy. His face was as red as a tomato—from straining, not from sun, because there was none that day. Herm was the type of person who stood too close to you when he talked. Thea was always taking a step back, trying to create a space between them.

"Hi there! Looking good!" she called as she got out of the car and followed the stepping-stones to the front door.

"When you have a minute, I want to show you something," he said, pushing himself up. He was probably close to her age but, because he was heavy, he seemed older. "Ever see jack-in-the-pulpit? Not necessarily a church pulpit, of course! How 'bout a synagogue pulpit?"

"I wish I had time, Herm. I'm in a big hurry. Maybe tomorrow when I get home from the station." Why did some non-Jewish people insist on letting her know that *they* knew she was Jewish, when all she really wanted was to blend in and be like everyone else?

"You got a date," she heard him say.

She dropped her pocketbook on the ottoman on the porch and picked up the package with Mickey's return address. It was heavy. She caught an edge of the packing tape and ripped it off as she sat in the rocker. When she opened the box, packing popcorn went everywhere. She dumped the rest on the floor around her feet. The gift inside was wrapped in paper covered with purple irises. There was a note tucked under the ribbon: *Happy, happy birthday! No matter what, I'll always be here for you, Mickey.* Even though her birthday was several weeks away, she put the note in her pocket and unwrapped the gift.

It was a collage Mickey had made. On a background of yellow and white gingham, she'd glued an old-timey picture she must've clipped from a magazine of two ragtag little girls in the early part of the century posing on an ornate wicker love seat, each with an arm draped around the other's shoulder. Beneath the picture was an old photograph of Mickey and Thea in the same pose. It had been taken when they were young, for Mother's Day. Their father had had the photographer come to the house. They were in the white wooden swing in the backyard. Mickey's muscular little legs were crossed, left ankle resting on her right knee, the way her father always sat, and she was pressing forward, determined, sure of herself, her free hand gripping her left knee. Her hair was thick, dark, and straight, and hung in her eyes. She was grinning her preorthodontia grin, with that space between her two front teeth. Thea was pale and thin and looked solemn next to her. Thea's hair was light, fine, parted on one side, combed tight into the teeth of a plastic barrette. Her free hand was hidden in the pleats of her skirt.

Mickey had outlined the photograph of the two of them in silver foil twisted into a shiny braid. Woven through the whole collage were flowers she'd cut from fabric and lace. There was a real butterfly, orange and papery, in the corner.

Thea would call her and tell her how much she loved the collage, how much she loved *her*. After she got it up on the wall. All of a sudden, she realized her headache was gone. She raised her eyebrows, wrinkled her forehead, felt her cheek. No pain.

She went to the drawer in the desk in the kitchen, the one Reid was always neatening and she was always stuffing. She rummaged through the appliance warranties, takeout menus, magnifying glass, wooden rulers to find the hammer and pack of picture hooks.

In the bedroom she stood on the padded bench of her mother's old dressing table and hammered in a hook above the mirror. Carefully, she hung the collage. When she stepped down, she backed all the way to the bed to see if it was centered. Humming, she got back up on the bench and shifted the frame over about a quarter of an inch. Reid was usually the one to hang pictures, but she didn't want to wait for him to get home. She was humming the song she and Mickey used to sing in cracked voices on car trips—"Side by Side"—back when they thought they sounded like singers on the radio.

Now the collage was centered over the mirror, but it was hanging crooked. It looked like everyone was leaning on everyone else. She tipped the left side up. Now. Both pairs of girls were upright. Two generations in a family, two sets of young sisters caught by the camera—a mother and her sister, the mother's two daughters. Each pair had stopped their play long enough to pose for the camera, waiting that one split second for something to happen.

. . .

Most nights before going to sleep, Thea and Reid read in bed. Two weeks after Mickey sent the collage, Thea was holding her book in one hand—a psychological novel written by a woman therapist whose research she knew—and twisting and untwisting her nightgown strap with the other. She followed the strap down to the white cotton lace that lined the top of the gown, smoothing the fabric over her breast, stopping at what felt like a doubled-over place in the gown. She slid her hand underneath. It was not a doubled-over place in the fabric.

She laid the book facedown on her stomach, careful to keep her place, and moved her hand over the spot, pressing in one direction, then another, with her fingertips. It was a lump and it was the size of a marble.

"Reid, feel this," she said, taking his hand and guiding it to her breast. She pushed his fingers into her flesh, like someone trying to make a seashell disappear back down into the sand. When she let go, he raised his hand and passed it over her breast, barely touching her skin, once, twice, almost timidly—this fact-finding mission in no way related to an act of intimacy.

"If this huge thing is malignant, I'm a goner," she said, trying to be the type of person who reacts to frightening things with humor, though she knew that he knew she reacted to frightening things with fright.

"How long have you known about this? For a while?" He sounded like something was stuck in his throat. "Did you just find it?" He cleared his throat, making a sound like a motor that wasn't catching.

"While I was lying here."

"You mean this minute?"

"For some reason, my hand went to that spot."

"You need to make an appointment. It's probably fine, but still—"

"It could just be a gland or something." She picked up her book. It was quivering. She laid it back down again. "Maybe I should wait and see if it'll go away by itself."

"No, I don't think you should." He turned toward her, grinding his shoulder into the mattress.

"Maybe it's tied in with hormones or . . ." She let her voice trail off, pulled the top of her gown to the side, and looked at her breast. In the lamp's small circle of light, her flesh appeared translucent, like a peeled pear.

"No, I think you should go as soon as you can. You don't wait with something like this." He was staring hard into her face, keeping his focus from her neck up.

"Okay. I'll call sometime this week."

"Call tomorrow. First thing tomorrow."

She sighed and ran her fingers over the spot again. There was a milky taste in her mouth. Her tongue and teeth felt coated.

He dropped their books on the night table and slid down, letting the pillow bunch under his neck. Gently, he pulled her to him. "I hate this for you," he said. "I wish I could take it away." He touched her forearm lightly, as though her whole body might give off danger signals.

"But it could be nothing. Don't go being an alarmist. Let's think positive." That whole speech of hers was so phony.

They rolled away from each other and switched off their lamps. Then they settled in, Thea flipping her pillow to the cool underside, both of them lying on their sides, facing out, like backward parentheses. When her eyes got used to the dark, she saw the shimmer of the silver oval in the collage on the wall across the room. Reid reached behind to pull her close, and they soon fell asleep with their backs touching. During the night, his fingers would move to her leg or arm. Her fingers moved to the lump.

The next morning she slept late, until eight-thirty. He'd already left for his eight o'clock class. She hitched herself over to his side of the bed, opened the drawer, and looked up the number in the phone book.

An answering machine. "This is Carolina Women's Breast Clinic. We open at nine o'clock. For appointments, please call back then. If this is an emergency . . ."

Insistently, Thea kept dialing, getting the answering machine over and over, eventually memorizing the number, until the receptionist finally answered.

"We can work you in tomorrow at ten-thirty," she said cheerily.

"I'll be there." Thea matched her cheeriness.

. . .

At the clinic, Thea tried to hold her paper bolero in place as the technician shuttled her from room to room, from mammogram to ultrasound. First, it felt as if her breasts were being pressed with an ice-cold iron, then scanned with a device that made her think of those old men who strolled the beach at Wrightsville, where she and Reid rented a cottage every summer, the way those men nosed their metal detectors over the sand. Finally, the technician told her to get dressed. The radiologist wanted to talk to her.

She stood outside his office, waiting for him to turn around and notice her. She toyed with her belt buckle, nervously sliding it left, then right, as though getting it centered mattered. He was slapping X-rays in the light boxes that lined the wall and frowning into their wintry landscapes. When all the X-rays were in place, he turned and motioned her in with one hand, tapping a picture with the ballpoint pen in his other hand. When she got closer, she could see that he was tapping a clotlike spot.

"It seems we have a suspicious mass in the left breast, located at one o'clock. You can see it here," he said, his pen now circling the air over the X-ray. "I think we're going to have to take it out in order to find out what we're dealing with." Not a trace of emotion in his voice. She was so stunned by what he was saying, in that plain monotone, that her thoughts clicked back to a gynecologist who'd told her she should do a monthly check of her own breasts, adding, in the same plain, monotone voice, she was lucky there wasn't much there to check.

. . .

At home there was a message from Mickey on the machine. They hadn't talked since the conversation about the letters. "Hi, it's me and it's eleven o'clock Tuesday. Call back when you get in. I've got something to tell you." Maybe she'd heard Thea had gone ahead with the letters. Maybe Florence told her.

"Mickey, hi. What's up?" Just begin as though everything were normal.

"Thea, I'm so glad you called back. I've got something to tell you."

"What?"

"I have to have a breast biopsy. I went to the doctor yesterday and at first I thought I wouldn't tell you until after the biopsy because I didn't want you to worry, but then I decided it was better to let you know what's going on."

Thea suddenly felt heavy, tired. Her clothes even felt heavy although all she had on was a long-sleeved T-shirt and jeans. The shirt felt as weighty on her breasts as a lead X-ray apron. "*You* have a tumor, Mickey?"

"Not exactly a tumor. More like sprinkles. Calcifications, they call them. It's not something you can feel."

"Thank goodness you called to tell me. You're not going to believe this — I'm not sure *I* believe it — but I just this minute walked in from the radiologist's office and I have a *lump* in *my* breast!" Take a breath. "How did you know . . . how did you know you had . . . something?"

"I can't believe it! What are the chances, Thea, of this happening to both of us at the same time? Well, here's what happened: I went in for my regular mammogram two weeks ago — it'd been a year — and they called me back to have another mammogram. Then they sent me to ultrasound. I had no idea anything was wrong. I was shocked. Yours is a lump? Did the doctor find it? This is so bizarre . . ."

"*So* bizarre! I just had my mammogram and ultrasound this morning. My biopsy is day after tomorrow."

"So the doctor found it?"

"No, I happened to touch there. I was reading in bed and

my hand went to it." Thea slipped her fingers inside her shirt, inside her bra. Still there.

"Your biopsy is so soon. I wish mine was. I have to wait till the end of next week. At least you'll know right away if it's benign."

"What if it's not? What if it turns out to be something . . . serious?" Mickey had probably already looked into all the possibilities and knew exactly what she would do.

"Well, you realize there are a lot of different ways to treat breast cancer . . ." Mickey's voice suddenly turned formal. It was the same voice she'd used years ago when Thea had asked her about sanitary napkins after seeing a Modess ad in a magazine. *Modess . . . because,* it said. At first, Thea had thought the sentence would continue on the next page. When it didn't, she said out loud, "Modess . . . because. Because why?" Mickey would know; she knew everything. But she took on a stiff, professorial tone: "Thea, when a girl becomes a woman—" Before she could finish, Thea was on the floor laughing. She thought Mickey was doing one of her imitations. But it wasn't a joke and Mickey got so angry she told Thea never to ask her anything again; that was it for those dumb questions of hers.

". . . a lot of different things you can do," Mickey was saying. She could be as formal as she wanted this time. "Some doctors believe you should just remove the lump and treat the breast with radiation. And some doctors think it's a risk not to take the whole breast. I believe it depends on the situation."

"Probably so."

"And then there's the question of chemotherapy. And reconstruction. There are a million decisions. All of a sudden, your whole life is about this. When I was in the doctor's office, I asked for more information — they tell you so little! — and they gave me a bunch of pamphlets. I called all the numbers and that's how I got this information. I'll go to the post office right now and mail you everything. Don't worry, I'll make sure you know exactly what I know. In fact, why don't you call your doctor and get all the details, then call me back and let me try to find out what I can for you. I don't mind. Oh, and I also went by the health food store and talked to this woman there about vitamins, and I bought some books and here's what I learned . . ."

Thea felt herself wanting to rely on her sister, to let her take over, just like when she'd beat up Bullet Jackson. Thea wanted Mickey to do whatever she had to do to make everything okay. For both of them, this time.

. . .

Thea had her lump removed. And waited.

The pathology report came back normal. No malignancy. She received her report the day her sister went in for her biopsy.

Mickey's was malignant.

Five days after she received her report, she was in the hospital having a mastectomy.

The doctor said the prognosis was good. Malignancy contained. No lymph node involvement.

Recuperation smooth. Thea took care of her after she was home until she was feeling better. Fast recovery.

Still. It was cancer.

. . .

Thea had a theory about how each daughter in a family occupies a place according to the trait she's known for. So-

and-so is the pretty one. So-and-so, the smart one. So-and-so, the sweet one. When a slot is filled, the next child to come along has to be something different.

In this family, Mickey was the brave one. And Thea was the sensitive one. When they were young, Mickey hated that Thea was so afraid of everything. In sports, it didn't matter what kind of ball it was—softball, kickball, basketball—she flinched and covered her face instead of trying to catch it. One day Mickey said she was going to teach Thea how to stop being afraid. Mickey and Bullet tied her to the oak tree in the front yard and threw every ball they could find at her. Thea screamed and flailed about, but the jump rope stayed tight across her chest.

. . .

She knew from her journals how people who narrowly escape feel guilty, undeserving of their good luck. She, who had always been afraid, was safe. Mickey, the one who was so strong it seemed nothing could harm her, was in danger. What had Thea done to deserve this?

Chapter 5

Every other week, late in the afternoon after leaving the radio station, Thea went to a massage therapist. She started going right after Mickey had her mastectomy. It helped Thea relax. It even seemed to help her headaches. Most of the time she could just lie there and make her thoughts disappear.

Today she had a four o'clock appointment. She parked on the side street, beside the 1950s-contemporary, U-shaped office building with its concrete geometric trimming. As she walked through the building, alongside the atrium open to the sky, she noticed for the first time a "waterfall" made of stacked slate. It bubbled over in choppy little spurts. Bamboo made flickering, fingerlike shadows on the wall as the breeze lifted its leaves. She remembered reading how the Japanese liked to plant bamboo next to a wall so they could see the wind as well as feel it.

She opened the door to the therapist's office. The front room was empty.

"Come on in," Coral called from the massage room. "I'm back here."

When Thea had come the first time, Coral told her that most clients liked to disrobe, but if she wanted to keep her underwear on, that'd be okay, too. What a wonderful word "disrobe" was, Thea had thought. So respectful.

"Just let me know when you're ready," Coral was saying. She closed the door, leaving Thea alone.

Through the window overlooking the street, she could see daffodils with their blunt noses sniffing the air. It had been a mild winter and there were signs of spring everywhere. Bradford pear trees were breaking out in white at every apartment complex in town. Pansies were gearing up for their big show. She could hear a lawn mower in the distance.

She twisted the rod to close the mini-blinds and took off her clothes—disrobed—and laid them across the cane-bottomed chair. Her long skirt with the tiny beige and white geometric print, her beige V-neck cotton sweater, white tights. Tan loafers under the chair. Bra and panties stuffed under the sweater. How odd to stand there naked. Posters showing the skeletal structure and the muscular structure of the body hung side by side on the wall. Two teddy bears huddled together on a big square floor pillow in the corner. The fern on the table under the window needed water; its dead fronds had fallen all over *Warm, Special Thoughts*, one of those books you see next to the cash register in the type of store that sells scented soaps and candles. In the center of the room an angel mobile hung over the massage table. She climbed up and covered herself with the sheet and handmade patchwork quilt.

"Okay," she called. "I'm ready."

"You want music, right?" Coral asked, opening the door and gliding into the room. She was lean and long-legged and wore ballet slippers, which made it look like she was pointing her toes with every step, like a dancer.

"That'd be great," Thea answered, closing her eyes.

The first visit Coral had asked if Thea wanted music. When she'd said yes, Coral turned on the tape, then proceeded to talk over it. She told about how she liked to set up her massage table in the family room at home and put a movie in the VCR and work on her husband for two straight hours while she watched a movie, how she originally was going to be a cosmetologist which is what her mother had wanted her to be but she decided to go into massage therapy instead, how she and her husband knew from the day they got married they didn't want children. Then she started asking Thea questions.

"Do *you* have any children?"

"No," Thea had said.

"Do you have any pets? Like a dog or a cat?"

"No."

"Well then"—she sounded like she was getting desperate—"do you have allergies?"

"What do you mean, do I have allergies?"

"I mean if you don't have a dog or a cat, you must have allergies."

When Thea came for her second visit, she got up the

courage to say that she'd just as soon listen to the music quietly. Without talking is the part she wanted to add, but didn't.

Today—her third time—the music was especially soothing, soft bells and a harp, like how the waterfall out front was supposed to sound. The massage oil had a lavender scent, and Coral—silent, at last—was rubbing her back with long, deep, wonderful strokes.

Maybe she'd let herself fall asleep. She'd been sleeping a lot lately anyway. Sleep was an old family remedy she was very familiar with. When she and her sister were growing up, they'd come home from school and the house would be so quiet it felt as though it were holding its breath. No bottles of Coke waiting for them on the kitchen table. No vanilla wafers on a little plate. Dishes from breakfast would still be stacked beside the sink. Mickey would make a face toward their mother's room, shrug, and go outside to play with Bullet. Thea would open the door to find their mother under a pile of blankets, her face buried in the pillow, venetian blinds drawn tight, the room so dim Thea could barely make out her outline under the covers. "Mother?" she'd whisper. But her mother wouldn't answer. Thea pretended that her mother was just tired. She'll feel better when she catches up on her sleep, Thea would say to herself. She'd sit on the floor outside her mother's room, just in case she needed her.

"Are you snoozing?" Coral whispered. "Time to turn over."

Thea stretched her arms and rolled over on her back. Coral began massaging her scalp. She let her head go loose in those strong, capable hands. And pictured her mother. Her extremes. The way she'd slip from minimal to excessive. Dark to bright is the way it had appeared to Thea as a child. At times her mother could be as invisible as a ghost; at times she seemed to be everywhere. She could be asleep in her room in the middle of the afternoon. Or she could be in the kitchen baking one elaborate gingerbread house after another, determined to create one perfect enough to suit her, candy-studded houses popping up all over the counters like a sprawling suburb. She could disappear into the quiet hum of heat coming on in the house, or she could be out shopping all day, day after day, searching for a certain wide-brimmed hat with cherries or a particular dress with a piqué collar. If she found the hat or dress she wanted, she'd buy two just alike, sometimes three.

There was even a famous story in the family about her shopping. Thea smiled when she thought of it. Coral must've seen her expression change because she stopped smoothing out Thea's forehead and reached under her to knead her shoulders, her generous palms digging deeper and deeper.

Thea's mother had been having a hard time deciding whether she liked a certain white straw pocketbook enough to buy it, so she told the saleslady to loop the straps over her wrist and hold it while she left the store. When she came back in and saw the purse as though she were seeing it for the first time, the saleslady was supposed to read the expression on Thea's mother's face and report to her whether her expression showed that she liked it. She walked out of the store, then sashayed back in, acting as though she'd just happened along. She must've looked as pretty and blasé as a movie star in a career role. When her eyes fixed on the pocketbook, though, her excitement hit one hundred and she grabbed the poor, bewildered saleslady, practically knocking her over, exclaiming, "It's gorgeous! What an absolutely *perfect* bag! I *have* to have it!"

When her spirits were high, they could always foresee the inevitable fall. All of a sudden, she would begin speaking softly, instead of in her usual, animated voice. Thea's father, hard of hearing in his left ear, would try to jolly her into talking louder.

"A what?" he'd tease. "A who? Speak up, Mollie, I can't hear you!" But teasing didn't help.

If Thea had to choose between the extremes of her mother's behavior, of course she'd pick the up periods. In the middle of all that intensity, there'd be laughter and fun. That's when her mother would get excited over every little thing happening in her older daughter's life, and all her sentences would end with exclamation points. That's when she and Thea would spend the afternoon shopping, without Mickey, who'd be off somewhere playing tennis. Sometimes, during the up periods, she would take both girls to Good Drugs on Main Street for ice cream—even after five o'clock, the normal cutoff time for snacks.

Coral's stomach growled a little. She was pressing into Thea's shoulders. Every probe seemed to draw another memory—

Thea and Mickey, eight and seven, sitting with their mother on the dark, wooden stools at the soda fountain, the girl behind the counter making a cherry smash for a customer at the far end, pressing down on the lever with her whole body, squishing carbonated water into the pointed paper cup in the metal holder. Mickey and her mother would finish their ice cream quickly. Thea was a slow eater—she was known in her family for eating green peas one at a time—and that day she was doing everything she could to make the ice cream, and the afternoon, last. The only time she licked was to catch a slow rivulet melting down the cone to her hand. Her mother was becoming impatient. Sometimes it was hard for her to sit in one place for too long. She had that expression on her face, her scarlet lips tight, the half-wrinkle above her eyebrow deepening. She took the ice cream from her daughter's hand and laid it on the counter.

"I'm so, so sorry, darling," she said. "You're going to have to leave the rest. I didn't have enough money, so I only paid for two and a half cones. Yours was the half."

Thea watched the ice cream pool on the marbled surface and wished she'd brought her Indian-beaded wallet so she could chip in the extra coins for the other half. Mickey hopped off the stool, grabbed her mother's hand, and tried to pull her along. Their mother shook Mickey's grip loose and waited for Thea.

Years later, her mother would remember that lie and apologize. Thea forgave her though, for everything, over and over.

The up moods would build slowly, but the low ones came on abruptly, as though her mother had suddenly wound down, like a clock that needed repair. She could be at the kitchen table peeling carrots, the garbage can at her knee, and in a split second, she was motionless, the peeler in one hand, a carrot half-scraped in the other. She'd sit, her determined shoulders pressed forward, staring out the window as though she were tracking the sun as it crept across the sky.

She could be in the backyard, in her Bermuda shorts and sleeveless blouse, arms and legs suntanned and sleek. She'd be waving the garden hose over her roses like a wand, turning the water into an arc that kept crossing itself. Then she'd block half the spray with her finger to make it reach the privet hedge in the back. The next instant, she was just standing there, the hose coiled on the ground beside her feet, the nozzle jerking around as if it were having a fit.

The music on Coral's tape player stopped. Silence. The memories stopped. Then the music began again. New Age music, not really music, more like sounds. Gentle sounds. With quiet, clicking rhythms in the background. Like the sound of marbles clicking, Chinese checkers, the game she and Mickey were playing lying across the rug in their parents' room that Saturday night. Their mother was sitting at the dressing table wearing a slip, her brown hair pinned up in back with a tortoise-shell comb. She took a sip from her Coke and ground out her cigarette in the little brass ring in the ashtray, her gadget for keeping foul smoke from escaping into the room. Then she began smoothing delicious-smelling cream on her face and neck. Thea's father stooped behind her to look over her shoulder in the mirror as he looped the tail of his necktie over his fingers. He stood back up and tightened the knot.

It had been one of those smooth evenings—her parents getting ready to go out, she and Mickey concentrating on the game. But then there were whispers between her parents, harsh whispers, imploring whispers—whose were the harsh ones, whose imploring? Suddenly, from out of nowhere, their father's reverberating voice: "Girls, you're going to have to leave the room."

"But—what—?" they asked, fumbling with the playing board and box, marbles rolling everywhere, their father edging them out of the room.

"Go downstairs. Both of you. Now. And don't start asking questions, Thea. Just go with Mickey," he said.

His body blocked Thea's view of her mother and she

couldn't see what had happened or what she was doing. As he pushed them out, Thea was sliding stiff-legged across the floor on her heels, digging them in, her head turned almost all the way around, like her doll, whose head Mickey had taken off and snapped in backward. Her mother was completely hidden.

How many times had this happened—the afternoon or evening abruptly interrupted, their mother not able, for unknown reasons, to follow through with plans. Mickey could shrug it off as just more proof of their mother's changeableness, instability. Thea never got used to it; she felt worry in every part of her body.

And then, the usual ending—their father downstairs, still dressed to go out, sitting on the brown leather sofa in the den, reading his newspaper under the lamp with the nappy linen shade, the expression on his face as dark as the headlines. Their mother in the bedroom, the door shut.

. . .

"That's it," Coral whispered, softly patting Thea's foot. "Take as long as you like before you get up." She closed the door behind her.

For a second, Thea wondered if she'd been asleep, dreaming. But no, she'd spent the entire hour in that state somewhere between waking and dreaming, drifting in the past. She lay there, on the table, trying to come back to the present.

. . .

That night, after dinner, she and Reid were in the den watching television. She was on the love seat, her legs stretched across the pine trunk they used as a coffee table; he was in the wing chair turned toward the TV.

"Reid," she said, "I got really hooked thinking about Mother today. She was so real she could've been standing there, right beside the massage table."

He didn't seem at all surprised at what she'd said. "It happens with me, too. Seeing my mother. Never my father. Maybe it's something about mothers."

"Maybe with you it's because your mother died when you were so young."

He draped himself over the arm of his chair in her direction. "You know, I just had a thought: If your mother came back, say, for an hour or so, which would you want to do—ask her things or tell her things? I guess I have a pretty good idea what your answer would be."

"I'd ask. How about you?"

He spun the glass paperweight on the glass-topped side-table. The sound was like chewing picnic food coated with sand. Then he put the paperweight down and started cracking his knuckles, one hand, then the other. "I'd want to tell her things. So she'd finally know what my life is about. I'd try to get in everything that's happened since she died—" Crack. "—about you and about my teaching, about our house—" Crack. "—about not being able to have children."

"What *I'd* do is get all the big questions answered first, and then ask the other things."

"What other things?"

"Well, for instance, I'd want to know more about the clinic in Massachusetts."

"Now when *was* that?" His eyebrows were so bushy that when he raised them, they made a straight line across his face, like a hedge.

"Right after Mickey and I went to camp, that Jewish camp Daddy sent us to, the one I left because I was so homesick. I guess I was twelve, I'm not positive." She leaned across her outstretched legs to poke a finger in the pitcher of pansies on the trunk. Almost dry. She'd take them in the kitchen later and add water.

"How'd your mother end up there? I mean, I know *why* she went, but how'd she actually end up going?" The television was flashing its too-bright, artificial colors behind him.

"She'd been spending a lot of time in her room, not talking, just sleeping. Aunt Florence came to Rock Hill, and she and my father were in the living room talking for hours. That night, after Aunt Florence left and Mickey and I were in bed, he came up to tell us to turn out our light." She thought about how she and Mickey had propped the Monopoly board between their mattresses and were building a house on it with playing cards. When their father sat on Mickey's bed, Mickey slid toward him. Their house fell in, but nobody bothered to pick up the cards. "He told us Mother was not well and he was taking her to a place in Massachusetts—a place, he said, that had a 'fine reputation.' The Hillberry Clinic. Mickey was winding that one strand of hair around her finger the whole time he talked." Thea had sat there, silently making bargains, promising that from then on she would do everything in her power to keep her mother "in the middle," where it was safe. She'd do everything her mother wanted. Get along with her sister. Whatever. "Mickey asked him if he was going to stay in Massachusetts with Mother." Thea pictured him, the way the lines in his face softened as if he were drawn in charcoal and everything had been smudged with a thumb—his usual reaction to Mickey, the way his whole body eased up when she was talking.

"What did he say?" Reid tried his knuckles again but they were cracked out.

"These exact words: 'I'll be right here. You can count on me.' "

"Sounds just like him."

"I was petrified Mother was going so far away I'd never see her again."

"How long did she stay?"

"Six months." When she came back, it was as if she'd been smoothed out, like fabric, with all the folds and creases ironed away. She wasn't depressed and she wasn't manic. No extremes. As if she'd been left in Massachusetts, and somebody they didn't know was unpacking the old, familiar, blond Samsonite suitcase.

"Did it help?" Reid asked. "Because I remember her seesawing back and forth during the years I knew her."

Thea got up and walked over to the window. She looked at a broken branch that had fallen and gotten caught in a bigger branch in the pin oak. She went back to the love seat. "What happened is that, as time passed, her moods returned. But not as severe as they'd been before she went to the hospital. It was like the borders had been pulled in. I never knew if it was the sheer terror of being hospitalized or maybe she had shock treatment there or maybe it was the result of medication she was on—but the extremes she swung between were definitely not as wide." Thea remembered how relieved she'd been to see the swings return, the way you'd be glad to see an old friend who was far from perfect but at least you knew what you were getting.

"Did you and Mickey go to see her?"

"Oh no, it wasn't allowed. My father didn't even go. Mother wrote to him pretty often though. He'd read the letters to himself, then immediately put them away. All he'd say was, 'She's doing all right, girls. Doing all right.' One afternoon while he was at work, Mickey said she was going to find those letters if it was the last thing she did. She told me I could come if I wanted. She knew I'd be right there beside her."

"Of course!" he said. A commercial had come on and it was loud, but then commercials were always several notches louder than programs. He hit the Off button on the remote.

"I followed her up the stairs to our parents' room, and she started opening drawers in our father's dresser like it belonged to her, beginning with the wide bottom drawer. She rummaged through his pajamas. Then the next drawer, his undershirts and boxers. Then his handkerchiefs. And tennis stuff. And then his socks . . . I remember they were rolled up like dark fists . . . and underneath them was the stack of Mother's letters. Mickey pulled out one and handed it to me. I was shocked. The writing was just a string of blocky, stunted little words." Thea had studied that envelope as if her own address would tell her everything. Mickey slid down to the floor and sat there, reading, her back straight against the dresser, knees bent, feet planted like roots. Thea lay across the bed, curled her toes in the bedspread fringe. "I've kept the letter all these years, but I haven't looked at it since that afternoon. Do you want to see it?"

"Of course I want to see it. I can't believe you've never shown it to me."

She heard him click on the TV as she went in the bedroom. It sounded like an explosion. People were screaming, sirens going off. When she came back, he clicked it off again.

"Okay. Now. Here's how it starts: *My darling family, you, Florence, and you, Mike.* Did you catch that? My aunt first. Then my father. And Mother must've mailed my aunt the original, because, see, this is a carbon copy." She held it out to him. "The handwriting is pretty shaky and hard to read, but here—"

Reid took the letter and squinted. "I don't think I can make it out. You read it."

> *It is brutal. It is a living hell—I am so weak—it is hard to walk. I am trying so hard to keep control—for both of you as much as for myself. I am very aware of the trouble I have caused you both but oh my God, how am I going to do it? I am so afraid—awash with fear—my skin is crawling, I am shaking inside & hands too. No matter how "pleasantly" they try to disguise it, you are a prisoner here—doors locked everywhere you turn, the feel of it is in the air even tho you are allowed (some are) to leave & enter the bldg. thru the one open door. Being here has drained me—I have already lost 2 lbs. & can't believe it's not more. I need to gain weight, not lose it. But how can I eat? Even if every door were open—all the time—it would still be Institution life & only one who has experienced it truly knows—it is indescribable & the same everywhere—"fine reputation" or not.*
>
> *Yes, Florence, I am reacting exactly as you expected. I hate the food, the people, the staff, the Clinic atmosphere. Already—almost right away, in fact, this place's "personal odor" came at me & I have to force myself to touch things & even wear my clothes. It has gotten into all my possessions. It nauseates me dreadfully. Florence, you're going to think I'm making this up but as if all this weren't bad enough, one of the nurses on my floor is even named Carter.*

"A nurse named Carter? What does that have to do with anything?" Thea said over the top of the letter. Reid gave a slow shrug.

> *No, this place won't get any better—I know that's what you're going to say—that it will get better—but the people staying here*

will remain the same, mostly crackpots, kooks, depressing just to look at & the teenagers awful. There are only 4 women near my age—2 are real nuts, 1 much older & the 4th the only one desirable for a friend. The whole unit is mostly teenagers—a tough, rough bunch—a shock to me. So different from my girls, nothing like my gentle little Thea.

As you can well imagine from this long "megillah" it got too late to finish last nite—& now I'm glad because your telegram just came, Florence darling, & I can include my feelings on receiving it—No, I can't—never could—express what a wonderful, wonderful brainstorm sending that telegram was—just what I needed. I love every word of it—I have held it close & kissed it. Yes, Florence, darling, I will remember every encouraging word you wrote & I will try—as hard as I can—& I promise to pray with all of me & open my mind & attitude, as you suggested.

But how can one deny physical facts? Where am I going to find the strength to stick it out? Oh, Florence, Florence, what can I do? I want you to promise me, on everything we hold dear together, that you will not make me stay here long. If I am not exactly what you want me to be in a bearable length of time, promise me you'll let me come home anyway with whatever improvement has been accomplished. Please promise—& keep it, my darling—else I cannot try as I should & as I want to.

Your bewildered, seeking-the-answer, but so loving sister,
Mollie

"That's so tragic," Reid said.

"I didn't want to stay up in that room with Mickey. I told her she could read every last letter if she wanted, I was going out in the yard to wait for our father to get home from work. Mickey didn't even look up. Her hair was hanging in her face. Can't you just picture those straight, saw-toothed bangs of hers? I sat on the front steps the rest of the afternoon, the letter folded into a tight little wad in the pocket of my shorts, like a boil on my skin. I sat there, watching for the Oldsmobile to come around the curve, hoping with everything that was in me he would get home in time to catch Mickey up in his room reading the letters."

Chapter 6

Thea still hadn't told Mickey she'd gone ahead with the translations. With the mastectomy and the recuperation, there hadn't been a good time to tell her. She would though. Soon.

Now the second letter was here. This would be the letter written on January 6, after the wedding, the seven-page one. The one she'd been waiting for.

She chewed her bottom lip and tore open the envelope.

Bit the soft flesh inside her cheek.

Until she read Helen's note: "The order of the letters is a bit juxtaposed. We have yet to come to the one describing Mollie's wedding . . . but all in due time. Because the wedding letter is so lengthy, it will take me a while to translate it. I would rather leave it until I am totally comfortable with your grandmother's idioms. Anyway, it is better to wait until the last to read the most important one. We will take the letters in order, skipping over the wedding letter for now. Enjoy the unfolding of your family."

Thea heard the sounds from down the street—a mother calling in children, a dog yapping, a burglar alarm set off in a house probably for no good reason.

January 20, 1938

My dear sister Celia leben with your family leben:

I received your lovely letter.

You want to know if Mollkeleh (Mollie) is already home? Yes, she has already fixed up her little apartment. Very nice, outstanding, and they are both ecstatic. So long since we have seen our Mollkeleh. Last Sunday we all drove to see her, also Florence and Mr. and Mrs. Rubin from Norway came with us. Our machine was packed. Also took along packages, bound up on both fenders and around the car. No side, no place to move. We had two tires to go flat on the road because it was so rough. Easy and Mr. Rubin fixed them.

Thank God, we arrived in Newberry, with mazel.

We found Mollkeleh fine, looks good and also her Mike was awaiting with pleasure. There was a great tumult . . . being with her mama and papa, Mollkeleh kept shouting. Mama this, Papa that. You have never seen such an outburst in your life. You know Mollkeleh has been always quick to excitement.

In a while everything quieted down and we began to look around her rooms. They fixed them very nicely. The bedroom looks like a lovely hotel. Everything is outstandingly pretty. She received very nice gifts that bedeck her room. Lamps, pillows, other things, pretty spread on the bed with small rugs to match. The floor is very pretty, you must be careful not to slip when walking. The kitchen, stove, in gray with blue. Everything is gray with blue. The pots on the stove match, also two sets of dishes. She tells me the man comes with ice for her icebox three times a week so the food stays fresh. So many beautiful gifts, she needed to buy very few things. She has a very nice breakfast set also matching. And a kitchen table with a stool for working. A large kitchen with three windows. Curtains from oilcloth, blue with gray I made for her. Everything is nice and fine. If business will be good with them, they will be all right.

Mama, she told me, do not worry about me, I am very lucky and pleased with my lovely home and with my loving husband. Better times are coming, she said, and we will be fine. Such a thoughtful daughter, my Mollkeleh, trying to make her mama to stop worrying. So much worry, I cannot begin to explain certain events.

They have a Negro who was supposed to start cooking for them this week. Mollkeleh goes every day to the store to help her Mike. That is what she wants to do. She says she is sometimes very tired and sleeps long hours, which she has always done.

Thank God for everything, what God does for us. No need for worry.

Mollkeleh and Mike live very lovingly, he keeps on kissing her and calls her baby honey and other such loving words.

I would pray to see Florence happy and married like her sister, but Florence does not as yet have a fellow. She was excited on Friday, traveled to Columbia on a date. To a show in the afternoon and in the evening to a party, to a wiener roast. Do you know what a wiener roast is? I do not . . .

We hope for better business. It is a bit better. We do not look for riches and since we have not found it we remain in the same place. It pleases me that we remain in the same place.

It has become cold, for the first time it snowed yesterday. I remain at home, not very keen on going out in the cold. I have a cook to come by and she uses the telephone to order groceries and that is how the winter goes. I do not feel in the best of health ever. My stomach troubles me. Dr. Wyman says to me that the same ailment I have, he has. Regardless of what my complaint is, he has the same always. He ordered me to eat a lot of greens. He must have found out that I am a cow and must have in me a lot of greens. Some days at home I feel a little better and I am able to eat. I will try to do what the doctor asks.

That is why I have become weak, a little too weak to do anything . . . immediately I become weakened. Believe me, Celianke, the way I take care of myself I should not have to lie in bed until ten o'clock, my breakfast in bed. The whole day either I lie in bed and read or I sleep a little.

With regards from my family to you all.

Your sister, Bella

P.S. Do not worry. Everything will be all right.

She dialed her aunt, doodling little boxes in the margin of the letter while she waited for her to answer.

"Hello?"

"Aunt Florence? Hi. The second letter from your mother just came."

"I've been waiting for it! But first, tell me how Mickey is feeling. I haven't talked to her this week."

Thea wondered if Florence had said anything to Mickey about the letters being translated, but Thea wasn't going to bring that up. "Mickey's really doing fine. One more week and the doctor says she can start playing tennis again." She drew little roofs on the boxes, then front doors and windows.

"Tennis? So soon? Amazing the way they get you moving so fast. Now. Let me hear!"

Thea read her the letter, then asked, "What *was* wrong with your mother?"

"Well, all I remember is Mama had been in the hospital for an operation—exploratory, they called it. But they couldn't find anything wrong. Then she came home and she still wasn't feeling well, so the doctor thought she had an ulcer and put her on a special diet. But see, she only had one kidney and later she got uremic poisoning, and that's what she died from. Your mother always argued with me that she died of cancer, but your mother was wrong. I don't know why your mother thought that. Mama died of uremic poisoning. I know. Let's see, Mama wrote this letter in January 1938, you said? So she died not long after that, less than a year. In fact, it was in the fall, right before the High Holy Days. Mama told Papa she had to lie down for a few minutes. It was in the afternoon. She wasn't feeling well. When Papa woke up from *his* nap—he always took a nap, no matter what—he was surprised to see Mama still lying beside him and not already down in the kitchen fixing supper. Then he noticed the bed was wet and he said, 'Bella, Bella, wake up!' but she wouldn't wake up. He shook her and shook her. But she'd died while he was sleeping."

"She was young, wasn't she?"

"Fifty-seven."

"And, Aunt Florence, one more thing—why all the worrying? I mean, I understand my grandmother was not well, but it sounds like there were other things going on, too. Over and over in the letter she says not to worry. Worry about *what*? And I know this sounds crazy, but does the name Carter have any significance?"

"Thea, darling, don't ask so many questions. It's bad for your digestion."

. . .

The following weekend, Saturday afternoon, the sun was warm on Thea and Reid in the side yard. He was bearing down on the shovel with his right foot, pushing it deep in the soil, making neat trenches around all the hostas. Then he lifted them out, their chartreuse leaves iced in white, and gently placed them behind him. His legs, khaki shorts, Hornets T-shirt were flecked with dirt and bits of leaves. He kept pulling a handkerchief from his pocket and brushing himself off. Thea was on her knees, taking the hostas he'd dug and separating them with a butcher knife into smaller clumps. Then she set them in a messy, uneven row along the edge of the bed of toothed-wood ferns, where they would plant them.

He stopped digging and bent around her to straighten the line of hostas. "I think it looks better if we plant them like this," he said. "And you've got them way too close."

"No, you're wrong. Look," she said, putting them back where she'd had them, "it's better if they're not in such a perfect line. And they *need* to be close so they'll fill in and be more of a mass."

"Where is it written that it has to be this way? I didn't realize it was *your* garden. I mistakenly thought it was *ours*." He rubbed the crease between his eyes, leaving a muddy smudge. "When do I get a say in how we do things?" He wasn't kidding.

The mailman came walking up the front path and spotted them beside the house. "Bills for sale!" he called, laughing his jolly laugh, the words muffled because he always talked as though he had a mouthful of marbles. "Gotcha plenty of bills!" He knew everyone in the neighborhood and he knew everyone's business.

Thea got up and met him in the front. He shifted the dark blue sack on his shoulder and gave her the mail.

"You can keep the bills, Howard. Just let me have the check from Publishers Clearing House!"

"Kept that in my back pocket, thank you very much!" He slapped his hip—his hand was as big as a book—and cut across Herm Proctor's ivy bed. "Mr. Proctor better get out here and do a little weeding. Getting sort of thick. I mean the weeds, not Mr. Proctor. Ha! Ha!"

"Anything interesting, boss?" Reid asked, coming around to the front, wiping his face with his forearm. He laid the shovel, caked with dirt, facedown in the grass, carefully, as though it were expensive china.

"Letter number three! Can you believe another one has come so soon?"

"I can't believe Mickey actually told you to forget about them."

"She's always so darn worried somebody's going to say something negative about our father. Heaven forbid there should be one tiny thing in these letters that puts him in a bad light. Of course, it wouldn't bother her a bit if they were filled with stuff about Mother, especially about her craziness."

"Well, to be fair to your sister, I have to say you're probably just as concerned with your mother's image as she is your father's." He squeezed her shoulder.

"And why is it necessary to be fair to my sister?" she said, fanning away the gnats sticking to her face.

"Here, give me the rest of the mail. I know you want to read your letter."

She was glad to take a break from yardwork. And from Reid. On the top step, she could lean back against the screened door and stretch her legs down the bottom three steps.

Helen had written: "Presenting more of this delightful lady, your grandmother. Enjoy!"

February 15, 1938

Dear Celia leben, with your dear family leben,

Celianke, you should not be disturbed with me if you do not receive a letter. I thought that the beginning of the week I would write to you, to answer your letter. But now it is already Thursday. Certainly you will receive my letter now, around Monday, and you, my dear, will think God only knows about me. I hope not too bad.

I am feeling, the last few weeks, much better, since I last saw Dr. Wyman. I try to do everything he asked of me. I take good care of myself and eat all kinds of greens. It is doing me some good.

I go to the store every day for a few hours. Work very little. I do not need to work but I am used to working.

Today on Main Street much tumult. President Roosevelt traveled through our town on the train to (or from—who is to know?) Warm Springs in Georgia. When the train stopped at the depot, he brought on Mr. Shillito, the postmaster. Mr. Shillito, everyone knows, is a Republican. There are two of those families in Denmark. Knowing this, the President, on the spot, fired him. Do you understand Republican? Easy explains to me. Much talk up and down the street about this.

The Sunday before last we were in Newberry, together with Mollie and Mike. We had a very large and good dinner. A delicious brisket with beans, potatoes and turnips. It was a jolly Sunday. It had been a long time since I have had such pleasure as this time, for I felt well. We spoke of you and your dear Meyer.

Mollie told me that she wrote to you. Everything is happy with her, a good husband, thank God for this. Everyone likes her in her town. She rests as she should. Perhaps you did not receive my last letter. Written only a few weeks ago. About Mollie and the baby. Much excitement regarding the upcoming event. How could you think that I would not write to tell you of this? If my last letter does not arrive, I will fill you in on many happy details, if not in this letter in a later one. No need for you to ask questions. I will explain everything in due time.

Did I inform you yet about the play Mrs. Ness and I attended at the Dula Mae Theater? Can you believe? A play in Denmark? I said to Easy I would like to go. To see a live play in person. He said it was nothing to go to. So, Celianke, I myself purchased two tickets and invited Mrs. Ness. We are sitting together in the balcony and she whispers to me, Isn't that Easy's head in the light, shining down there? When we were again home I asked him and he explained that he was walking on the street and saw all of the excitement and became right away curious and went in to see the play. What do you think of that?

I received this week a letter from Mollie. She writes that she had a chicken one day and used my noodles with the soup that I cooked for her and enjoyed very much. Her Mike likes this. One evening she had company, bridge players, and served the cake that I also brought, a plain chocolate with filling between the layers of nuts (pecans) and topped with a few cherries I bought at the store. The price is 10 cents a jar now. Expensive because they are from last summer but it is worth it for the flavor. I am sure you would love this cake.

This is one cake you wanted to know about in your letter. The second is also a layer cake, but between the layers are bananas, split lengthwise, only use white icing, plain. Making two layers is very good. If you wish to adorn with nuts and cherries, it will be the same.

You must have thought that only God knows what sort of cake my sister is making there. My cook makes very often lemon pies with coconut at dinner for dessert. I speak often about your pie, how it used to turn out. She answers that you must have a better oven than we have. You guessed it, I tell her.

Well, sister dear, only healthy we should be for, thank God, food is not lacking for us, no one. There should be better business, then everything would be good. The spring should only be a little warmer, then we will do business.

If you hear of storms, they are not in our area. It happens not far from us but, thank God, not in Denmark. The town is too small for the large storms. In Columbia, all of the telegraph lines were wiped out. God should help, let it become still and we should not know from this.

It is not good weather, too cold. We must warm our home.

We all wish you much goodness and health. Let me know much good from all of you.

It pleases me that Florence lives with us and helps her papa in the store although I worry. She does not have a husband as yet but she is having good times. Older sisters should marry before the younger.

Mollie and Mike look fine, happy. Everyone who sees them says they are a lovely couple.

Easy and I are getting older, we feel this. More there is not to write. I hope to see such a long letter from you, that I am not the only sister to write long letters.

We send regards to your family, certainly heartfelt.

Your sister, Bella

Her mother was pregnant with her! These letters were incredible. She'd call her aunt now and let her launch forth with her stories. This could easily become a pattern, calling Florence after each letter, but then Thea was the type of person who loved doing the same thing over and over. She could be like a car stuck in mud on a rainy night, wheels spinning deeper and deeper.

She went in the house to get the portable phone, then headed back outside. "Hi, Aunt Florence, what're you up to this pretty Saturday afternoon?"

"Oh, Thea dear, I'm up all right. That's the main thing. At my age, it's good just to be up!"

"Are you ready to hear another letter?" She sat on the top step again, straightening her shorts beneath her.

"I'm all ears!"

Thea read it, leaving out the part about Florence not having a husband and older sisters marrying before younger sisters.

"My grandmother sounds so happy about my mother marrying my father," Thea said. "That must've made Mother feel good that her family approved of her choice. But I just keep getting the feeling that my grandmother is holding something back from her sister—"

"Thea." Her voice was an octave lower. "When Mama was in the hospital for her operation, your mother and I were there with her. She was so weak that day. She motioned for your mother to come closer to the bed. Did your mother tell you what she said to her?"

"No, I don't know about that."

What she did know was that she was getting ready to hear something important. Finally. She concentrated on her breaths, air pushing in and out. Inhale. Exhale. A bright yellow bird flew by, from one side of the yard to the other. It was as yellow as a slice of lemon, like a canary someone had let loose by mistake. It flew back across the yard in the opposite direction and then was out of sight. She waited for it to cross the space between the pin oaks again.

"I don't know," her aunt was saying. "Maybe it's not a story for the telephone."

"Not a story for the telephone?" Forget the bird. "You can say anything you want on the phone. It's totally private. And *I* called *you,* so you don't have to worry about the expense. Go ahead. It's perfectly okay. Tell me."

"No, I really don't think this is the right time. I'll tell you when I see you."

When she saw her? At her aunt's age, anything could happen. "But we might forget about it. You've got the time right now, Aunt Florence. I've got the time. Please tell me."

"Thea, dear, this'll have to wait until I see you."

She wasn't going to budge. Thea had the feeling that the harder she pushed, the farther away her aunt would sound. The conversation started off between two people in the Carolinas. Now her aunt could be in Wyoming, she was sounding so distant.

"But you—"

"No, no," Florence said, "this just isn't the time. I'd rather tell you in person."

End of conversation. They said good-bye and Thea looked for the yellow bird. Robins, sparrows, and bluejays were flying everywhere, making their ragged music. No yellow bird. She wondered if Reid had seen it. She wondered if the whole thing had been her imagination.

Reid came loping around from the side of the house. "What'd you do, call Florence?"

"Yeah. And she came close to telling me something big. I'm sure of it." She repeated the conversation to him, how her aunt had closed up so quickly.

"You should drive down to Columbia." He'd dug up the azalea that died during the winter and was holding it away from his body, its leaves brown and crisp, a tangle of roots exposed. "I wouldn't wait. She's not getting any younger. You could ask her everything you want to know. Obviously, she's ready to talk. Hell, she probably knows things you've never even thought to ask, and with everybody gone, she's your only hope. You ought to do it. Soon."

How could someone so totally wrong twenty minutes before be so right? She'd call her aunt back.

Which she did. All set for the following Saturday, one week away, late morning. Florence wanted her daughter, Evelyn, to be there, too.

Chapter 7

They looked slightly uncomfortable crammed together on the hard Victorian love seat. They both had on navy—Evelyn, a knit tunic and pants; Florence, a silk suit with the skirt cut just at her knees—and because they sat so close, it was hard to tell where one ended and the other began.

Thea sat in the brocade chair across from them.

On the table next to the love seat was a Meissen lamp with winged cupids and flowers. Under the lamp was a photograph of Florence and Jack at their twenty-fifth wedding anniversary party. She was unwrapping a sterling silver pitcher—her heart-shaped face turned to the camera—and he was beside her, smiling, his gold tooth showing, a hearing aid in one ear. She'd been the *baleboosteh* of the family, the one who took care of everyone, the homemaker, the one who always wore an apron, whose house smelled like brisket or roast chicken. In the photograph, she was plump and soft, wearing a shapeless print dress, something someone much older should wear. She had always been pretty, but in those days, she didn't do much to fix herself up and she'd appeared almost dowdy.

When Thea's mother died, though, Florence changed drastically—both in looks and personality. Suddenly, she cared about her appearance, and she *was* beautiful. Her hair was silver and "done," her figure trim and shapely. She now wore the latest fashions. She'd buy clothes, change her mind, take them back, as though it was a game and she was determined to come out on top. She said the trick to exchanging things, even after keeping something for months, was to stay on good terms with the salespeople. And, in fact, in shops all over Columbia, they loved her.

She buried two husbands after Jack died—she said his heart stopped for no good reason—and she wanted to get married again but would not date a man who couldn't drive at night. *She* still drove at night and did not want to be the chauffeur. Most men her age weren't driving anything, she liked to say, day or night!

Beside the picture of Florence and Jack was a framed snapshot of Thea's grandparents, posed in front of a dusty car, her grandmother wearing thick cotton stockings, a coat with a wide velvet collar, and a cloche, one side pulled down to her eyebrow. She was smiling sweetly for the camera, almost beatifically. Thea's grandfather wore a suit, the elk's tooth hanging from his vest. He held a cigar in one hand. The thumb of his other hand was hooked rakishly in his vest pocket. A suitcase was on the ground between them. The dirt was hard-packed beneath their feet, not a blade of grass in sight.

On the table next to Thea was a sepia photograph she'd never seen before. Florence must've just had it framed. Across the bottom was a hand-lettered banner: *Key Club Dance, 1937.* She spotted Florence in the back row, even though she faded into all the other girls in the picture, with their pale, nondescript gowns. Thea's mother was in the front row, her tight, dark, bias-cut, taffeta gown pulled above her knees as she stooped to balance. She held a tasseled dance card in one hand and her date's hand in the other. He was turned toward her. No wonder; her smile was blinding. It looked as if the camera couldn't stop staring at her either, though dozens of other young women and their dates were posed for the picture.

Florence was telling how Thea's and Evelyn's grandparents, Bella and Easy, had met. "See, they were first cousins but they never knew each other. They both came over to this country from Eastern Europe and were staying with their aunt in New York. That's the way they did back then. People doubled up. You'd come over and stay with a relative. They'd take anybody in who needed a place to live, and they'd keep them till they could get on their own feet. Well, Papa and Mama met and fell in love. The family didn't want them to get married, since they were first cousins and all. I think Mama's sister, Tante Celia, was very opposed. She was living in the aunt's house, too. But oh, your grandparents were stubborn and they went ahead and got married anyway."

"My grandparents were first cousins? I never knew that. How could we not know something that important?" Thea said. What she didn't know about the family was like a stain, spreading wider by the minute.

"Mama, tell her the story about Grandpa's pants," Evelyn prompted, winking. Her lashes were long, like a child's. She put on her lipstick a little outside her lips, which gave the impression she was pleased even when she wasn't. "You know, Grandpa Bogen could charm the birds out of the trees."

Thea was still thinking about her grandparents being first cousins and wanted to ask more about that. On the other hand, she was afraid of using up her questions too early in the day. She looked from her cousin to her aunt. Florence was laughing before she even began the pants story. "Back in those days, men didn't have zipper trousers, they had button trousers. And Papa lost a button in the middle of a gathering of ladies in the house on Palmetto Avenue. *Mittender-enen,* he wanted Mama to sew the button, right then and there. He didn't even take his pants off. He just stood in front of Mama and she was sewing and he would turn to the company and say, 'Excuse my back, my front's engaged.' I thought it was awful. I was just a teenager then and that, to me, was very embarrassing. She could've sewn up his . . . you know!"

Florence and Evelyn were laughing. Thea tried to laugh, but it sounded forced. She wished Mickey were here, wished she'd been interested in the letters. Mickey would know how to bring up a tricky subject. She pictured her sister sitting across the room, twirling her hair.

"Well, Aunt Florence," Thea began, uncrossing her legs and stretching her neck, rolling her head to one shoulder, then the other, "on the telephone when you and I were talking about the letters, you said you were going to tell me the story about the time my grandmother was in the hospital and you and Mother were there—"

Her aunt looked at Evelyn. It was a look that said, See, I told you she wouldn't forget about it, now what do I do?

Evelyn looked at Florence. Her look said, Don't do it.

Thea had witnessed an entire conversation taking place only in their eyes.

"Well, that's something that doesn't need to be talked about," Evelyn butted in. Even though she was five years younger than Thea, she had always treated Thea and Mickey as if she were years older. Evelyn's favorite childhood game had been "queen," which meant Thea and Mickey had to do everything she wanted. The only good part was seeing someone, *anyone,* even Evelyn, boss Mickey around. Evelyn belonged to Florence, clearly the caretaker in the family, which made Evelyn feel she was something special; Thea and Mickey belonged to Mollie, the one who had to be taken care of. Thea wasn't sure what that made them.

"Why is this something we can't talk about?" Thea asked.

"Because it's not even a funny story," Evelyn said. "We've been talking about happy times and happy memories, and it's just water over the bridge to go into things that'll make somebody feel bad."

Water over the bridge? Evelyn and her malapropisms. When Thea had told her about Mickey's and her mammograms, Evelyn kept calling them monograms. Another time she'd said she didn't want to get too emotional about whatever they were talking about because she didn't like to wear her heart on her cuff.

"But, Evelyn," Thea said, with a slight rise of tone, "your mother is the only one left who knows these things. I want to hear all about our family, not just the happy parts and not just the funny stories. I don't want my own family stories censored. And besides, make *who* feel bad?"

Evelyn didn't look at Thea. She looked at the ceiling, then at her shoe. She twisted her left foot around in a tight little circle, the size of a dessert plate. She wasn't going to give an inch.

Thea decided to try her aunt again. "I'm so disappointed. Please tell me what happened. One day I won't have the chance to hear these stories."

"Sometimes you say things. You know. Sometimes you talk and you don't realize you *shouldn't* talk. There's no point in talking. Believe me, you wouldn't want me to tell you. Evelyn showed me the rightness of it, but don't worry, when I'm gone she can tell you the story."

Evelyn, the person who never got her words straight, was the keeper of Thea's family's secret, the one she was going to have to depend on.

"And why does Evelyn know this? And I don't?" Thea's voice didn't even sound like her voice. It was thin and shrieky. She was becoming aware of the aura that always preceded a headache—not a visual aura, more like a feeling that something wasn't right in her head, a warning, like what animals might experience before an earthquake.

Evelyn crossed her arms over her ample bosom and began another story. "Did Mama ever tell you about Grandpa and the train trip?"

The idea of her cousin trying to distract her with a new story, as though she were a child reaching for something breakable and Evelyn were the adult handing her a toy instead!

"I wish you wouldn't try to change the subject," Thea

said to her, spacing her words for extra emphasis. Her aunt stuffed a small needlepoint pillow behind her back. "How would you feel if *my* mother were the only one left and she knew something about *your* mother, but I didn't want her to tell you?" How much higher would the pitch of her voice go? She now had a full-blown headache. "Think about it. How would that make *you* feel?"

"Thea, darling, the past is past. Take my word for it," her aunt said, in a voice so much like Thea's mother's, it felt as if *she* were talking. "It's not the type of thing we ought to discuss. Why I even mentioned it on the telephone I couldn't tell you." Florence leaned back on the pillow and nodded at Evelyn, who was smiling, and went on, "I made a promise to your mother that I would never say anything to you about this. And if you ask me to tell you this thing, you're asking me to go against her, to betray your mother, and I know you would never want me to do that. I didn't know whether your mother ever told you the story or not, but I figured by my sending you these letters you might learn a few things. Not that I wanted to betray your mother . . . I can't read Yiddish so I didn't know what was written there. But I know one thing for sure, *I* could never be the one to tell you. Never."

. . .

Through the glass, Thea could see Tim in the next control room, drumming his fingers on the arm of his chair. People walking up and down the hall were laughing and talking. The receptionist, holding a fingernail file and a pink phone message slip, was knocking on the station manager's door. Two interns from the university were having a conversation outside her door. What was nice was that not a single sound came through those sealed walls. She loved that. It felt so protected. The President of the United States could declare war on all of Asia and she wouldn't have to know. All she heard in there was somebody talking about a rottweiler or a man complaining about his boss or a woman worrying about a son obsessed with the Grateful Dead. *She* was grateful. Grateful for that place she could escape to. Control room was a perfect name. An insulated world where she was in control of how much came through.

Tim was giving her a thumbs-up. Even outside the control room, he communicated mostly by giving cues, as though they were on the air every minute of their lives.

Caller number two was ready. The first caller had been a woman who wanted to talk about her husband's drinking problem. Thea suspected the woman also had a drinking problem. It had not been an easy conversation.

"Hello, Jan. You're on the air."

"Hi. I'm calling about my son."

"Uh-huh."

"Are you there?"

"Sure, go ahead."

"Well, my son is thirteen . . . I mean, fourteen . . . and has several very nice friends, but he feels like he's just not well liked because he's not in what they call the popular crowd. I went to have lunch with him at his school yesterday and it made me heartsick. This little 'in group' was gathered around a table in the middle of the cafeteria, talking away, and the kids at all the other tables in the room were practically facing them. It felt like the whole place was leaning . . . sloping . . . in their direction."

"That sounds like such typical behavior for teenagers," Thea said, pushing her hair up off her neck.

"But that's not the whole reason I'm calling. The part that

bothers me about all this is what my son says about himself." The woman's voice was gentle. Thea liked her. "He feels very different from everybody else. He's not at all interested in sports. He's real artistic. In fact, he's an excellent cartoonist. The boys in his class are always making fun of him for not playing sports and for sitting around drawing these funny little characters. What do you think I should be saying to him?"

"Well, first, let me mention something: I have a theory about this very thing you're talking about. I believe each of us, in some way, feels different from everyone else. Either it's because we're artistic—or not artistic—or we have curly hair or we wear braces on our teeth or we're a different religion, but there is something we see in ourselves that sets us apart. And what we do with this difference is, instead of simply saying, 'we're different,' we take it a step further and say 'we're less than.' "

"This is true," the caller said. "While you were talking, I was thinking about when I was growing up. I sure felt different. I was five foot nine in the ninth grade. I towered over everybody, even the teachers."

"And it's not just when we're young. We carry this sense of being different—of being not as good as—right into adulthood. So much of our behavior, whether we're children or adults, is aimed toward establishing or maintaining relationships that fulfill our need to belong. This very minute, I'll bet every adult listening can name precisely what it is that makes him or her feel, at times, like an outcast. This feeling becomes something we cave in to whenever we face a difficult maturational task or a core issue."

"So, is this what I tell my son?"

"Probably nothing you tell him is going to take his feeling

away. But helping him see that he's not the only one going through this might be reassuring for him. Have you ever told him of your experiences as a teenager?"

"No, not really."

"That might be good to do. Also, are there art activities outside of school he could participate in?"

"That's an idea. Maybe. I don't know . . ."

"Not only would he be spending his time doing what he loves but he'd have a chance to meet other kids like himself and form friendships based on a mutual interest. This would take the pressure off *having* to make friends."

"I'll see what I can find out. Well, thanks, thanks for taking my call."

One more caller. A man whose wife hadn't been interested in sex since before their first child was born.

. . .

Tim saluted Thea as he backed out the door and disappeared down the hall. She sat there, picturing the scene in the school cafeteria the woman had described.

Maybe all we ever want, she thought, is to belong. Now there's a subject she could call a radio therapist about. She'd know exactly what she'd say:

It's about my father. And the strong connection he had with my sister. You should've seen them. They looked like bookends. Their hair. Eyes. Chins. Sturdy build. She had his looks, his personality, his name. Mickey, Mike. She had his everything.

This was crazy. Here she was, in the control room, going through an imaginary phone call to some imaginary radio therapist. Her grandmother's letters had put her over the brink!

I didn't look like anyone in our family. It would've been so even, so parallel, if I'd looked like my mother. True, I was aligned with her—she practically ignored Mickey—but a connection with Mother was a fragile connection. We sure didn't look alike. She was small-boned, slight, and so am I, but that's where the resemblance ended. My hair's blond—not yellow like cornmeal, more like the white of a blank page. My mother had brown hair. My eyes are round, like I'm surprised or sad, clear and ice blue. Somebody once told me they're the color of glass. Mother's eyes were almond-shaped, dark. At times my face is so pale in the mirror, it looks like some of my features have been erased, as though I'm going through life anonymous. I wish I had my mother's hair and eyes. I wish I had her color.

She realized she'd been mouthing words. Had anyone seen her? She glanced over her shoulder. Tim hadn't come in.

There was the night my father took me to the circus, and for some reason, my mother and sister didn't go. Just before we went into the tent, he bought me a bag of roasted peanuts. After we found our seats, I started eating the peanuts. The first one was rotten. The second one, too. Before long, I realized all the peanuts were rotten.

She was really getting into it now. She let her chair rock back and clasped her hands behind, raising them as high as they would go. The stretch felt good.

My father was enraged. The idea, he said, selling rotten peanuts to children! He took the bag and spent the whole evening hunting for someone in charge to complain to. I sat there, watching the trapeze artists swing at dizzying heights, the high-wire walkers lurch forward and backward with their toes closed around the wire, and the trained animals balance on those little blocks their masters whipped them to. The seat beside me, where my father should have been, was empty.

She couldn't stop. But she knew any minute Tim could come in the control room next door and begin taping. She swiveled her chair so that her back was to the soundproof window separating the rooms.

And the time Reid and I had just gotten back from our honeymoon in Dorado Beach and we wanted to show my father the pictures we'd taken . . . He was only interested in the ones with tennis courts in the background. "Soft courts?" he asked. "Good players there?" It was the first, and last, time I ever got angry with him. I grabbed the pictures from him and said, "Never mind! You don't give two hoots about our trip! All you care about is tennis! Too bad these aren't pictures from Mickey's honeymoon!"

She couldn't remember his reaction to her outburst. Had he said anything at all? She was spinning her chair in circles. Around and around she was going.

There was one time, maybe the only time, I felt very connected to my father. I was a senior in high school, and my homeroom teacher, Mr. Westbrook, stopped me in the hall. I was chewing gum so I thought I'd been caught, but it turned out he wanted to tell me I was class valedictorian and would give a speech at graduation.

At dinner that night, I told my father.

"Well, well," he said, his face brightening. He patted me on the back as if I were choking on a fishbone. "That's grand, Thea. Just grand. I'll help you with your speech."

My father had never helped me with anything. He'd taught Mickey to ride a bike in one afternoon, but knowing it would take me longer, he turned the job over to Levi, the one-armed yardman. Mother taught me to swim. Aunt Florence taught me how to drive on her stick-shift Studebaker. But now, here was my father saying he'd help me write my graduation speech. There was no way I could stop the smile from taking over my face.

My speech became my father's speech. Night after night, he and I hunched over the breakfast table with his dictionary and book of famous quotations, crafting the speech I would deliver. It felt like we were pals—no, it felt like I belonged to him, finally.

Graduation night, I stood on the stage, facing a darkened audi-

torium, and began the speech with one of my father's favorite sports quotes: "It is not the size of the dog that's in the fight; it is the size of the fight that's in the dog."

Giving that speech was like borrowing my father's jacket. It felt nice and warm, and I was perfectly happy letting it swallow me whole.

Chapter 8

Mickey and Joel were going to be in Charlotte for the day. She would drop him off at the shoe show in the Merchandise Mart and come by the house that morning. She'd stay till Thea had to leave for the station.

Mickey had mentioned offhandedly on the phone that Joel would be in Charlotte, and Thea had asked her to please come with him.

This would be a good time to tell her about the letters. If Mickey wanted to read them, she could have copies of the three Helen had sent so far. Whether Thea would tell her about the incident with Florence and Evelyn in Columbia remained to be seen.

Thea was just finishing making up the bed when the doorbell rang. She shook out the white feather comforter and pulled it over the sheet, letting the comforter collapse into itself like a balloon with a slow leak. Then she threw the pillows in place and ran to the back door.

Mickey looked healthy—tanned and fit, her back straight as a tree. Hard to believe she'd had surgery so recently. She was wearing a short-sleeved, loose-fitting cotton dress that came down almost to her leather sandals. The dress was a tangerine color, not bright, sort of a dusty shade. Thea wished she'd thought to wear a dress. Plus, her yellow shorts and top suddenly seemed too yellow.

They hugged. Mickey always hugged with the top part of her body. Her middle curved backward into a C.

"So-o? How *are* you?" she said, dropping her ropy, sack-like pocketbook on the floor.

"I'm fine. I'm so glad you decided to come. How are *you*? You look great."

"Thanks. I feel so back-to-normal now. Look how I can move my arm." She circled the air like a windup for a pitch. "Isn't that amazing? And I really feel like I've got my strength back, too. You should see my serve. I told Joel the surgeon must've inserted something to give me all this power. I'm better than ever. At least on the tennis court!"

"Well, don't stand there like a stranger," Thea said. "Come on in. Want some coffee, or a Coke? Is it too early for a Coke? Sounds like I'm offering you a martini, the way I'm asking if it's too early in the day to drink!"

"How about a glass of water? No ice." She felt behind her for a chair and sat down at the kitchen table.

Thea brought the water and sat across from her, sliding the glass over.

"You're not having anything?" Mickey asked.

"I may have a Coke in a little while. Not yet. So . . . what've you been up to?"

"Not much. I told you pretty much everything that's been going on the last time we talked on the phone. You tell me. What's new with you?"

"What's new . . ." Thea looked out the window. She thought about the yellow bird she'd seen in the yard. Someone had told her it might be a wild goldfinch. But that would be a dumb subject to bring up. "Well, things at the station are good—" Not such a good subject. Could lead to a discussion of delving and psychologizing. (Like one of Mickey's jokes, the one about Southern Baptists and sex, but all Thea could remember was the punch line: *Not good. Could lead to dancing.*)

"Is Reid here? I was hoping I'd get to see him."

"He's helping somebody out at the university move all day today. He owes this guy a big favor."

"Is he going to teach this summer?"

"For the first time for as long as I can remember, he's not. He has a million projects he wants to get to."

"Like what?" Mickey coughed dryly and took a swallow of water.

"Well, the yard. He wants to put in a fish pond out back. And get rid of all the monkey grass in the bed by the back door. We've got the kind that travels underground by rhizomes, these little hemplike roots that are hard as anything to pull up. It's like kudzu. Never, ever plant monkey grass in your yard! I keep telling him we've got it, let's just live with it. But he hates how messy it looks growing up under the azaleas."

"I agree with him. Sounds like it's time to pull it up."

"Maybe so. Listen, come sit in the den. Let's be comfortable. I want to tell you about something."

They ended up sitting beside each other on the love seat by accident. They'd sat down at exactly the same time, expecting the other to sit across in the chair. But there they were, squeezed in tight like Florence and Evelyn that day in Columbia.

"You know our grandmother's letters?"

"Well, yeah, what about them?" Mickey inched away from Thea, tossing the plaid throw pillow on the rug to give herself more room. She hit her glass by mistake. It wobbled, but she grabbed it before it fell over. "Good hands!" she said.

"Here," Thea said, leaning close so she could use the hem of her shorts to wipe the bottom of the glass. "Mickey, I have to tell you, I, uh, the woman I told you about is going ahead with translating the letters. The truth is, I really was going to tell her never mind, not to bother doing them, but it was a real busy time and before I had a chance to call her, she'd already—"

"No big surprise there." Mickey drank the rest of her water and set the glass resolutely on the pine trunk.

"Oh."

"What I mean is, I expected that. Knowing you and the way you are, you just couldn't stand not to find out what was in them. Maybe for you it was the right thing, but—"

"Aren't you curious? I've made copies for you. She's done three, so far. You were right, by the way, they're really charming." Thea tried to smile at her.

"Am I curious to see them?" Mickey picked up the glass, realized it was empty, set it back down again, gently this time. "Well, let's put it this way. I've gotten along okay without them so far and I'm sure I can make it to the end of my life without knowing what's in them. But as long as you've gone ahead and made copies, I wouldn't mind taking a look. I don't mean right now, of course. How about giving me the copies and I'll take them home?" She coughed again and scratched behind her knee. Then, with her finger, she pushed her bottom lip between her teeth and nibbled, twirling her hair at the same time.

Thea went in the bedroom to get the letters. When she came back, Mickey was lying across the love seat, her feet still on the floor, her head propped on the arm, eyes closed. There was no room for Thea beside her.

"Everything all right? Want some more water?" Thea asked.

"No, that's okay. I was just resting. Sometimes a car trip makes me a little tired."

"Well, it hasn't been that long since your surgery, so naturally you get tired. Here. These are yours to keep." She handed the letters to her, one sheet at a time. "This is the letter before Mother and Daddy's wedding. And this letter and this letter were written after the wedding, but neither is the one written immediately after the wedding. That's a really long one with all the details about the ceremony and the reception. Helen said she's going to save that one for last."

"How do you know it's telling about the wedding?"

"When Helen was looking through the letters to find out whether she could translate them, she read me a part about silver dishes and candlesticks in the long letter. She *said* it was describing a wedding." Thea decided not to tell her about the P.S. Helen had found so strange.

Mickey pushed herself up and walked out to the back door.

"Thanks for making me copies. I'll put them in my bag right now," she called from the back hall, "so I won't forget them."

"You're going to love reading—"

"Do you have any peach-colored lipstick?" Mickey called back. "For some reason, the only color I have in my pocketbook is bright red, which wouldn't exactly go with what I have on."

Had she heard what Thea started to say? "Yeah, come back to the bathroom with me."

The two sisters stood in front of the mirror at the sink, as they'd done so many times growing up. Thea combed her hair with her fingers, pulling a few strands down for bangs like Mickey's, then pushing them back off her forehead. She touched the half-wrinkle above her left eyebrow, so much like her mother's. Mickey examined the lipstick, holding it up to the light.

"This is just right. It has some brown in it," she said, outlining her lips, then filling in. She tore off a square of toilet paper and blotted, one clearly defined imprint.

Obviously, that was it for the letters. Thea wondered if she should bring up the meeting with Florence and Evelyn in Columbia. Mickey checked her front teeth for lipstick.

"I'm starving," she said. "What's for lunch?"

"Something new, an eggplant dish. I hope you'll like it. Slices of eggplant broiled and topped with basil from my garden and mozzarella, goat cheese, too, and then you roll them up and pour homemade tomato sauce over everything. Doesn't that sound good? But before we eat, I want you to see where I hung your collage. Over the dressing table. It's so wonderful. I really love it."

"Oh, great! I want to see it." Mickey screwed the lipstick

back down, put on the cap, and stood it on the counter. "Why don't you keep your lipstick in your dressing table?"

"Well, I do. I just had that peachy one in the bathroom. It was one of those 'free gifts with purchase' and I just haven't put it away yet."

Mickey walked over to the collage and straightened a corner. Then she backed away from it. "What a perfect place for this."

"Isn't it? Take your time looking," Thea said on her way in to the kitchen. The story about Florence and Evelyn would wait for another day. "I'll put lunch in the oven."

"Sounds good. I want to look at your pitcher collection in the den one more time, too, while you're doing that."

Thea heard her picking up different pitchers in the old corner cupboard that had belonged to Reid's mother. "Is this one new? The red and white creamer shaped like a cow? It's my favorite."

"No, I used to keep it in here," Thea said from the kitchen, "so I could use it when we have company, but then I decided it was too cute to be hidden in a cabinet. It's my favorite, too."

So often Thea and Mickey were attracted to the same things. Thea thought of another time Mickey and Joel had come to Charlotte, and Reid and Joel were wearing the exact same burgundy wool crew-neck sweaters their wives had bought them for gifts.

While the eggplant was heating, they walked around the yard, Thea showing Mickey her roses and the new bed of laurel, their pointy leaves closed like hands in prayer. Thea showed her where the pond would go and what they'd plant if they got rid of the monkey grass: wild ginger here, a lace cap hydrangea back there. Bleeding heart and loosestrife.

The day was all greenness and sun.

They ate lunch on the screened porch, the ceiling fan throwing shadows, riled wasps occasionally batting the screen, trying to get in.

"Guess who I ran into the other day? Right on King Street in Charleston?" Mickey said. "Miss Althouse."

"Miss Althouse? As in 'Miss Outhouse,' home ec teacher in high school?"

"Yep. And the two of us were standing there on the street talking and talking. Can't you just picture the home ec room in the school basement? With those four little kitchens all set up in that one big room? The girls learning how to make iced tea! And the boys taking 'shop' down the hall."

"Well, how'd she look?" Thea asked. "She must be about ninety!"

"No, actually, she looked good. The same, in fact. She was old then. And she's old now!" They both laughed. "She brought up that time she told us about Coca-Cola taking the enamel off our teeth, when she said they'd done experiments and Coke ate right through the skin of a pearl. She said she'll never forget how you went home and dropped Mother's good pearl earrings in that glass of Coke—"

"*Me* drop Mother's earrings in Coke? It was *you*!" Thea broke up a spiderweb under the table beside her chair by sliding down low and taking a quick swipe with the side of her foot.

"Are you crazy? Even Miss Althouse said it was you."

"No, Mickey, I remember it perfectly. You made me wash the things before Mother got home."

"Look, the reason *you* had to wash them is because *you* were the one who got them sticky in the first place. Thea, you have a very interesting way of rewriting family history!"

Mickey was laughing. "Meanwhile, this eggplant is fantastic. I want the recipe." She rose with a cough to take her plate into the kitchen.

"Do you really like it?" she called after her sister. "Meanwhile, I want to go on record as saying it was you on that kitchen stool watching Mother's earrings sink in Coke! I can still see you turning the glass around and around. You know you always had more nerve than I did. Oh, the way memory is constantly being reconstructed!" She picked up her plate and followed Mickey inside.

"Here we go. A little psychologizing!" Mickey turned around and put her hand on Thea's arm. "Just remember, there were times you had nerve, too." She was now in the kitchen. "Weren't you the one who said to me, when I was already feeling as awkward as anyone could feel, 'You wear braces and glasses—what next, a hearing aid?' "

Mickey put her plate on the counter.

"I hate to admit it, but your memory about that is absolutely correct," Thea said, setting her plate next to her sister's. "The question is, what had you done to provoke me?"

Later, after Mickey left, Thea scraped the dishes. She noticed they'd each left the last bite of food untouched. It wasn't something either of them consciously set out to do, just one of those little things they both did. Sometimes, the ways they were alike seemed to be highlighted with a thick yellow pen; other times, you couldn't see anything but differences.

. . .

There was that one big fight when they were a junior and senior in high school. Actually, there were a number of fights in those years, but this was the one Thea remembered best.

It was a Saturday and Mickey was on the phone in the back hall downstairs, talking to one of her many friends. Thea was listening in on the upstairs extension. Mickey said to hold on a minute, she wanted a Coke—but instead of going in the kitchen, she sneaked upstairs. There was Thea, lying on her back on the cedar chest in the landing, one leg casually crossed over the other, dangling a sandal by the strap on a big toe, the telephone to her ear. Mickey flew into a rage. She ran in their bedroom, knocked the screen out of the window, and pulled the top drawer all the way out from their dresser. It hit the floor with a crash. She floated every piece of Thea's underwear—panties, bras, a sock, its mate, the rest of the socks, slips—out the window. It all came to rest on the front lawn like litter, for the entire neighborhood to see. Thea immediately hung up the phone, marched downstairs to the piano, and when Mickey got back on the phone, she began banging out the scale: C . . . D . . . E . . . F . . . G . . . A . . . B . . . C. Over and over. Mickey went on with her conversation, screaming over the racket. When she hung up, Thea played one last scale, slowly, loudly, deliberately: C . . . D . . . E . . . F . . . G . . . A . . . B . . . *C-sharp*. The off ending was meant to drive her sister crazy.

That night Mickey was drawing sports figures in her artist's pad and Thea was writing in her diary. Their mother came up to kiss them good night and sat on the edge of Thea's bed. Thea hoped Mickey would feel left out, with Thea and her mother sitting so close, the floor lamp separating the two beds like the tall brass branch of a family tree. Their mother began her familiar lecture about sisters and how important they are.

"Friends are just friends. But a sister is—blood! Blood!"

Mickey erased and brushed away the dust, erased and

brushed away the dust. Thea decided to act disinterested, like her sister, and started underlining everything she'd written.

"Hand me your diary and your pencil, darling." Their mother's dramatic voice. "I want to write down a prediction—so you'll have it the rest of your life! Some day you'll both understand what I'm talking about."

She flipped to the inside front cover and wrote something in her opulent, looping script. She read it out loud: *Years from now, my two daughters will be very close*. When she said the word *very*, she closed her eyes.

Then she said what she always said when Thea and Mickey had a fight: "Did I ever tell you girls about Florence and the oatmeal?"

Mickey tucked herself around her pad, hiding the exasperated *yes* she was mouthing, still erasing. Thea could see there was nothing left to erase. She decided to abandon her sister and her sour attitude. She hugged the diary to her chest and wormed closer to her mother.

"It doesn't matter," Thea said. "I want to hear it again."

"Well, you know your aunt Florence likes a lot of salt on her food—" Her voice was settling into a rhythm, as though she were reading a mystery story. "—and whenever the two of us would be eating together—and I don't just mean when we were little, I'm talking about even after we were grown—she would first sprinkle salt on her own food, then reach across the table and, without asking me, sprinkle salt on mine. One time—oh, I guess it was a few years after we both got married—she and Jack and your father and I took a vacation together. We went to Myrtle Beach, to the Ocean Forest Hotel, which, of course, we've always adored! It was early spring and it had turned very cold, so Florence and I ordered oatmeal for breakfast. When the waitress brought it to the table, Florence took the salt shaker and sprinkled salt on her oatmeal and then, sure enough, she stuck her arm across the table and sprinkled it on mine. I don't know what came over me! I heard myself all of a sudden speaking up! 'But I don't *like* salt on my oatmeal,' I said. 'I like sugar.' Now you see, *that's* how close sisters should be, close enough to put salt on the other one's oatmeal!"

Mickey loved to remind Thea that this story did not say what their mother thought it said. Thea would never admit to her sister that she was right. After all, Thea would tell Mickey, their mother and Florence *had* been close. How many times had their aunt driven the hour and a half from Columbia to Rock Hill when their mother was having one of her bouts with depression? Sometimes Florence would stay for days, cooking, taking care of the whole family. It had never occurred to Thea or Mickey to ask who was taking care of Evelyn.

Here's how it would go: First, Florence would get Mollie to sit on the side of the bed and swing her feet to the floor. That would be the beginning. Then she coaxed her out of the bedroom, into the kitchen for a bowl of soup. Thea's mother would slowly sip the split pea and barley soup Florence had made, looking up every now and then, the unspoken words of love and appreciation written across her face as clearly as if they were in neon. When the soup was finished, she'd stiffly cross the room and put her arms around Florence, who would be watching over every spoonful. They'd hug for a long time.

Then Florence would talk her into getting dressed and putting on real shoes instead of bedroom slippers. She'd sit at her dressing table and Florence would hand her a lipstick, then a powder puff. Florence stood behind her, brushing her hair, and her head would tilt in the direction of the strokes as if she were in the shower and hot water were streaming through her hair and falling over her shoulders. Then Florence buttoned the hard-to-reach buttons on the back of her blouse.

When she was ready, they walked down to the end of the driveway and back.

After several days of short strolls in the driveway, they walked all the way to the end, turned right, and headed up the street, their arms linked like two women going shopping—it looked like nothing more serious than that—the two of them finally disappearing around the curve.

Chapter 9

Monday, and the mail came early. Another letter from Helen. Thea folded it, slipped it in her pocketbook, and left for the radio station almost an hour early.

Instead of going left at the fork beyond the Handy Pantry, she went right, headed up the hill to the light. A man she always saw walking in the neighborhood crossed in front of her, swinging his arms expansively in perfect synchronicity with his feet, as though he were doing a tap dance. He was attracting as much attention as a blind person in traffic. The light changed. She turned left, then into the parking lot of the new Northern Moose coffee place. She'd pick up some decaf to take home, have a cup of coffee, and read the letter there. Now that's a sophisticated thing to do, she thought, sit at a table in a coffee shop and read a letter.

"A cup of Emerald Cream to drink here," she told the girl behind the counter, who had on a tan-colored Northern Moose T-shirt. "And a pound of the House Blend decaffeinated."

The place was large and open and empty, with big plate-glass windows and rock-and-roll music from the fifties playing in the background. Thea took her coffee to the "fixings" table, poured cream right up to the top, and went to a table in the center of the room. She stirred with the little wooden stick, licked it, dropped it on the table. Reid would've gotten up to put it in the trash can.

Ellen Proctor, from next door, was suddenly standing over her, swiftly tapping her shoulder. "Don't you just love this place? And it's so close. So close." She was dressed all in black, very smart-looking.

"Hi, Ellen." Thea crunched the letter into her lap.

"Are you waiting for somebody? I don't have much time—I have to pick Herm up at the car place, the Volvo's on the blink—but I could get a latte and keep you company for a minute. Just for a minute." Ellen was one of those people who say everything twice.

"Ordinarily, I'd love that, but I've got some work to do before I go to the station. Have to get ready for today's program." Ellen had never mentioned the show. Sometimes Thea worked it into a conversation just to remind people.

"Oh, of course. Of course. I ought to get what I came for and head on out anyway. Of course." Three *of courses*?

"Let's do it another day," Thea said. "Say hi to Herm for

me." Maybe she was being too abrupt. "Oh, and how're the kids? What do you hear from Herm Junior? How's summer school? Is his job at Applebee's any better?"

"Hates it. Now he's a prep cook and he chops lettuce for an entire eight-hour shift. Every shift, he has to fill one of those huge plastic garbage cans with chopped lettuce! But it's good experience. And he loves the class he's taking. Just loves it. Susan is talking about wanting to go to State. Still dying to be an architect, you know." The Proctors had good kids. Herm and Ellen were very involved parents; Thea imagined she and Reid would've been that way, if they'd been able to have children.

"Give Herm Junior my love when you talk to him. And tell Susan to come over sometimes."

"Sure will." Ellen walked sideways, like a crab, to the counter. "Oh, and I heard your show last week. When that woman called about her son not being popular. Your answer was good. Real good." Now she was at the counter, asking for the Colombian blend, paying with a handful of change, then out the door. Thea took a sip—too hot to drink—smoothed out the letter and began to read.

April 10, 1938

Dear sister Celia, leben, with your dear family leben,

Surely you have received my long letter. It was only last week that I was able to write it, excuse me. It happens sometimes. It will straighten itself out between us, sister.

I with my family are, thank God, well. I feel fine, thank God. I do not suffer and work a little.

It is Pesach . . . everywhere clean. Gave this week a good clean-

ing. When I told my help that they made everything very clean for Pesach for the seder, they do not know about that, they just know about doing good work. Spring cleaning, that is what the people here call it, but what I say (Pesach) they do not know anything about and do not understand me. They only know Easter.

Well, sister, I am very pleased that we have finished the job. My Negro is sick. She did not show up two weeks ago Saturday. Sunday we drove to visit her and find out what her sickness is. Easy sat in the car and I went in to her little house. On entering I asked her what is with you, what is your sickness. She became mute . . . then said I cannot tell you what happened to me . . . and uncovered the quilt cover to show her baby, born on Saturday morning. What do you think of that?

When Easy came in and saw the situation, then we both became without speech.

Her husband is dead almost a year. She has six children from before, now again. Seven babies. And she is supposed to be the cook, makes $3.00 a week from me. She sent me another in her place until she is able to come back. Then I do not know if I should take her back. She is the best I ever had in all respects though.

This week I had help and did everything at one time. My house shines. Now everything is clean, clean curtains, waxed floors, the kitchen. Only the oven needs to be koshered, that is for next week. On the porch white covers look good for the seder. We are driving next Sunday to Columbia, everything for Pesach to bring home from the city.

From Mollie a letter last week. They cannot come to the seder. She wishes to travel to be with her loving family but since this is not possible, she does not worry about having a seder. For Mike not to have a seder is something he cannot think of. God blesses those who want to be observant, I tell my daughters often. Today I received a postal card from her . . . that they have been invited by an elderly couple, very religious people, and prominent people, rich. I am overjoyed. She will take pleasure, she will see. Of this I am certain.

As I am writing this letter I hear the ice man passing up and down the street calling, "Ice, ice, made in the shade, sold in the sun."

All for the best in its fullest sense.

Yours always, Bella.

Thea took a swallow of coffee and reread the part about God blessing those who want to be observant. She had her own theory about religion. She believed it was mostly a matter of nostalgia, a matter of comfort. People have a longing to repeat the patterns of childhood and re-create what feels like home. It's the familiar hymns, the litanies from long ago, that keep bringing us back. If we have warm memories of being Baptist, Catholic, or Jewish when we were growing up, then we'll probably feel good about being Baptist, Catholic, or Jewish when we're adults.

The synagogue her family went to in Rock Hill was on the wrong side of town—on the other side of the Southern Railway tracks—in a low-rent, boarded-up area near the Coca-Cola bottling plant. Inside the black iron gates at the entrance, a dark, dungeonlike hall led to the sanctuary, which was small and bare-walled, and always cold.

During Friday night services in the fall of the year, she could hear the cheering at the football stadium across the back field, and she would sit there trying to figure out whether it was her school's team or the other, trampling its way into the end zone. Her best friend, Martha Jean Aycock, would be at the game, along with everyone else. No matter how loud the congregation sang "*Adon Alom,*" Thea could hear the marching band at halftime—the saxophones, drums, the crushing notes of the tuba.

For the High Holy Days, a student rabbi from a New York seminary would come down to lead the services. Thea and Mickey would ride to the train station with their parents to meet the young man and bring him back to stay at the house. It was always an Orthodox Jew. Why they sent Orthodox Jews to South Carolina was beyond her. Their skin would be pale as milk. Her father said it was because they spent long hours inside studying the Talmud. They wore tight-fitting black suits, very different from the blue-and-white-striped seersucker that puckered across her father's shoulders. Those rabbis didn't look or act like any people she had ever seen before. When she and Mickey were teenagers, their mother would remind them not to offer to shake hands with the young men because they weren't allowed to touch a woman who might be menstruating. Thea wanted to separate herself from them, pretend they weren't sleeping in the guest room across the landing.

Even so, being Jewish hadn't really made her feel different from everyone else. Jewishness was just another personal trait—like hair that was too fine, or shyness—a pesky characteristic she'd be better off without, but nothing that ever caused any serious problems. Well, maybe that wasn't *exactly* the way it was. Jewishness was more like a blemish you tried to scrub away with lemon juice, or conceal with the slightest dab of cover-up. She didn't know what would happen if it was obvious, if it showed too much, but she knew she didn't want to take that chance.

In the sixth grade—the first day of the school year, in fact—Miss Craig had written the daily schedule on the board, a schedule that included Bible class once a week after lunch.

"Now, you," she said, waving her hand in Thea's direction as though she were swatting a fly, "you can go to the library when Mrs. Daniels comes, if being in the room for Bible will make you uncomfortable."

What makes me uncomfortable, Thea wanted to say, is being the only one asked to leave. I think I'll just stay, is what she did say.

Mrs. Daniels was a stout woman with an unusually large, open face, which gave her the appearance of being able to look everywhere at once. She walked to the front of the classroom and, in a strong, hypnotic voice, said, "Boys and girls, picture yourselves back in the days of the Bible. Here's Ruth, walking away from the river. She is holding her head high and very steady." Mrs. Daniels walked back and forth in front of the desks, holding *her* head high and steady. Her footsteps were like gongs. "Can anyone tell me why Ruth is holding herself so straight?"

"Is it because she's proud of being a Christian?" one person asked.

"No . . ." Mrs. Daniels' voice went up at the end of the word, making no sound like yes.

"Is it because she knows Jesus loves her?" someone else asked.

"Good try . . . but no, dear . . ."

There was a growing excitement in the room and Thea was getting caught up in it. Her arm shot up and began waving, in spite of the fact she wasn't even supposed to be there in the first place. How could she possibly presume to know the answer when no one else did? They'd been going to Sunday school and vacation Bible school all their lives and probably knew every word of the Bible. She and Mickey had gone to Sunday school maybe half a dozen times, when the circuit-riding rabbi from North Carolina traveled south over the state line. And then the emphasis had been on learning about Jewish holidays.

The whole class turned toward Thea.

"Is it because she's carrying a jug of water on her head?" she guessed.

Snickers from everywhere.

Then, "Yes! Yes! Yes!" from Mrs. Daniels, who reached her hands up to steady the imaginary weight she'd been carrying, her words thrumming like organ chords.

Thea was saved.

But not for long. In seventh grade, the boys were playing kickball in one corner of the school yard and the girls were playing Red Rover in another. "Red Rover, Red Rover, let Alma come over," one line of girls chanted to the other. Alma Brunson was the roughest girl in the grade. Thea hated when she was called because she always went for the weakest link—where Thea's hand held her best friend's. She and Martha Jean were both skinny and frail, and, once again, Alma threw her entire body against their arms, breaking their hands apart like twigs.

Miss Craig blew her whistle, calling everyone in. Martha Jean and Thea dawdled along the concrete walk leading to the building, both of them shaking out their arms and rubbing the sore places.

"Hey, how about what happened to Ed!" Martha Jean said, her tiny lips puckered, eyes wide as small suns.

"What?" How could anything happen to Thea's boyfriend she wouldn't know about?

"You didn't hear? Some boy from Northside School called him a"—she swallowed—"a dirty Jew-lover. Ed beat him up."

Ed—his name no bigger than a fist—loved Thea, a Jew. A dirty Jew. Suddenly, she could see him hiding her family in the basement of his house on Myrtle Drive. In the hollow of night, he'd bring leftover scraps of potatoes and bread. If the soldiers came, his beautiful older sister would keep them occupied in the living room while he sneaked down the hidden stairs to wave Thea's family back into their musty, mildewed corner.

. . .

Thea looked up. The girl in the T-shirt was wiping a table near the front door, a wet rag in one hand, a dry one in the other, both hands circling the surface like the rotary brushes of a floor polisher. She was singing along with the music. *Shoo-doot'n-shoo-bee-doo . . .* Thea turned back her sleeve to check her watch. She had five minutes to make the ten-minute ride to the station.

. . .

Her first caller was a woman whose seven-year-old daughter had stolen a doll from a friend's house. The rest of the callers talked about their own troubled childhoods.

When the program was over, Tim poked his head through the door, his neck extended. "Could I see you a minute in my office?" he said. Then he drew his head back in, like a turtle.

"Sure. I'll be right there," she answered. Now what? She had *not* gone on and on that day. True, she'd been a little late and he'd had to do some of the preliminary things she usually did, but she'd been ready when the program began. Plus, she got to a lot of callers, which was what he was always wanting.

She followed him into his office. His stringy arms held a

stack of loose papers, a notebook, eyeglasses, and a mug all in a jumble. When he closed the door, the papers fell everywhere, like flecks of dandruff. He and Thea almost bumped heads on their way down to the floor to pick everything up.

"Just have one thing to say," he said, piling it all on his desk. He pulled his chair around and slid his long, slender column of a body downward in it as though he had a hundred things to say. He stretched his legs out across the tweed carpet. "Good show today. Good pacing. Good answers."

"Thanks," she said, still standing. "Thanks a lot." But?

Then, abruptly, he stood up, bowed slightly, and made a chopping motion with the side of his hand in the direction of the door, as though he were signaling a plane to the gate. They were back to cues.

But he'd actually given her a compliment! There had been words! A conversation! She hurried out of his office, singing *shoo-doot'n-shoo-bee-doo* . . . underneath her breath, feeling light, lucky.

. . .

"That's not a word," Reid was saying that night, his hand poised on *The Official Scrabble Players Dictionary*.

"Go ahead and challenge, if you want," she answered, grinning, still in a good mood from that afternoon. "Be my guest."

"Abey?"

"Yes, abey. It's a form of the word *abeyance,* meaning to set aside something. You know. The legal term. But you're the English teacher, why don't you challenge me? If I'm right, though, you'll lose your turn."

"What makes you so full of piss and vinegar when you're playing Scrabble—and such a wimp in real life?" He winked and picked a shimmery stray hair off her black T-shirt. The last few days had turned hot and sticky. The air conditioning was going full force, frosting the windows and chilling the black and white linoleum in the kitchen. Thea had put on socks before they started the game.

"You make me sound like I have a split personality."

He picked up the paperback dictionary and watched her while he shuffled the pages with his thumb, the sound like a small motor. She knew he was testing her, threatening to look up *abey* to see if it was, in fact, a word. He searched her face for a clue as to whether she was bluffing. She made her face opaque, locked her eyes in an expressionless gaze.

"Not only do you have a split personality," he said, "you've also inherited your grandfather's poker face."

"Let's leave ancestors out of this. You've got a few skeletons in your closet I could pull out and rattle around."

"This dictionary is for the birds anyway. Any dictionary that lists—what was it?—*eng* as a word . . ."

"Oh yes, *eng* is a word. It's a phonetic symbol."

He tucked the dictionary under his hip—they were sitting catercornered at the pine table—and rotated the board toward him. The far corner of the board knocked over the snapshot that had been propped against the salt and pepper shakers. Belle had sent it a couple of weeks ago—she and Ann standing up in the boat in the lake behind Mickey and Joel's house, both girls tall like their parents, tanned. Ann, strong and athletic like Mickey. Belle, willowy, graceful, like Joel. They both had their father's earnest, narrow face. Reid set the picture straight again.

"All right," he said. "I'm not going to take a chance on this one. No challenge. I'll probably kick myself later for letting you get by with it. How many points do you get?"

She tapped out her score on the tiles with her fingernail. "One, two-three-four, five, six-seven-eight-nine. Triple word score. I get twenty-seven, total. Not bad." She added her score on the yellow pad.

"And I'm sitting here with practically all *i*'s." He rearranged the tiles in his rack. "This is pitiful."

"Want to hear the score so far? A hundred and eighty-eight to one-oh-one."

"And you're the hundred and eighty-eight, I gather. Which is why you're so eager for me to know the score."

"Right." With a pen, she traced over their names, printed in small, plain letters, as different from her mother's out-of-bounds alphabet as anything could be.

"And they say only children are competitive. Speaking from experience, an only child can't hold a candle to a firstborn!" he said.

"I'm not at all a typical firstborn."

"You don't *think* you're a typical firstborn. But it's highly debatable. Firstborns never feel they got their due. Which makes them fierce competitors. Always trying to recoup what they think was taken from them. Hey, that sounded pretty good. I ought to be on the radio!"

"It's your turn. Go." She kept her head down so he couldn't see her smiling. He wanted fierce competition? She'd give him fierce competition.

He pinched high on the bridge of his nose in the corners of his eyes with his forefinger and thumb, a gesture she'd fallen in love with on their first date, then put four tiles down on the board, picked them back up, checked to see if there was anything better he could do, then put the same four tiles down again.

"*Fire*. A measly six points," he said. "And I only got rid

of one of my *i*'s." He felt around in the velvety bag as though he could avoid the vowels and pick only *z*'s and *x*'s. "I don't believe it." He placed the new letters on his rack. "Another *i*. How many are there in the whole set?"

"Your word reminds me—whatever happened with those students who got caught with the sofa in their room?" She picked up five of her tiles and cupped them in her hand.

"The administration kicked them off campus."

"Are you serious?"

"They can still go to class, but they have to find off-campus housing, and they're on probation. Violated the fire code."

"Of course, it doesn't matter that it's been twenty years since a couch caught fire in a dorm room." She placed her tiles back on her rack.

"Well, sofas are against the rules."

"Sofas with upholstered arms, right? Most people are worrying about drugs and alchohol with young people, and your administration is kicking kids off-campus for upholstered arms! What's wrong with this picture?"

"The parents of the students are pretty upset, I hear," he said. "Writing letters to the dean and to the president. I think they're making a mistake. They're just teaching their kids to avoid taking responsibility."

"I don't know about that. Sounds to me like the administration is overreacting. I can understand the parents' side. I'd probably feel the same way if it were my child." She watched the lights go on in the daughter's room upstairs in the Proctors' house next door, the gold shine through the tops of the pines so bright Thea had to look away. She reached over to pull the café curtains closed.

"I don't know, maybe it *is* pretty hard for parents to accept," he said. "But let's not go into it. I've heard enough about that at school."

"Here." She added an *s* to *fire* and put down the other letters, moving vertically up the board—*m*, two *o*'s, and *z*. "*Zooms*. The *z* is on a triple letter so that's thirty. Thirty-one, thirty-two, thirty-three—thirty-four—thirty-five." Tapping out her score on the tiles, this time with the pen. "Thirty-five."

"Actually, you get thirty-six. You forgot to count the s."

"Actually, I get forty-two. We both forgot to count *fire*."

"I'm hungry." He leaned back in his chair to see the clock on the stove. "It's after ten." He pulled away from the table. "How 'bout some popcorn?"

"Oh, darn. I bought some green peanuts at the farmer's market this afternoon and forgot to boil them. Wouldn't they taste good right now? I hope I can remember to cook them tomorrow when I get home."

He was in the pantry. She could hear him taking down the popcorn popper from the top shelf and getting the jar of popcorn. He put the pot on the stove, turned it on, poured in the kernels, went back to the pantry for oil. She would've hurried to get the oil, to keep the kernels from burning. He was taking his time, stopping to straighten the herb picture on the wall beside the pantry door.

She turned his rack to sneak a look at his letters. He had four *i*'s, an *o*, and two *u*'s. No wonder he was thinking of food.

"Let's forget the game," she said, turning his tiles back before he saw her looking at them. "You've suffered enough!"

The snap of the kernels breaking out and their toasty aroma were filling the kitchen. She'd heard that people trying to sell a house sometimes popped popcorn right before a prospective buyer came, to give the house a homey, welcoming smell. Or was it that they baked Pepperidge Farm apple turnovers? Now she couldn't remember which it was.

"By the way," she said, looking up at the strong, sure curve of his shoulders, "F.Y.I.—for your information—*abey* is *not* a word. You should've challenged me. But I have to admit I do love that you were willing to go along with me, no matter what." She walked over to him, took his woolly arm, and held it to her face, the scent clean and sweet as light perfume.

Chapter 10

April 19, 1938

Dear sister Celia,

I am letting you know that I am, thank God, well. I do not suffer. I helped to make everything ready for Pesach and feel fine.

Sunday we were in Columbia. Easy and I bought the Pesach order. Then we, with Florence, traveled to Newberry to see Mollie and Mike... They looked very good, a very happy couple. On their whole life I pray they have much happiness. Mollie dressed very nicely with spring clothes, looks very pretty. She will try to come to Denmark soon and stay a few days.

Surely you have received my long letter as I have received yours and thank you. Write again but write a little more. It is good to tell your sister how the days go in your life, to write a longer letter. You are a little miserly with your words.

My Florence worked for her papa for two weeks, perhaps I wrote to you about this. I write to you so often it is difficult to know what has been written. Soon Florence will finish her two weeks of work and has already spent her wages, $30.00 in two weeks. Bought herself two dresses, fancy shoes, white with brown, stockings, good underwear, $1.00 for a small bottle of perfume with more things that she wanted very much. Now she will stay at home to rest for two weeks before she will come back to work. Those are her plans.

My cook is back to work and I have become free again.

I wish you to have a happy Pesach with everything good, that we should live to next year and all of us be together for the seder. And if we cannot be together to write more often. We thank God for this, that we should not be disturbed with one another, two devoted sisters with our families, one from the other, please God. This is my prayer.

I received from Cousin Yetta a letter with a small picture to show me her Pearl's two children which I send to you, according to her wishes.

Pearl's little girl is very pretty and the little boy is handsome but looks different with his olive skin. I did not remember that she had a little son. My thought was always that she had one child. Whoever asks me I tell them, one little girl. But now I became surprised. They should have long years with her two pretty children. When I showed the picture to my children on Sunday, they all cried out, Mama, whose boy is he? Who is his papa? We had a bit of fun. Mollkeleh did not join in the fun. I believe from working so hard she is sometimes not in good humor. She became angry at our good fun and left the room.

Everyone be well. Have regards from my entire family and from myself.

Your sister Bella from the South

Thea turned down the water on the stove to keep the peanuts from boiling over and went to the phone above the desk. She was still eyeing the pot. Simmering now. Safe to turn her back.

"Hello?" Florence's sandpaper voice. How Thea loved it.

"Hi, Aunt Florence. It's me. Guess what I have for you!" Maybe after she finished reading the letter to her, she'd call Mickey and see if she wanted to hear that last one, and this new one.

"Another letter? Let's hear it!"

"First, let me ask you, did Mickey say anything to you about her not wanting me to get the letters translated?"

"Honey, I've lived long enough to know to stay out of those sorts of things. I figure you're both grown and can work it out for yourselves. *Without* me. Meanwhile, I can tell you, *I* don't mind hearing them one bit!"

Thea read her the letter, knowing neither of them would mention Mickey's reaction to the letters again. Or the meeting in Columbia. Or the part in this letter about Florence spending her salary on clothes for herself before she'd finished working the two weeks—because Thea didn't read her that part. Family stories had a way of taking on new truths, depending on who was doing the telling. This story was slightly different from Florence's version where she had to buy clothes for her sister with her small paycheck.

"I wish you could have heard Papa," Florence said. "He put on a Passover seder that was . . . mmm . . . really something. He had a beautiful voice. He'd close the store late at night and it would be twelve, one o'clock in the morning before he'd finish *davening*. We'd lie on the floor right by the table and fall asleep, your mother and me, listening to him. One time he tried to sing like Caruso and he hit a high C and tore something in his throat and had to go to bed. It was the only time I ever saw Papa sick in bed!"

"Aunt Florence, can I change the subject for a minute? Why do you think it said in the letter that Mother became so angry? That just doesn't make sense to me." The only time Thea had ever seen her mother truly angry was the afternoon she'd slapped her.

"Your mother . . ." Florence said. Thea turned to check the peanuts. Still simmering. "Your mother . . . well, let me tell you a different thing. Your mother was very religious at one time, you know."

"My mother was religious?"

"Oh yes. She even studied with Rabbi Kline when she was a young bride. In the beginning of her marriage, she would travel from Newberry to Columbia to learn Hebrew two days a week. She even went to the Orthodox *shul* in Columbia, which surprised me, because she'd always said she wasn't going to travel from town to town after she got married like our mama and papa did. You know, back in the old days, we were always driving to Columbia from Denmark or whichever small town we were living in, driving to the closest city for services and to be with Jewish people. And with Papa's gambling, we had to move so much . . . Your mother always wished we could stay in one place. But anyway, in the Orthodox *shul* in Columbia, your mother sat upstairs with the old women. That's the way they did then, the men downstairs, the women up in the balcony. And, on Yom Kippur, the very religious people didn't wear shoes with hard soles.

One Yom Kippur, somebody made the remark to me after services about my sister sitting up there in her bare feet. When I said to Mollie, 'They noticed you sitting like you're so religious,' she said, 'What do you mean? My feet hurt so I took my shoes off!' "

That story didn't have anything to do with Thea's question. As an experiment, she decided to ask a question that she knew her aunt would *want* to answer. "Did your family keep kosher in Denmark?"

"We started out that way. We ordered meat from Charleston, but one time the truck got lost and by the time it got to Denmark and they found our house, all the meat was spoiled. You know, they didn't have refrigerated deliveries or that sort of thing. So, Papa said, 'This is the end of kosher, as far as we're concerned.' But you know, Mama and Papa didn't stay in Denmark that first time we lived there."

Nothing wrong with her hearing. "They didn't stay in Denmark? You mean they lived there two different times?" Thea uncoiled the phone cord and walked over to the stove to stir the peanuts, taking one out and dropping it on the spoon rest. She'd let it cool before she tasted it to see if it needed salt. She'd also let her aunt go on for a while before she tried to interrupt again.

"Oh yes. Well, you know Papa and Mama moved to Denmark from New York not long after I was born. Of course, they wouldn't let us in Denmark at first because of polio. They called it infantile paralysis back then. They would quarantine a whole house and make the people fly a flag outside to let everybody know. We had to stay in St. George with a friend of Papa's till they checked us out and gave us permission to enter the city." Florence laughed. "The city! Well, Denmark *was* a city compared to St. George! You know how your mind jumps from one thing to the other? For some reason, I just thought about how they didn't have screens on the windows in those days. We slept under netting. And God help you if a mosquito got in under the netting with you!"

"Netting on the beds? Sounds like the tropics." Maybe if Florence keeps talking, she'll slip and tell something she doesn't mean to tell.

"It was a hard, lonely life, especially for Mama, in such a small country town. They pumped water from a well. Mama barely spoke English. Papa learned English quickly because he was in business, out in the world with people, and it was easier for him. But Mama, it was hard for her. So many new ways, people with such different customs. Papa's cousin, Abe Bogen, who persuaded Papa to move south in the first place, couldn't even speak English when he first went into business. Abe was a peddler, traveling around the countryside selling dry goods. He learned one thing to say in English: 'Look in the basket.' When the person would ask him, 'Do you have this or do you have that?' Abe would say, 'Look in the basket.' He figured if they saw what they wanted, they'd buy it. I don't know why I'm talking so much. I hope you don't think all this is boring."

"No, no, you're never boring," Thea said, cracking open the peanut with her teeth. It was good and salty. She stirred the pot again and cocked the lid halfway. Almost done. "I *would* like to ask something about Mother though."

"Well, there's another story about Abe Bogen I want to tell you. He also learned the English words, 'Can I sleep with you?' See, he'd be traveling around the countryside and sometimes he'd need a place to stay. So one time the farmer's wife came to the door and he asked, 'Can I sleep with you?' The husband came after him with a shotgun!"

That sounded like an old joke Mickey used to tell, but Thea laughed anyway.

"After we lived in Denmark the first time, Papa bought a store *and* a house from a man in High Point. Papa heard he'd made a lot of money. The grass was always greener on the other side. If Papa heard someone was making money in another town, he would just pick up and move us there. And he was always playing cards. Why he gambled, I don't understand. All those years it was his ambition to accumulate enough cash to go back to New York and open a big department store. E. C. Bogen's, he was going to call it. He even told each one of us what we would do in the department store and we believed everything he said. He said I'd be the floorwalker."

"That sounds like a streetwalker!"

"No, no, dear. A floorwalker was very important. A floorwalker walked around the store making sure everything was all right and that the salesladies were doing their jobs. Mama and Mollie were going to be salesladies. Well, anyway, Papa bought this man's whole life—lock, stock, and barrel. We moved to High Point into this man's house. We slept in his beds, slept on his sheets, we ate from his dishes. Everything that man owned Papa bought. And Papa started running the man's store. High Point was a bigger town and we liked it better. There were Jewish people there and we all had a good time. But it didn't work out. Business wasn't so good. No wonder that man wanted to sell everything to Papa so cheap. Papa was a dreamer. He'd get in the gin rummy games with his friends, trying to turn the cash he had into more, and he'd lose it all. Soon Papa heard about an opportunity in Blackville, so he closed the High Point store and sold our house and we moved to Blackville. From there we moved to Barnwell. Then Columbia. Then Bamberg. And then we moved back to Denmark, where Mama and Papa stayed, even after Mollie and I were married and gone."

"I can't imagine moving around that much," Thea said. "Didn't your mother mind living like that?" Another question Florence would like.

"Back then, the husband was lord of the house and the woman did whatever he said. The only person who seemed to mind was your mother. Every time we picked up and left a place, your mother would be so sad. Her voice would get very soft. Sometimes she would be talking and I could hardly hear her. Sometimes she wouldn't talk at all for long periods. She'd take naps. Of course, she was very popular and always made friends fast. A lot faster than I would. But that didn't seem to help. It took her a while to get used to a new place. Making friends wasn't the problem. It was that she needed to be in the same house, the same *place*. She needed that security."

Thea dumped the peanuts in a colander in the sink. The opal-white steam rose, fogging her glasses, and she couldn't see a thing. She pulled them off. The nuts were not only done, they were soggy.

"But talking about all this reminds me," Florence moved on, "one time there was a disease going around, an epidemic, and I hadn't caught it. So Mama and Papa sent me to Norway to be with the Rubins until the epidemic passed."

"To Norway. Sounds so exotic!" Thea laughed. She could win the Miss Congeniality trophy.

"It was nice in Norway with the Rubins. One evening at sunset, I was walking down this dirt country road with Mr. and Mrs. Rubin, and Mrs. Rubin had her arm around my shoulder, and I was enjoying being the only girl there, and I was thinking I wish I was their child, you know, because I'd be the only daughter. And she, at that point in life, wanted another child, a daughter. She had two boys, Jake and Sammy. Well, she turns to her husband and says, 'Uh, Rubin'—she called him by his last name—'wouldn't you like to have a little girl just like this?' I looked up in time to see his face, and he was making a terrible grimace. It was no mistake. I saw it. And listen to this: When she finally did have a girl, to my satisfaction, that little girl was really ugly! I'm going to tell you something, he got paid back for making that face about me."

"I can't imagine anyone making a face talking about you."

"Well, back to Papa and Denmark. His business was finally good enough for them to buy a house. The house he bought had been a small hotel. It was two stories, plus a basement. There was a long hall upstairs with lots of rooms branching off. Mollie and I used to hide in the rooms from each other. You know how little children play hide and seek."

Okay, Thea was catching on. Florence was cagey. If she gives me enough details, I'll forget about asking my tough questions.

"We lived in the house that used to be a hotel for several years until we had a fire," Florence was saying. "The house burned completely to the ground. Mollie must have been about seven and I was ten. She and I were in bed asleep. It was early Sunday morning and Mama and Papa were in the kitchen. All of a sudden, I heard Mama screaming, 'The *kinder*! Easy, get the *kinder*, the children! The house is on fire!' I heard Papa screaming, 'The *gelt*! Get the *gelt*, Bella, the money!' See, Papa always kept the store open late Saturday night and came home with the money from that whole week, so this being Sunday morning, the week's earnings were upstairs in his and Mama's room. Papa ran upstairs and got the money and then he raced down to the basement and saw that the whole furnace was about to explode. So he and Mama together ran back upstairs and took Mollie and me out on the porch up there. By that time, we couldn't go down the stairs because of all the smoke. Mollie was crying, 'I'm not going outside in my onion suit!' See, we were still in our bedclothes. In the winter your mother and I slept in union suits. The firemen and the people from the neighborhood were gathered around in the front yard. There was a man standing down there holding his arms open and Mama was going to throw Mollie down to him—from that height! But I stopped her. I wouldn't let her throw your mother off the second-floor porch like that. Can you imagine what would've happened if I'd let her *throw Mollie off*?"

Regardless of what Florence would or would not reveal, she *was* Thea's mother's caretaker. More than that. She'd saved her life over and over. After having to look out for her for so many years, it made sense that resentment would eventually replace concern. No wonder Florence changed. It was probably her way of marking the end of taking care of someone else and the beginning of taking care of herself.

"So, all the firemen and people formed a human ladder—"

"A human ladder?" Thea asked. "Do you mean they were on each other's shoulders?" She wasn't going to let her get by with everything.

"All I know is they handed us down one person to another. Right after we all got out, Mama ran back in the house to turn the light off under the pan on the stove. She'd been frying herring for Papa's breakfast. One minute after she was back outside again, the thing in the basement exploded and the whole house went up in flames. Papa paced back and forth. Mama held onto Mollie and me, one on one side, one on the other. I could feel Mollie trembling. I know that sounds impossible. But I could feel her shaking *through* Mama's body. We watched while everything we owned burned up."

"It must've been so frightening. Mother never told me. I can't believe I haven't heard about something that important in your lives."

"Your mother didn't like to talk about it, even right after it happened. She was like Mama in that way. Mama always had an expression, 'The last word you keep to yourself.' And your mother kept certain things to herself, too."

Florence was making sure Thea knew there were certain things she was going to keep to herself, too.

"But I'm going to tell you something else. A short time after our fire, maybe a year, no more than that, your mother's best friend, Kat, died in a fire in her house. The way it happened with Kat, she was standing near an open fireplace in her house and she backed up to it and her skirt caught fire. They couldn't put it out and she burned up. Losing Kat was very, very hard for your mother. You'd always see the two of them, Kat and Mollie, jumping rope, playing paper dolls, walking home from school together. So. Kat burning up. Coming after our fire. It was not good. Not good at all."

Thea didn't hear another word. She was back in the house in Rock Hill, in the hall outside her mother's room, easing the door open, looking at her mother in bed in the middle of the afternoon, blankets and afghans piled high, her hair loose and spread out on the pillow like dark knots of rope.

. . .

Saturday night, a week later, Thea and Reid were getting ready to go out. She emerged from the bathroom, wrapped in a towel, wearing a poofy plastic shower cap, dripping water across the bedroom carpet. When Reid saw the shower cap, which he always said looked like a hair net a woman working behind the counter in a cafeteria would wear, he said with an exaggerated Southern drawl, "I'll have the butter beans, ma'am, and some o' them mashed potatoes an' gravy."

He smoothed down his shirttail and pulled on his khaki pants. She took off the shower cap, dropped it on the floor, and shook out her hair. "There you go," she teased, crossing the room to him, "tucking in your shirt like they taught you in the Army, tight across your belly. The side seams are supposed to line up under your arms, not around your back!" She tried to loosen his shirt, picking at the blue chambray fabric with her fingers.

"Ow, you're pulling my hair!" he said, laughing, twisting away, then toward her. He leaned down and kissed her as though they would not be going out at all. His hands were wide across her back.

"I like you, Miss Cafeteria Person," he whispered, his lips right at her ear. He unraveled her towel and let it fall around their feet. "I like you very much."

"Ditto," she whispered back, first feeling the flannel warmth of his body, then the bare chill of the air in the room. "But let's not get distracted. We've got dinner reservations in twenty minutes." She reached down for the towel, pulling herself away.

. . .

The hostess at Independence Café showed them to a table. They settled into the garlicky smells and soft, festive chatter around them. Thea laid her pocketbook on the floor beside her chair and picked up the menu. Her mother used to carry a little gadget with her, a brass hook she'd slip onto the edge of the table to hang her pocketbook on. When a waitress commented on it, Thea would smile apologetically to acknowledge that she knew this person was overly extravagant but there was absolutely nothing she could do about it.

"You painted a toucan at day camp today? A *toucan*?" It was the woman at the table next to them. She was talking to her daughter, but making sure her husband—and everyone else within earshot—knew how smart their little genius was. "One of the colors, you say, was *indigo*?"

Thea made a J with her forefinger and thumb for Reid's benefit, her signal that a person close by was Jewish, a signal he always pretended, with a mock scowl, to disapprove of. He thought it was funny that Thea could tell when someone else was Jewish, and that it mattered.

She sometimes joked she was sure she'd been switched in the hospital nursery, since it was obvious she was meant to be Presbyterian or Methodist. A joke, but not totally. It wasn't that she was denying her religion, it's just that something was wrong from the inside out. She'd read about people who have sex-change operations, how they always felt they'd been trapped in the wrong body. She understood exactly what they meant.

But she didn't want to get into that conversation tonight, so she pulled out the letter from Helen Feinman that had come that afternoon.

"Number six," she said, shifting her chair to the left so the family at the next table was behind her and out of her line of vision. "Only two more to go."

"Has Mickey said anything about the letters you gave her?"

"Not a word."

"But then neither have you, right?"

"I don't know whether I should be curious about what she thought of them or relieved we don't have to discuss it."

"Like getting your eyes examined and the optometrist asking, 'Which is better, one or two?' " What did that have to do with it?

The waiter was standing beside the table, ready to take their drink order. He wore one small gold loop earring and he blinked a lot, as if he were wearing new contact lenses. She said she'd have a glass of the house white wine; Reid wanted a beer. And they'd like to go ahead and order dinner. Lemon chicken for her. Steak for him. The same things they always got here.

"Sixth one, eh? I think I look forward to reading these letters as much as you do!" Reid held the pages near the candle so he could make out the words, but before he could begin reading, the waiter was back with their drinks, ceremoniously placing the glass of wine beside Thea's plate, and with a flourish, turning the bottle of beer completely upside down in an empty glass, the mouth against the bottom of the glass. Then he raised the bottle—straight up—filling the glass. When he finished, there was only a thin halo of foam.

"It's the Wisconsin way to pour beer. That's where I'm from and I can tell you, there's plenty of beer up there!" The waiter was proud of his trick.

"I'll bet," Thea said, no enthusiasm. She didn't bother to look up.

"Hey, aren't you that therapist on the radio?" he asked.

"Well yes, I am."

"Wow! I thought I'd heard your voice somewhere! Your accent! It's very distinctive. Doesn't exactly sound like Charlotte."

"I grew up in Rock Hill. Maybe it's a South Carolina accent you hear. So, you listen to my program?" She was smiling now, really smiling, and her face was eager and turned toward him.

"Oh sure. It's great," he said, blinking at her.

"Well, thank you! You're nice to say that." It was her radio star-to-fan tone of voice. She didn't have many opportunities to use it, but when the occasion arose, she didn't hold back. By the time he left the table, her back was straight and her head high, as though she were in a parade. She glanced around the restaurant to see if anyone else recognized her. She felt like Elizabeth Taylor.

"You love that attention, don't you?" Reid said. "You weren't going to give that guy the right time of day—until he told you he heard you on the radio! Admit it!"

"Sh-h. Somebody'll hear you. And anyway, you're wrong." She glanced around again. "Just read the letter."

May 12, 1938

Dear sister Celia leben, with your dear family leben:

Surely you have received my writings in which I wrote to you from everything. I have your letter also received and it pleased me that you all enjoyed this Pesach. Thank God for this.

Now I can tell you that we feel fine. I feel very good lately. Work in store and rest after dinner a little, not much.

My Florence does not want to live with us in Denmark. She wishes to tear the string that binds her, she is strong, thank God. Stubborn, also. She has always been too certain of what she thinks. You know this. In the past you have taken her side against me when I have spoken with you about her, do you remember this?

Last Sunday we traveled to Newberry because Mollkeleh wanted this and because she has been a little unhappy of late, of which I will not go into now as it is not necessary. Do not keep asking. My thinking was that we should go to be with her, to cheer her. That we should come together on Mother's Day. So we came, Easy and I and Florence. We traveled by train because the car is broken.

My Florence had packed a valise, not telling anyone. She said . . . I am not going back. It did not help to speak to her. She remained with Mollkeleh and told us that she will find a job working in Newberry, not in Denmark. Today I received a letter from her, that Monday she is going to work, has a job with Jewish people, office work in a jewelry store, bookkeeping and such. A jewelry store will make her happy. She likes pretty things for herself.

I am pleased, only God should help, that she will work at a good place, they should be pleased with her and she with them. What should we say? We cannot sway her, Easy would want her here in the store because he can use her. But she does not want to be at home. Why so important that she should be with her sister? When her papa asks her to stay at home? Yet I am glad for her to be with her sister. Sisters should be together, yes? Back and forth, my feelings.

My children presented me very finely with gifts for Mother's Day. Mollkeleh with a pair of pretty slippers, black with white trimming, special, a fine shoe, with a pair of silk stockings, an added present. Florence, a white slip, a flat crepe, a good one. Easy, a compact with everything that makes one pretty and young.

Business with us is a little better these few weeks because of the school's closing. They buy a little to dress up the children.

We close the store 6:30, it is a pleasure. We come home for an early supper. We have a long evening for ourselves. We never had this to happen. Only I and Easy are home, it appears to me funny. I have already told Easy, at supper, that I do not feel myself yet that old to be so alone, two plates at the table. Where I was accustomed to have the whole table ringed around with plates. Much was cooked and fried. Now. Now, a little bit and a little bit, no one here to eat . . .

A terrible thing happened in this town I almost forgot to tell you. A Negro was digging in a gravel pit and the mound suddenly gave way. Under the gravel and rock the man was buried 5 or 6 feet. Other men in the pit worked to immediately pull him out and he was still alive but it was found that his entire back split open. He died on the same day that the accident occurred. So much to be sad about.

This is all the news that I have to write. I await from you also a letter with all that is important to know.

I am writing this at home. Soon it is time to go to sleep. It has become very windy this evening and I feel like writing.

With regards to you all from,
your sister Bella

P.S. Please write much and give an answer . . . what do you think of what I write to you? What is your advice about Florence?

Reid folded the letter evenly, ran his finger along the creases and handed it back to Thea. Then he spread his napkin across the table and with slow, wide, sweeping motions, began smoothing out the wrinkles in the cotton.

"Interesting," he said, "Florence was telling you the truth. She *did* give her mother practical gifts. A good slip, it said, unlike your mother and her silk stockings present. Maybe your mother did have an ulterior motive in giving her mother the stockings."

"Maybe," she said, not meaning maybe at all.

"Look, we can talk about Florence being stubborn or her job in the jewelry store and how she wanted pretty things for herself. Or the man in the gravel pit. Do you like those topics better?" He laughed and dropped his napkin in his lap.

The waiter was back with their salads. He rotated the plate at Thea's place as though it had a front and a back. He finally settled on placing the side with the artichoke heart next to her. He plopped Reid's salad in front of him without fussing with it at all. Then he was off.

"Your grandmother sure sounds upset about Florence leaving," Reid said. "And why would she move in with your mother so soon after your mother's wedding? I'll bet there's a lot more to *that* story. And what's all this about your mother being unhappy and your grandmother not wanting to discuss it?" He took a long drink of beer. Thea tasted her wine. He was finally coming around to the right response.

"Families!" he said, raising an eyebrow and tipping his head toward the table next to them, the couple and their daughter, then toward the letter in Thea's hand. That's more like it, she thought. He'd known her long enough to understand that at the heart of everything were the phantom halves of her family's stories, the ghost of what was not being told.

Chapter 11

Reid had known her since college. But the year before they met, she'd been engaged to someone else. A boy named Richard Raab, who was tall and broad like Reid, but dark, with black hair as thick as an expensive carpet. He looked like one of those mobsters in *Life* magazine. Sounded like one, too, with his heavy Bronx accent. His family had moved south to Charlotte just before he started college. He was abrupt when he spoke, but he seemed strong and sure of himself—qualities Thea had been drawn to.

She met Richard at the University of Georgia her sophomore year, his junior year. He gave her an engagement ring the next year, on her twentieth birthday, but by Thanksgiving, she was having second thoughts and tried to give it back. He talked her into believing that she was in love with him but she just didn't realize it yet. He said everybody got cold feet. He was convincing and she wanted to believe him.

But her doubts didn't go away. It seemed as though her mother knew something was wrong, but she brought up the subject only one time.

"Are you sure you're in love?" she asked, fussing with scraps of paper covered with estimates and other details for the reception at the Andrew Jackson Hotel.

"Yes, I'm sure," Thea lied.

She wanted her mother to ask again. She wanted to tell what a huge mistake she was making. She wanted her mother to be the type of mother who could sense what was going on with her daughter. But her mother was so caught up in making plans and operating at such a high pitch, she couldn't possibly focus on something that would bring it all down.

Invitations had been mailed and R.S.V.P.'s were coming in. A white gown and veil hung in Thea's closet; the matron of honor, Martha Jean, and the flower girl had their matching azalea pink taffeta dresses. All over the house, damask-covered tables displayed gifts. It looked like a store—salt and pepper shakers lined up in pairs, sterling Revere bowls, ornate trays propped on their sides, china and silverware laid out as though the whole town were coming for dinner. Richard had made reservations for the honeymoon, a cruise to Bermuda, and they'd signed a lease on an apartment in Charleston, where he'd start medical school in the fall. Thea liked that part—moving to the town where Mickey and Joel lived. She and her sister would probably get along great, Thea thought, living so close. She wasn't sure, at this point, what she would do about her last year of school.

There were a lot of things she wasn't sure about. She felt as though she were in a speeding car passing one landmark after another. Every time another arrangement was made, she said to herself, Oh well, it's too late now.

Then it was a beautiful June morning and she and Richard were driving up to Hickory to buy furniture. The air had a pure scent, as if the whole world were getting ready for a wedding.

Inside the warehouse, the salesman led them from one fake room to another, thumping the tops of tables with his hairy fingers to demonstrate the quality. They tried out dinette sets and sofas, armchairs and love seats, but when they got to the bedroom area, she began to feel dizzy, disoriented, almost drunk. Bureaus and dressing tables, stacked on top of each other, were on the verge of toppling. She could hardly make her way between the beds.

The salesman left to find a catalog. She said quickly to Richard, "This is not what I had in mind. There's nothing here I like so let's just come back another day." She heard herself sounding certain, like him. Her left hand was a fist on her hip.

"Another day? The wedding is in three weeks!" Richard's gravel voice was suddenly high-pitched and tinny. "There's no way we can make another trip to Hickory."

"Well, it doesn't make sense to live with something that's not right," she said, lifting her limp hair off her neck and fanning herself. The warehouse was air-conditioned, but perspiration coated her face like a second skin.

Minutes later, they were in the car headed for home. The air now was stale, as if the pollution level had skyrocketed while they were in the warehouse. She knew it was time to call off the wedding. She also knew she had to do it on his turf.

When they got to his house, luckily, his parents were out.

"Richard," she said in the back hall just inside the door, "I can't go through with it. The wedding, I mean. We're not going to get married. I'm sorry, really sorry. I feel awful doing this, but it's not going to happen."

He looked like a cartoon character who'd just been robbed. His mouth and eyes were hollow circles, zeros. He knew she meant it this time.

They stood there, staring at each other as if they were committing the other's face to memory. She thought about the night before, how once again they'd been together on the den sofa in this same house and come close to having sex, but—once again—Thea had stopped him. Lately, it had been easier to put him off, with the wedding so near.

The back door opened and Richard's parents walked in. They all stood there, in that tiny space, jammed together.

"She just told me the wedding's off," Richard said, his accent as different from hers as anything could be. They were continents apart. Always had been.

His mother's mouth dropped open. She headed into the den and sat down on the sofa. The others followed her in, Richard and his father ahead of Thea, trudging, as if they were making their way through mud.

"You sure you aren't just getting butterflies, with the wedding so close and all?" his father said to Thea, though he was looking at Richard. "Maybe you need a few days' rest . . . last-minute details . . . overwhelming . . . nerves . . . running a fever? . . . getting sick?"

Things were becoming blurry again and voices were turning to static.

"I think I want to go home," she said.

"We'll drive you back, dear," his mother answered.

The four of them rode in silence. Nothing felt real. They were like stick figures drawn in a hurry, not fleshed out, quick lines substituting for people. The half-hour trip from Charlotte to Rock Hill—just across the North Carolina–South Carolina line—seemed to take months. When they finally pulled in the driveway, Thea let herself out and walked across what seemed like a huge expanse of lawn to her parents' house.

When she opened the front door, she heard television laughter. Her father met her in the hall, looked at her face, then went back in to turn off the TV. Her mother put down her book. "What're you—why are you home so early?" she asked, eyebrows squeezed together.

"I called off the wedding." All of a sudden it was so easy to say that she said it again. "I called off the wedding."

"Oh, oh, darling . . ." Her mother patted the cushion next to her on the leather sofa, but her father motioned for the two of them to change places so Thea would be next to his good ear. After they'd finished arranging themselves, Thea started talking. Her parents leaned into every word, something holding them both in place, her mother still and attentive, no soaring or dipping, her father staying close, no disappearing. Her mother actually seemed relieved, almost pleased. Her father had a serious look on his face. Smoke from her mother's cigarette drifted over their heads.

Richard made one more try at holding on to Thea. The next morning he called and asked if his uncle, whose granddaughter was going to be the flower girl in the wedding, could come talk with her to see if this were something that could be fixed. That's not what he said but Thea knew it's what he meant. The uncle was a sweet man, but she wanted to ask what a neurologist, who specializes in the brain and nervous system, could possibly know about matters of the heart.

Three days later he came. Thea's mother greeted him at the door with a hug, not exactly her exuberant greeting, but friendly enough. Thea hung back, wanting her mother to stay with them, but she hurried into the kitchen, mumbling about a pot of something on the stove. The uncle pulled his white collar away from his neck with one delicate finger and followed Thea into the den.

"Uh, Richard tells me you're unsure . . ." he began, as if it were his duty to begin, ". . . uh, about going through with the wedding . . ." He sat on the edge of a chair, appearing ready for a sudden takeoff.

"Actually, I'm becoming more and more sure as I go along."

His round peach of a face brightened.

"Well, what I mean is," she said, "I know now that marrying Richard would be a big mistake. I'm just not in love with him." She was surprised, for the second time in three days, at how certain she could sound. "I wanted to be. He's a good person, and since he loved me, I thought I could learn to love him back."

The conversation was making her think about the visit from Martha Jean Aycock (now White) the night before. Martha Jean had been married for a year, and she and her husband, Billy, were living in Colorado. She was in Rock Hill for a family reunion and had come by the house. Originally, she'd planned to stay over at her parents' house after the reunion for Thea's wedding. Martha Jean and Thea had been friends from kindergarten through the twelfth grade. Martha

Jean's face still looked the same—those wide, speckled-green eyes and tiny, flowerlike mouth—but she seemed tired, older, and Thea noticed she bit her fingernails to the quick.

Thea's mother had phoned Martha Jean before she left Colorado to tell her the wedding was off. Still, the two girls talked about everything *but* that. Until right before Martha Jean left—when she said quickly, as though making it brief and last-minute would reduce the shock, "I wish I'd had the nerve to do what you did."

. . .

Richard's uncle was pulling at his collar again.

"There's nothing wrong with you or what you're feeling," he said, pushing on his knees to stand. "You're just not in love. Nope, there's nothing wrong with that. I think you're a mighty brave young woman to do what you did."

Brave was not what she felt. It was more like she was in mourning. Whenever she thought about the furniture store, Richard's face, the drive home, she cried. How could she have hurt so many people? She began sleeping long hours, a cold, wet washcloth pressed to her forehead to numb the ache. How had she gotten herself into this situation?

Years later she came up with a theory:

When she'd graduated from high school, her father wanted her to go to a college where there were a lot of Jewish students. Her mother said that she should go to a school with a good drama department. "Think of all those Opening Night parties!" she kept saying. "It's marvelous to major in drama, darling! And if you stay all four years, people will *know* you! You'll become *somebody* on campus!" Thea wasn't sure about Jewish boys *or* drama, but she knew she didn't want to venture far from home. So, she went to the University of Georgia, with its large number of Jewish students and reputation as a party school, a reputation built on panty raids and vats of Purple Jesus. In every way, it was the wrong school for her, but she stayed all four years, organizing committee after committee to try to raise the academic standards and make it a more serious place. It never occurred to her to transfer; she thought it was up to her to make the school fit her. Hadn't her mother said it was important to stay there?

Right away, Thea saw that she'd made a mistake. Jewish students were funneled through Jewish Rush; boys went to rush parties at the three Jewish fraternity houses, girls at the two Jewish sororities. Thea had pictured herself an Alpha Delta Pi with the friend she'd met during orientation, but it was as if all the students had been lined up and the Jews had to march through one door and everyone else through another. The friend disappeared from Thea's life.

She also learned, her first week, that Jewish girls were expected to date Jewish boys. Growing up, she'd known only one Jewish boy, Barry Shinner in the grade ahead of her. Barry once bragged he'd gone all the way with Olivia Pursley, the retarded girl who still wet her pants in junior high. Thea had hated that everyone assumed she and Barry were cousins just because they were both Jewish.

The Jewish students at Georgia came from Atlanta, Savannah, or Jacksonville—big cities to Thea. Even the ones from small towns seemed "citified," different from the slow-talking, Southern, Gentile kids she'd grown up with. The popular Jewish boys at Georgia would never have been popular in Rock Hill. The standards for Jewish boys, she decided, must not be the same as for non-Jewish boys.

When she started dating Richard, it was easy to make

herself believe she was in love with him. He was the first boyfriend she'd had since Ed in the seventh grade. Martha Jean and Thea had not been in the popular crowd, but Martha Jean had always had a boyfriend, one boy after another. The rare boy who showed an interest in Thea usually had acne or was shorter than she was or had the reputation of being a terrible kisser. Then, there was Richard—interesting and smart and not bad-looking *and* very much in love with her. Before she could get her thoughts clear, they became engaged. But wasn't that the reason a Jewish girl went to college, to find a nice Jewish boy to marry?

. . .

After she broke her engagement, the days passed. Summer eased into fall, and days and griefs began to shrink into detail. She went back to the University of Georgia for her final year, the year she would get her diploma and fall wildly, madly, unmistakably in love with non-Jewish Reid McKee.

. . .

She sat in front of Reid in geology class, fall quarter, senior year. They'd both put off filling that last science requirement. He asked her out the second day of class. They went to the Holiday Inn restaurant for coffee and stayed so late talking—it was after three in the morning—the manager told them he was going home and for them to flick the switch on the coffeepot before they left and shut the door tight, that it would lock behind them. The next night they went back to the Holiday Inn restaurant for a steak dinner—this time, the manager sent over a bottle of Chianti—and they stayed late again, talking. Thea felt totally at ease with Reid. She told him all about herself, about her mother, her unpredictability—all the way back to when Thea had found the wedding gown. She told about her sister. About her father.

Reid talked about his mother's death the summer before his freshman year at Georgia, how everyone in Spartanburg had thought she was so wonderful, the way she was always giving. She'd been a "self-appointed social worker," he called it. No degree; she'd just decided to help other people. He talked about the afternoons he sat on the granite steps outside school, waiting for her to pick him up. She was always late—but mostly, not there at all. Never at his baseball and football games, never at school events, just not there. The night she died was rainy, close, and foggy. She'd driven out in the country to check on a fifteen-year-old girl and her baby. A truck carrying timber crossed the center line, and Reid's mother was dead before she could be pulled from the car. He and his father had huddled in the doorway of their house while a patrolman, hat held reverently over his heart, told them the news. In one night, Reid said, they'd gone from being a family—even if they weren't an especially close family—to being just two guys, a father and his son.

After dinner at the Holiday Inn, Thea and Reid went to his apartment and had the kind of sex she'd only read about in books, sex so smooth there would not have been a stopping place even if she'd wanted there to be. They said the words, "I love you," over and over.

On their third date, they became engaged.

. . .

Now came the hard part. How could she tell her parents she was marrying a non-Jewish boy?

But nothing in this family was ever the way Thea thought

it would be. On the telephone, she told her mother and father about Reid, and her mother immediately exclaimed, "He sounds wonderful, darling! Just wonderful! When do we get to meet him?" Her father didn't say much, but then he never said much.

She was ready to take Reid home to meet them.

Her mother gave him her big hello and hug right at the front door. Her father shook his hand, reserved but cordial. Then her mother threaded her arm through hers and crooned, "Darling, come look at my new pantry! You won't believe how just adding three new shelves and shifting everything around has given me so much space! Excuse us, please, Reid and Mike. You boys get to know each other and we'll be right back."

Come look at her pantry? Thea had just walked in with her future husband and all her mother could say was come look at the new pantry? Thea couldn't imagine what Reid was thinking. As her mother walked her away, she glanced back at him, crisp and pressed in his new navy blazer and white shirt, standing next to her father, whose arms were folded.

Her mother pulled her toward the kitchen and into the pantry, which had always been as well stocked as a grocery store, as if her mother was afraid of not having enough. Thea looked around. Now there were twice as many mason jars of vegetables. The towers of canned soup were taller than ever. The potato bins overflowed. But her mother was not focused on the new and shifted shelves.

"He's *gorgeous*! And you're lucky as you can be!" her mother whispered feverishly, her face beaming, teeth shining like strobes in the narrow, dark room. "Don't you dare let him get away!"

After graduation, they had a small wedding in the rabbi's study at the Reform temple in Charleston. Mickey arranged everything. Their mother never would've been able to plan a wedding after the one that had been canceled, and Mickey convinced Thea, who convinced Reid, that this particular rabbi was sensitive to interfaith marriages and, with Thea's background, this was where they ought to get married. Thea thought it was smart to let Mickey make the plans so that she could get used to the idea of Thea marrying Reid. Little by little, Mickey was becoming fond of him; she didn't actually say that, but Thea could tell. Mickey brought flowers from her garden for the rabbi's study, planned a delicious lunch after the ceremony at her and Joel's favorite restaurant—an intimate, shuttered seafood place in the historic district.

The photographer she found took pictures of the bride and groom: Reid, level and steady in the hand-tailored navy suit he'd splurged on; Thea, in her short, white wedding gown, her curly hair pulled into a flower-entwined twist, her small face bright. There were other photographs, too: Mollie, wearing a strapless royal blue dress, a little too dramatic for the occasion. Mike, always somewhere in the background. Mickey, pregnant with Belle, busy, tending to the flowers, instructing the waiters. Joel, tending to whatever Mickey was tending to. Reid's father, jolly, a bear of a man. Martha Jean and Billy White. Reid's two roommates from college and their chatty girlfriends. Aunt Florence and one of her husbands. Evelyn, showing up in almost every photograph.

Just before the wedding, Reid had been accepted into the master's program in English at the university in Charlotte, so he and Thea settled there. She took a job as a secretary at a radio station. When he finished his master's and started teaching at the university, she began a master's in psychology but kept her job at the station because it was easy and stress-free and gave them a little more income while she was in school. After she got her degree, Tim asked her to host a daily call-in show counseling people on the air. Soon her program was picked up by other stations around the area, in North and South Carolina and in Georgia.

After she and Reid were married about five years, they were ready to start a family, but she could not get pregnant. She saw her gynecologist, then a specialist, then a specialist recommended by the first specialist. She went to so many different doctors during that time, it became practically a full-time job juggling the X-rays and test results and making sure everything found its way to whatever new office she was being sent to. Even making love became a job—the calendar, the thermometer, the charts, and through it all, the dark, gloomy blood of her menstrual periods.

She thought about getting pregnant every minute of the day. She became obsessed with babies. Once, she found herself following a woman with a newborn all the way through Giant Genie, beginning in the frozen-food department, past the bread and meat, up and down the aisles. Thea watched the woman put Pampers in her cart, tiny jars of strained apricots and spinach. Thea's arms ached because part of her was reaching for the baby, taking him from the infant seat, and part of her was holding herself back. She wanted to feel the baby's talcum-powdered skin, nestle his sweet head against her throat. She wanted to finger the damp wisps of hair curling over the neck of his terry-cloth pajamas.

She and Reid were trying everything anyone suggested:

a special poultry diet, cough syrup for him morning and night to speed up his sperm, and of course, a regimen of pills and injections, including hormones, for her.

Her mother said odd things during all this. Once, she almost sounded as though it were her fault Thea couldn't get pregnant, as though she'd done something wrong. "Oh, I feel so bad about this," she said. "If only I'd—oh, the Lord works in such mysterious ways."

When Thea asked what she meant, her mother resorted to her old standby: silence, then humming.

She sent Thea newspaper and magazine articles and telephoned constantly with advice:

"You need to exercise more, darling, get outside, move around."

"Why don't you take tennis lessons?"

"Maybe you shouldn't be so active. Take a break from everything for a while. Get more rest. Go on a vacation with Reid, just the two of you, some place romantic."

"I think you should keep busy so you won't think about things, darling. Work harder. Maybe get a second job."

Mickey did everything she could to avoid mentioning *her* little girl. If she happened to slip and refer to Belle, she'd change the subject in the middle of the sentence. "I didn't get to play in the tournament Saturday because Belle had a bad—speaking of bad, did I tell you Joel's manager quit?"

Worse, during this time, Mickey became pregnant again. Soon, the rounded stomach. The full, soft breasts. Again.

Then, miraculously, Thea's periods stopped. *Her* breasts became full and tender. A pregnancy test came out positive. Excited phone calls to her mother and Mickey, Aunt Florence, Martha Jean; telling everyone at the radio station. She started keeping saltines beside the bed to relieve her morning sickness. Soon she felt the baby move, a foot poking here, pointy elbow there, like lovers under a blanket.

But the pregnancy turned out to be a "false" one. A spurious pregnancy, pseudocyesis, the doctor called it. How could this be? Thea sat in the doctor's private office—the decor making it look like someone's warm, welcoming living room—shaking her head. The cortex of the brain, he explained, can have great influence on the pituitary, not uncommon in women who want so intensely to become pregnant. There can be definite physiological changes, he was saying, but unfortunately, no change in the size of the uterus. No baby, in other words.

False pregnancy. False start. False front. False pretense. False hope. False alarm. So many false things in this world.

But he wanted her and Reid to go to an infertility specialist in Baltimore. Which they did. They spent three days there. More tests. Yes, there was a problem with her, the doctor said, but he believed a minor office procedure would take care of it. Air would be passed through her fallopian tubes to open them wide for conception.

A minor procedure! After all they'd been through! This was truly a miracle. They were ecstatic. Everything was set. They were to come back to Baltimore in four months. All she had to do was have a routine physical with her regular doctor in Charlotte just before they returned.

The night before her physical, she went to sleep early. Sleep had become so pleasurable, with all those soft dreams of babies. But that night she tossed and pitched. When she woke, the sheets were a tangle around her feet and she was in pain.

"Reid! Wake up!" she cried, feeling for his arm. "Please, please get the heating pad."

"What's wrong?"

"My stomach is killing me. Hurry!"

"Oh, honey, I'm going. Hold on, hold on." He rolled out of bed and fumbled through the dark to the bathroom. She could hear him brushing the bottles of suntan lotion to the side of the top shelf in the linen closet to get to the heating pad. The pain was getting worse. She sipped instead of breathing, as though she'd had the breath knocked out of her, as though the only way she could get oxygen was through a straw.

He was back beside her, gently tucking the heating pad around her stomach. She pressed it tighter into her middle as if holding a cold heating pad could stop the sweeps of pain. He plugged it in. She changed positions, then changed back, from her side to her stomach to her side. She drew her legs in and heard herself making whimpering sounds.

"How is it now?" he asked.

"I've never . . . felt . . . pain like this . . ." she managed to whisper.

"Do you think it's something you ate?"

"I don't know, didn't you and I eat the same things . . . ?" Hard now even to whisper.

"We need a doctor, sweetheart. We've got to get you to the hospital. I'll help you put some clothes on."

She ended up wearing his big plaid cotton shirt over her jeans with the waist unbuttoned. She didn't want anything touching her. He half-walked, half-carried her out to the car.

It was two in the morning when they got to the hospital, but the lights inside were gleaming like blisters. People were lounging in chairs in the waiting area, drinking coffee, watching a black and white movie on TV. A tired mother was telling her son to behave, to stop rolling around on the carpet. He'd sit in the chair next to her for a few seconds, his little feet dangling, then he'd go back to rolling around on the carpet. A sulky teenaged boy wearing a backward baseball cap and unlaced hiking boots slumped in a chair, his long legs like a spider's. An older man in work clothes dozed in the corner, his chin buried in his chest. They looked like the same people you always see in a hospital. Don't they ever go home?

"Thea McKee?" a nurse in seamless white, pushing an empty wheelchair, called from the doorway.

She briskly wheeled Thea down the hall and into a curtained area, while Reid stayed back to fill out forms. She helped Thea into a hospital gown and onto a gurney, where she lay, waiting, holding nothing but her own arms.

Finally, a doctor came in to examine her. Probing questions, probing hands, probing instruments, a needle in her vagina. She was so exhausted from the pain and from no sleep that everything was feeling thin around the edges.

"And your periods?" he was asking. "Have they been normal?"

"No . . ." she said. "My last period lasted only a day . . . which was very unusual . . . just a little spotting . . . that was it."

"Have you been experiencing any discomfort in your abdomen prior to tonight?" He was pressing her stomach on the left side.

"Well, yes, some . . . but I thought it was just nerves . . . what I mean is, maybe a nervous stomach over everything that's going on."

"Vague discomfort . . . hmm . . ." he was saying, but his voice was now coming to her from a great distance.

Then Reid was standing beside him and the two men were looking at her with sad expressions.

"Mrs. McKee, I'm afraid we have an emergency on our hands," the doctor said. "There's blood in the cul-de-sac between your cervix and the floor of the vagina. I suspect that you have a ruptured tubal pregnancy."

The doctor was so young. He looked like he still had the flush adolescents have when they're bursting with hormones. Could someone this young possibly know what he was talking about? And did he say *pregnancy*? Was she finally pregnant? But pregnant in her tubes? Ruptured?

"We need to go in immediately, can't wait until tomorrow, getting an operating room ready now . . ." He and Reid were both nodding mechanically. Then Reid walked across the room, leaned down close, and shyly kissed her fingers.

After surgery, the doctor's words cut through the gauzy haze of the recovery room: "Indeed, Mrs. McKee, when we opened your abdomen, we encountered a copious amount of blood there. A small vessel at the rupture site was leaking fresh blood. We had to remove the fallopian tube on the left, the one that had ruptured. And there was considerable scarring, and adhesions, enveloping the fallopian tube on the right side, so we had to remove that tube, also, as well as the uterus. Otherwise, we would be inviting another ectopic pregnancy."

There won't be a pregnancy, he was saying. This was it. No trip to the doctor in Baltimore. No minor procedure to fix things. No pregnancy. Ever. No baby. Ever. No son, no daughter. No shaking drops of milk from the nipple of a bottle on her wrist to make sure the temperature was right. No crib for Reid and her to pull chairs beside to watch a small person sleeping. No damp curls at the base of a neck to kiss.

It was the curls that finally made her cry. The curls, she wanted to tell the doctor. But he was gone. A nurse was getting ready to give her an injection. Nurse, she wanted to say, you understand, don't you? It's the curls I'll miss the most.

But the nurse was holding a syringe up to the light and when Thea tried to focus on it, the dark took over, and all she could hear was a baby crying.

. . .

The On the Air sign was flashing, Tim was motioning, and someone was saying her four favorite words: *"What do you think?"*

How long had she been sitting here, waiting for the program to start? Had she completely missed the beginning of this call? She straightened. A caller was saying ". . . so I'd like to know. He graduated from college last year and has a job but doesn't make enough yet. A friend of mine said she thought I was keeping him from growing up by letting him come back home to live. Do you think I am?"

"I have a theory about young people who come back home," Thea said, probably a little too authoritatively, but she was trying to recoup. "I believe that when a young person moves back, he's there to get something he didn't get the first time. It might be to mend a ragged relationship with his parents, or simply to get more grounding."

"But you think it's okay?"

"Yes, I do think it's okay. Your son needs a place to live and you're fortunate to be able to provide it for him."

"Good." The woman was hearing exactly what she wanted to hear. Should Thea have gotten more information before she jumped in with advice?

"Does your son have friends?"

"Oh yes. He still hangs around with some of his high school crowd. A lot of them are living at home, too."

"And does he talk about saving to get his own place?"

"Actually, he's not real talkative, but he did say once that he hopes he'll get a raise soon so he can afford to move out."

"What does your husband think?"

"He travels, so he's not really around that much. Whatever I decide is okay with him, basically."

"Well, I think you're doing the right thing. It would probably be smart for you and your son *and your husband* to negotiate what the rules will be, before problems arise, because once there's a problem you'll be emotional and it'll be harder to resolve things. Your son is not the same person he was before he left home, and some of the rules you had when he was in high school may not work for you, or him, now. Also, you should require him to do some jobs around the house. And have you thought of charging him room and board?"

"I never thought of making him pay."

"Well, you might consider . . ." *Was* it an off-the-wall idea? Of course it wasn't. "Anyway, I think you'll know and he'll know when it's time for him to leave. Meanwhile, this could be a valuable time for all of you. A time for your son to establish a relationship with you on an adult level. And with his father."

"Well, thanks. I really appreciate what you said."

"On the other hand, I'm not recommending that he live there indefinitely. Don't make it too comfortable for him."

. . .

As Thea drove home, she worried about that last call. Sometimes it was so hard to keep her answers free from her personal feelings, to keep her own longings tucked away. She *tried* to get to that objective place where all she heard was the person's voice, but other voices had a way of getting in there, too. Voices that said no matter what the circumstances, let your children come back. Hold those children, love those children. Be grateful you have children.

Chapter 12

"Did you see this from Helen Feinman?" Reid called from the front of the house. It was a Tuesday night and Thea was washing the dinner dishes.

"What'd you say?" she called back, dripping soapy water across the counter he'd just wiped, on her way to turn off the radio.

"I said I just found a letter from Helen Feinman," he shouted, too loud now that the radio was off. He came in the kitchen. "I think it came today, but it was stuck inside a Lillian Vernon catalog. Here. I'll finish the pots. You take this."

"Just let the big pot soak. It's pretty bad. I'll do it tomorrow. Or this weekend." She wiped her hands on a dish towel, took the letter and headed for the other room.

"Don't go away. Keep me company. Stay and read it to me. It's been, what, two weeks since the last letter? What number are we—"

The short ring of the doorbell interrupted him. Thea left the letter on the counter and walked out to the back, flicking the lights on outside. Through the small window in the door, she saw Susan Proctor, Ellen and Herm's daughter, hands stuffed in her jeans pockets, shoulders hunched up to her neck. When Thea opened the door, there was a strong apple smell, fresh and autumnlike. But it wasn't autumn.

"Susan, come in!" Thea said. "Do you have on perfume?"

"Pardon?"

"I mean, you smell so good!"

"Oh, I bet it's my hand lotion. Country Apple." She fished out her hand and sniffed it, then held it up for Thea. "How're you, Mrs. McKee? Mr. McKee—hi, hope you're doing well." Susan, sixteen now, had been this well mannered at age three.

"Hey, Susan! Apple-flavored hand lotion? I can smell it from here. I hope a good-looking boyfriend gave it to you!"

"No, just Mom. Too bad!" She wrinkled her nose. "Listen, I hate to bother you, but do you have an extra onion? I'm making dinner tonight for my parents. Burritos."

"Lucky them!" Thea said, on her way to the pantry. She picked up a small onion with green shoots as spiky as crocus leaves. "This one's no good." She lifted out a bigger onion, soft and black. Not brown. Black. Rotten. "Oh, I hate this. I don't have a fresh one."

"That's okay. No problem. I'll run up to Giant Genie.

Sorry to put you to all this trouble." Susan was out the back door. "Thanks anyway. You two have a great evening!"

"Before you go, tell me what's new in your life?" Thea asked, poking her head out into the night.

"Not much. I kind of like somebody. He's in the grade ahead of me. A senior. We've gone out twice. Cu-u-te boy!" Susan cocked her face in a charming way. "I'll keep you posted, I promise." She disappeared into the camellias along the edge of the backyard.

"You are so funny! You did everything but give her candy! If you could bribe those kids next door to stay and visit, you would! By the way, add onions." Reid nodded toward the grocery list he'd started next to the phone. He was still washing. The list was organized into dairy products in the top right corner, produce in the lower right corner, chicken and meat in the top left. Thea wrote hurriedly, in the correct place, then looked around the kitchen for her glasses, found them behind the radio, pulled the tall wooden stool out from under the center island and climbed up. She ripped open the letter.

"Well, here's what Helen says on the Post-it note: 'The next Bella letter after this will describe your parents' wedding. Since it runs seven pages, I'll send it to you in installments so that you may savor the contents slowly. It will take us back to January 1938.' Not only does she sing when she talks, but she has a flair for the theatrical when she writes!"

"So this is the next to the last letter." He was scrubbing the spaghetti sauce–coated pot with a wadded-up Brillo pad, going after burned-on stains that had been there for as long as Thea could remember.

"The next to the last one," she said.

May 20, 1938

My dear sister Celia leben, with your worthy family leben:

Your letter received Wednesday at dinner and read to my Easy right after dinner. We enjoyed your writings. Also your dinner with Cousin Yetta. It is good to hear that it was good and your loving guests enjoyed it. It is very good to make a fine dinner for your family . . . everyone together, amused and enjoyed themselves. I long to be with you, sister, at such times. Was a little gossip spoken?

Last week we were at home and I spoke often to Easy that my sister Celia has guests and everyone is talking together, and certainly a few words about me as well.

God should give everyone good business with much good health . . . to make possible a trip, to be able to see my sister and everyone together. That is a blessing from our loving God. It should not be thwarted, even from afar. That we can meet together is our thanks to God for his help to us.

You recall that my Florence left to live in Newberry? She recently returned home for a few days to help in the store. Easy wrote to her more than one letter asking and asking her to do so and finally she answered yes. The reason she ignored her Papa? She met a fellow in Newberry and they are in love and are to be married in July. So quick she goes for him. This fellow, Jack. But that is why she says she did not want to travel home to help her papa.

We have a sale in the store since Friday, two weeks. The sale is not going well. We are not making money and we are not making out well. Do not know yet what we will do. Maybe we will sell the store and move to Columbia. Do not mention this to anyone. What time will bring I do not know. I will keep you informed in the next letter.

What Mollkeleh told me was that they had promised to send to you a photograph but have not as yet had it taken. You will consider this as their wedding photograph although you know that there were no wedding photographs, which I do not need to explain at this time. Too much explaining is not good. But not to make you feel bad, I am sending to you my photograph with Mollkeleh taken during the High Holy Days not so many months ago. Please forgive me that I did not wear my black kid gloves you sent to me. I was in a hurry not to miss the chance to be in the photo.

Easy brought me to Newberry to my Mollkeleh. We were with her from Friday on. Sunday we were all together as a family. Dear sister, you must picture my great pleasure to sit around the table with my two daughters who were so very happy to be together. Sisters are meant to be together always. In their hearts if they cannot be together in person.

On this trip, we also met Florence's Jack. A nice Jewish boy. From a good family. Everyone was happy for Florence to become a bride come summer.

My darling child, Mollkeleh, looks very pretty and happy. I was pleased to see how good both Mike and she look. Mollkeleh is very pleased with her Mike. Mike holds very dear his "Faygeh," that is what he calls her, Faygeh, little bird. And her cook also calls her Mrs. Faygeh. When she goes out to shop for Mollkeleh, she tells them that Mrs. Faygeh wants to have fresh bread, fish. Everything is Faygeh. We laughed long over "Faygeh."

The dinner was good. Everyone enjoyed it.

I wrote to you already that my cook is back with me. She does not mention giving birth to a baby and I do not say it either. I give her the order and she does everything well. My luck that I have such a good Negro. She cooks and cleans. Honest, clean, dressed in white. Her name is Mary. Everything is Mary, much like "Faygeh."

Take regards from me and my entire family to you with your family.

Your sister Bella

P.S. Will immediately to Cousin Yetta write and tell her that Mollkeleh will send her a picture soon also. Received from Cousin Yetta a letter last month. I did not have my glasses to read it. Cousin Sam Bogen read the letter for me. Isn't it a wonder that Sam is able to read Yiddish being in America for so long? He said that Cousin Yetta speaks to God often. With each word she reminds herself of God and God should really help her because she means this truly.

"Mrs. Faygeh!" Reid was saying, fitting the big pot into the already full dish drain beside the sink as carefully as if he were filing.

"That was really a sweet scene, wasn't it?" Thea said. "The lovey-dovey couple my grandmother talks about, though, is slightly different from the two people I knew. My father was so obviously in love with my mother, but she always seemed like she was holding back. *I* was more important to her than he was—do you know what I'm trying to say?"

"I do. Your mother treated your father like, well, like there was something missing. But then, there was something missing with my parents, too—my mother always off taking care of some other family, paying attention to everybody but my father and me. One thing, I never saw your parents argue."

"No, you wouldn't have. That was Mother's big rule. They didn't even *disagree* in front of us. Mother wanted more than anything to have a peaceful house."

"Did you ever see them have an argument?"

"Well, not exactly. But I'll tell you about one time when things were a little strange. Mother took us to the Ocean Forest Hotel in Myrtle Beach for two weeks. My father was going to come down the second week. Now you have to picture this place. It was like a big sandcastle, white, with low annexes spreading out from the main building. And terraces and balconies everywhere. On the weekends they had dances, with a band, in the outside ballroom and the first weekend—"

"Outside ballroom?"

"Actually, it was open on the sides but it had a ceiling, with one of those spangled balls that rotated and threw lights everywhere. Anyway, Mickey and I were wearing identical white cotton sundresses. She didn't like the dress because she said it looked like a tablecloth, but I knew the real reason was she didn't want to be dressed like me. I loved when we were dressed alike."

"That doesn't surprise me!"

"I can still remember what Mother wore, a strapless sundress with a black background printed all over with these splashy white gardenias. She'd bobby-pinned a live gardenia in her hair. Ver-ry carefully! You know gardenias immediately turn brown if you touch them, don't you? Anyway, she looked dazzling. Like Dorothy Lamour."

"Dorothy Lamour, huh?" He was sliding the wire rack out of the toaster oven, getting ready to clean it.

"As we walked into the ballroom, Mother was snapping her fingers to the music. Then a man appeared out of nowhere and they started dancing. Mickey and I just stood there. We didn't move. They were weaving in and around the other couples on the floor, and she was laughing at everything he said. He even dipped her—remember how people used to do that? It looked like any minute she could fall over completely backward."

"You and your sister were watching this whole scene? Did your mother acknowledge the two of you during any of this?" He'd finished the wire rack and it was hanging on the handle of one of the pots in the dish drain. Now he was washing the aluminum tray with a soapy sponge.

"She did not know we were there. Mickey and I didn't move from our spot next to the band. I can still see that man. Sort of short, with light hair. Very nice-looking."

"Interesting."

"Sad. Especially since I'd been so excited about the three of us going away together, without my father. He was never much fun at the beach — I don't think he even owned a bathing suit. All he ever wanted to do was play catch with Mickey or take her to some tennis court to practice. The week without him had been great, up until the dance. Mother, Mickey, and I would lie out on the beach in the hotel's striped canvas chairs, eating pecan logs and drinking Coke. Mother would read to us from *Little Women*. Have I ever told you that was her favorite book? She'd ask which sister we wanted to be, but of course, she'd pick first: the sick one. I think she liked the drama of being the one who died. Mickey always picked Jo."

"Naturally. The gritty, headstrong one," Reid said. "Who did you pick? *Whom* did you pick?"

"I never could decide who I wanted to be, so I just switched back and forth between the two sisters that were left." She thought about this for a second. "We'd go by our *Little Women* names all day, even when we were with other people. If one of us forgot and used the real name, that person didn't have to answer."

"Sounds like your mother was her old self." He'd found

two pencils and was sliding one under the rim of each wineglass he'd left to dry upside down on a dish towel, his invention for keeping moisture from collecting inside.

"But when I saw her dancing and laughing, I wished for my father. Mickey and I didn't see the man with the blondish hair again after that night. Mickey's opinion was that his vacation was over and he'd gone home. She said our father wasn't going to like what Mother had done. My feeling was that Mother had come to her senses and told him to leave her alone and our father didn't have to find out about any of it." Reid looked up. He was smiling. "In the mornings, Mother slept late. We had adjoining rooms, and Mickey and I would play Monopoly till Mother tapped on our door to let us know she was up and we could all go to the Toddle House for pancakes. One other thing I remember: When we got sunburned, she would sprinkle talcum powder in our beds so our arms and legs wouldn't stick to the sheets. The whole room would smell like roses."

"What happened when your father came?" Reid was taking off the knobs of the stove top and scrubbing with the Brillo pad. It occurred to Thea that he should have been the wife.

"Well, first of all, he looked totally out of place in his suit and tie and heavy shoes. His skin was chalk white next to Mother, who by then was practically the color of cinnamon. The first night he was there, Mickey and I could hear them talking in their room." Actually, she and Mickey had pressed their ears to the wall. Mickey kept telling Thea to stop breathing, that she was keeping her from hearing. Thea tried to hold her breath, but it came out anyway, in airy little spurts. "Mother was saying the dances were fun and it was a great way to meet people. My father said he didn't care about meeting people, that he came to the beach to relax and be with his family. She said there was a dance that night and Mickey and I liked dressing up and at the last dance we'd danced with each other. She didn't mention *she'd* danced with someone. Of course, he ended up going along with her."

"So what happened?" He put the knobs back on and rinsed and dried his hands. Nothing left to clean. He took a lightbulb from the top shelf of the cabinet.

"We all went to the dance. Mickey sat with her friends at a table set up for kids and they drank Shirley Temples. Balloons were tied to the back of their chairs. It looked like they could float away any minute."

"You didn't sit with them?" He was out of the kitchen.

"You know I didn't make friends that easily . . . I stood by myself next to the band—can you hear me?—"

"Keep going." He was in the bathroom. "I can hear you. I'm just changing the bulb."

"I stood in that same spot, next to the trumpet player, and watched my parents dance to 'Humoresque.'"

For a second, in her mind's eye, she could see her father take over, her mother follow his lead, the lights spilling over her bare shoulders like the moon cracking into pieces. Thea could almost hear the sad, lonely sounds coming from the brass throat of the horn.

. . .

Later that evening, she was crouched under the desk in the kitchen, talking to Mickey on the phone. She was telling Mickey about the caller whose twenty-something-year-old son had come back home to live, what did Mickey, who'd had experience with children that age, think? Mickey said Thea had good instincts and she should trust them, that however she had advised the woman Mickey felt sure was wise, and right. Thea thanked her sister, then thanked her again. Then she told about how she and Reid had finally gotten rid of the monkey grass in the bed by the back door and he had put in an oval fish pond. Mickey said she wanted to tell Thea something she'd been meaning to say for a long time. She wanted her to know what a wonderful husband she thought Reid was and that whatever she'd said about him before they got married, she did not still feel the same way. Grinning, Thea said, "You are saying so many things I love hearing!" Mickey said they were true and she should've said them a long time ago. Thea asked how Mickey had been feeling and how things were at the community center. Teaching children's tennis clinics every afternoon, Mickey answered, and men's and women's clinics on the weekends, and she hardly had time to work on her own game but she was hoping that in the fall, all this would change. Thea said Mickey was too good to neglect her game.

After Thea had read her grandmother's letter aloud to Reid and he'd finished changing the lightbulb, she'd dialed Mickey's number. He came back in the kitchen and pulled the plastic bag of garbage from the can to take outside, gathering up the two empty cardboard boxes she'd left beside the back door a week or so ago. He kicked the screened door open with his foot, and in that split second, a bird flew in the house, a bird so black its body looked oiled.

Thea had immediately dropped to the floor and crawled under the desk. She knew that what she should've done was tell Mickey what was going on and hang up so she could help Reid get the bird out, but she just couldn't interrupt the conversation—it had been smooth as hand lotion and felt just as good. Throughout the call, the bird was whipping through the kitchen, ricocheting off the walls and windows, trying to find a way out, but Thea crouched down, hugging her knees, staying with the conversation.

Then: "You'll never guess what's going on. There's a darn bird flying around our kitchen!"

"A bird? How'd a bird get in?"

She told about Reid, the garbage, the open door.

"A bird infestation! That reminds me of a story the rabbi told at Friday night services. Want to hear it?"

"Sure."

"Well," Mickey coughed and went on, "there are these three rabbis discussing a problem each of them has in his synagogue, a problem of mouse infestation."

Thea gave a little laugh even before Mickey got into it, because she was talking with a really funny Yiddish accent. Mickey had always been a great comic. When they were young, she could make Thea laugh any time she wanted by doing her imitation of the alteration lady in the store, a woman who had a thin upper lip. Mickey would tuck in her lip, making it stick to her front teeth, which were very prominent then—that big space between them—and she'd press her thumb and forefinger together, as if she were sewing, and pluck straight pins from the imaginary pincushion strapped to her wrist. Thea would be holding her stomach, laughing.

"The first rabbi says, 'Here's what I did about the problem: I took a big piece of cheese and walked around the synagogue with it to attract the mice's attention. Then I walked outside with it and all the little mice came scurrying outside, and the problem was solved. But, two days later, they were back.'

"The second rabbi said, 'I thought I had a wonderful solution: a Pied Piper. I got a man to play the flute and he walked around the synagogue and all the little mice started following him and he led them right out the front door. Problem was finished. Except that in two days, they came back.'

"The third rabbi said, 'I solved the problem once and for all.' The other two rabbis were amazed. 'You solved the problem?' they said. The third rabbi said, 'That's right. Solved. The mice left and they haven't come back.' The other rabbis asked, 'How'd you do it?' The third rabbi said, 'I made little mice *yarmulkes* for them. Then I bar mitzvahed them. They shook hands with me and left. And they never came back.' "

"You are so funny!" Thea laughed, picturing mice with *yarmulkes* on, then picturing the bird flying around her kitchen with a little *yarmulke* on. It did sort of look like one of the Orthodox rabbis who used to come to Rock Hill for the High Holy Days, in its dark, shiny suit.

All her life, she'd hated the feeling of birds flapping near her, their loopy swerves and dives, feathers flying off in all directions. When Mickey was a teenager, she'd bought two parakeets—one yellow, one green—with her allowance. She used to take them out of the cage and set them free in the house, which would send Thea screaming up to their room. One day Thea set them free in the yard . . . for good. By accident, she swore.

Last summer, birds had built a nest in Thea and Reid's chimney. For days they could hear the earnest little voices speeding up and slowing down. He'd joked that they sounded like a family quarreling.

Now he was trying to coax the bird out the back door with a broom, but the bird was so frightened it kept flying away from it.

"Come *this* way!" A gentle swat with the broom. "Hey,

aren't you supposed to be roosting at night? What're you doing in here anyway?" Another swat.

Thea's mother always said that a bird in the house meant bad luck. When a blue jay flew in the toolshed and Levi, the yardman, tried to shoo the bird out—that one arm of his poking the air with the tip of his shovel—Thea's mother wrung her hands like washcloths, muttering, "Oh, something bad is going to happen. Something really bad."

Tonight, a bird in the house was good luck. True, Thea didn't like the sinister whisper of its wings as it dipped and rose, but through it all, she and her sister were talking and laughing, being sisters.

For some time now, she'd felt that the prediction her mother wrote in her diary—*Years from now, my two daughters will be close*—was beginning to come true. It was as if she and Mickey were coming to an understanding of where one's province ended and the other's began. Maybe it was a matter of respect for the other sister's right to be different; maybe it was a respect for the fault line that was part of their relationship, that could cause disruptive shifts at any moment. They still ventured into perilous territory, but they knew to pull back before any damage was done. They both seemed to want to be close, though not necessarily in the way their mother had envisioned. They'd had to come up with their own version of closeness.

And now, Mickey actually had taken back what she'd said about Reid all those years ago. And wasn't that admiration Thea heard in her sister's voice when she'd talked about Thea's advice on the radio?

Their mother trusted luck more than anybody they'd ever known, but maybe even she would say that this time a bird in the house was not a bad sign.

Chapter 13

"I have a four-and-a-half-year-old daughter who has an imaginary friend."

She liked when callers got right into what they wanted to talk about. She wished they never told her they enjoyed the program or asked how she was. Then she had to thank them for the compliment, say she was fine—and what she ended up with was a very boring interval.

"At first, it was cute and my husband and I would just sort of humor her along. But now it's getting so we have to include her so-called friend in everything or our daughter gets terribly grouchy. I have to set an extra place at the table, and at bedtime we pretend we're tucking Sally in, too—

that's the imaginary friend's name. Is this normal? Should we start telling our daughter this person doesn't exist? Shouldn't she know the difference between real life and make believe?"

"I can understand your concern, but let me reassure you, it's perfectly normal for children your daughter's age to have imaginary playmates. Does she have a sister or brother close to her age?"

"No, she's an only child."

"Is she in nursery school or day care?"

"Not yet. We decided to keep her home an extra year. She'll start kindergarten at our church next year."

"That's when her imaginary friend will disappear. Because she'll begin to be very busy with her school friends."

"Right now, it's hard to picture her ever letting go of this imaginary friend. Really, you should see her talking to her. You'd think somebody was in the room."

"I know. In fact, I know from experience. I didn't have many friends when I was your daughter's age so I had an imaginary friend named Rose Black." Maybe a little humor would help here. "My mother used to tell about the time she was taking a bath and I came into the bathroom and pointed to her breasts and boasted, 'Rose Black has one of those.' "

The caller laughed, a bashful laugh.

"The point is, you can relax about this. Don't take it too seriously. We tend to think whatever stage our children are going through is permanent and we can't imagine they'll move out of it. We worry that the behavior is indicative of some deep, far-reaching problem. But, believe me, it won't be long before you and your husband will be telling 'Sally stories.' And laughing at them."

"Thanks. Really, thanks."

"Thank *you* for calling. And thank all of you out there for listening. This is Thea McKee. We'll be back tomorrow at the same time . . ."

She could've told about the time her family was sitting around the dinner table and Mickey was jabbering on about the father of one of her friends joining the navy. Thea had said, quietly, "Rose Black's father is in the navy, marines, *and* air force."

Rose Black had been her clout. Her one-upper.

. . .

The receptionist opened the door to the control room. "Thea." She pointed to the phone. "Line two. Your husband."

Odd for Reid to call her at the station. And so soon after her program. He must've dialed the minute it was over.

"Reid?"

"Sweetheart, are you on your way home?"

"Well, yes. But why?"

"I'll just talk to you when you get home."

"I can hear something in your voice. Go ahead, tell me."

"It's not good. I didn't want to tell you on the phone. The only reason I called, I was afraid you might leave the station and be out for a while running errands and . . ."

He stopped there. How many seconds ticked by? She waited for him to start talking again, going through a list in her mind of all the things that could possibly have happened: car wreck, illness, somebody dying. Who? Maybe it wasn't so bad. Maybe it was somebody they barely knew.

"Mickey went to the doctor today—she just called and is waiting for you to call her back—anyway, the cancer is now in her lung."

Mickey. "In her lung? What do you mean?"

"Well, you know that cough she's had? She went to an allergy specialist and he put her through all these tests and, in the end, prescribed an antihistamine. It seemed to help in the beginning but then not so much, and she finally decided to go to her oncologist. She didn't say anything about this to you because she had a feeling he was the one she should've been seeing all along. She was afraid it was going to turn out to be more serious than an allergy and she didn't want you to worry. Anyway, the oncologist ordered a chest X-ray and he got the results and they've done other tests, some pretty invasive tests and"—a pause—"it doesn't look good. It doesn't look good at all."

She sat down, stood up, sat down again. What she really wanted to do was crawl out of her skin. "Are you calling from home?" She didn't know why she asked this. Of course he was at home.

"Yes, I'm home. And I'll be here when you get here."

"I'm on my way."

. . .

The sky was low and rain was closing in. In the car, it dawned on her that Mickey had never shown her the scar after she'd had her mastectomy. She was so much like their father—the stoic personality, the way neither of them talked about their cancer. Thea wondered if she should've asked to see her scar. Would that have been the sensitive thing to do? There her sister was, having to deal with the loss of a breast and she didn't have enough compassion to ask about the scar.

She *had* gone with her to the plastic surgeon's office in Charleston to talk about reconstruction. The two of them had seen the film designed to inform patients about the procedure while protecting the doctors by spelling out all the things that could go wrong.

"Why in the world would anyone want to go through all that just to get back a breast?" Mickey had said to her, which was exactly what she was thinking.

When the nurse brought Thea into the room after the doctor had examined Mickey, he was naming all the benefits of reconstruction. It was a smooth setup. First, get the negative stuff out of the way. Then talk the patient into having it done. This didn't work with Mickey though. And Thea was relieved for her sister not to have to go through it.

But should Thea have asked to see the scar? Did Mickey wear a prosthesis? Was it uncomfortable? What was it like when she went to buy it? Thea didn't even know. Why hadn't she offered to go with her? What was she thinking? What did Mickey do when she wore a bathing suit? Thea was trying to remember that last time they all went swimming in the lake behind Mickey and Joel's house. Didn't her bathing suit have a ruffle across the top? What did she do about nightgowns?

There was a part of Thea that knew she was obsessing, probably because it was impossible for her to take in the enormous sweep of Reid's phone call. Easier to focus on one small thing, one single regret. But she couldn't stop. Even the rain on the windshield zigzagged across the glass like an uneven scar.

If Aunt Florence had had a mastectomy, would Thea's mother have asked to see the scar? If Tante Celia had had a mastectomy, would Thea's grandmother have asked to see the scar? What was wrong with her? Why couldn't she do the right thing where her sister was concerned?

Now it was raining so hard she could barely make out the road. The engine in the car was saying *MickeyMickey-Mickey*, the windshield wipers, *MickeyMickeyMickey*.

. . .

The days slowed to a long arc.

Driving to Charleston to be there for the 8 A.M. surgery. Getting to the hospital just as an orderly was taking Mickey away, the wheels of the stretcher a hollow whistle in the bright corridor.

Walking alongside her—Joel and Ann on one side, Thea and Belle on the other. Thea squeezing Mickey's hand with both of hers, leaning down to touch her sister's face with her face just before she was wheeled through the doors of the operating room.

Waiting. None of them talking. Turning magazine pages as though they were reading. The television, its cheap, easy stories and cheap, easy endings. The four of them looking like they belonged there, with the same people who were always in a hospital waiting room.

The surgeon coming out, saying he opened her, then closed her back up. Nothing he could do. *Inoperable*. Cancer everywhere. The girls crying softly. Thea staying in Charleston. Meeting Belle for lunch, near the frame shop where she was now working. Going to see Ann's eight-year-olds play in the city tournament. At night, sitting and talking with them, tickling their arms the way she used to when they were little, remembering how she would kiss the dimples on the backs of their hands. Holding them close, wondering who was comforting whom, knowing that when she held them, she was trying to wrap herself around a loss that had already occurred—the loss of children—and a loss that was imminent. The way losses can feel cumulative.

Sitting by Mickey's bed in the hospital, watching her sleep, keeping a cup of crushed ice ready so she could spoon the chips into her sister's mouth when she was thirsty. Wringing out washcloths and placing them across her forehead to bring her fever down. Holding a cold washcloth under her chin to relieve the nausea.

Carrying flower arrangements from the room while a nurse wheeled Mickey out to the car.

Cooking for her sister, making enough split pea and barley soup for the freezer. Taking her on short walks when she grew stronger.

Leaving a bowl ripe with peaches on the kitchen table, peaches so bright they looked as if they had taken all the sunlight from the rest of the room.

Kissing her sister good-bye, the long, slow hug, walking out her front door, across the yard to the car, turning to wave one last time, maybe to return to her for just a minute, to tell her one important thing, only to find she'd already gone back inside.

. . .

Days passing. Weeks. Months. Four months.

Back in Charleston with her.

The terrible, half-torn sounds of coughing, the choking, gasping. The glass by the bed to hold sputum.

In the hospital again. The snaky tubes. Harder for her to breathe now. Sleeping most of the time.

Coma. The machines, their insistent sighs.

The winter sky out the window lavender, like the beginning of a bruise.

And then one sister peacefully, irrevocably disentangling herself from the other. Breaking free.

All their lives Mickey had protected her. Spoken for her. Thought for her. Thea had studied Mickey's face to find out if she approved of her. Studied Mickey's face to find out if Thea approved of Thea. All their lives Thea had clung to her.

Now, for the first time, she could not follow.

She climbed into the hospital bed to lie beside her, pulled the blanket, stubbled after so many hospital launderings, over both of them, tucking it under their chins like a muffler. Thea's body was an outline of her sister's, their fingers scalloped.

. . .

Anyone who knew them growing up always said their names together—Mickey and Thea, Thea and Mickey—as if they were one long word, joined in some mysterious way. This was that unlikely instance of the older sister wishing she could blend into the younger sister.

As girls, they made their own paper dolls and all their clothes, and stored them in cigar boxes. But Mickey was the artistic one. When she crayoned full red lips on her paper doll's face, Thea crayoned full red lips on hers. When Mickey twisted a paper clip into a tennis racket for her paper doll and Scotch-taped cellophane across it for the strings, Thea did the same.

When Mickey made shell jewelry, Thea was right beside her. They'd sit at the card table for hours, squeezing the honey-colored glue onto the backs of tiny seashells, sliding the pastel blossoms into place. When Thea was finally able to copy her sister's design, her sister would dream up something new. Mickey turned the hobby into a business and sold her jewelry to La Petite, the beauty parlor in the converted Dairy Queen out on the highway, where they had their hair washed and set every week. The pins and earrings sold so fast, Pearleen could hardly keep them in the shop.

MickeyandThea. TheaandMickey.

Two girls doing somersaults and cartwheels in the front yard, wearing the lime and fuchsia crepe paper dresses with pinked hems their mother had made, the stiff ruffles like wings. In the spidery afternoon, they flicked themselves across the lawn, in and out of sunlight and shade.

Two girls playing the rock-scissors-paper game with Bullet Jackson next door in the empty henhouse, the platform that once held cages of plump, chattering hens now a place for competition.

Two girls pouring Mercurochrome on the roots of the dogwood tree in the backyard, believing, together, they could turn its white blossoms pink.

Two girls hearing the news on the radio that Ava Gardner had come home to Smithfield, North Carolina—Mickey finding the family's number by dialing random people in the town, determined that she and her sister would speak to their favorite movie star, right there in the next state, so close.

Two girls stretched across the fringed rug in their bedroom, the Sunday paper spread before them, the week's brides in black and white. The pointing, the debating over which was the prettiest, the negotiating, the compromising until they narrowed it down to one bride, their pick of the week—the search for perfection, something they'd be engaged in the rest of their lives.

Two girls walking to school together, Mickey pulling

Thea up onto the stone wall that lined the houses the last block before school, the wall their mother had warned them to stay off—each of them carefully placing one foot in front of the other, holding their arms straight out, balancing under the tremble of oak branches.

Thea and Mickey—like their paper dolls—one-sided girls in weightless clothes—one so flimsy she might dissolve without the other.

. . .

Sleep. Days, weeks after her sister's death, it was all Thea wanted to do. She got herself to the station, managed to host her program, came home as soon as she was finished, called Belle, called Ann, and slept. Reid grocery-shopped and cooked. They ate dinner together, quickly, usually in silence. Reid would run his fingers through his hair and smile gently in her direction—generous, understanding Reid.

She was usually in bed by nine.

In a dream, she and Mickey both had had heart surgery, and they were recuperating. Near the end of their hospital stay, they were invited into a room where there was a table covered with paper plates. Each plate held cookies baked by a different nurse. The sisters could each have one plate, a nurse informed them.

Mickey chose quickly, saying she wanted one with both "grown-up and children things on it." What a good idea, Thea thought. She now saw the situation through Mickey's eyes and realized that her sister had come up with a perfect way to make a distinction.

Thea began looking over all the plates to determine which had that combination of "grown-up and children things" Mickey had talked about. Thea tasted a cookie, although she knew she was not supposed to eat from a plate she might not choose; it wasn't polite. Still, she kept taking test bites, moving from plate to plate, becoming more and more anxious because she couldn't make a decision and time was running out.

What she really wanted was Mickey's plate.

Chapter 14

A month later, Thea had to leave for work early to do some publicity for the station's fund-raising drive coming up the next week. She'd overslept, but she'd told Reid she'd fix dinner that night and there was still time to rinse off the slick Pic-of-the-Chix legs, breasts, wings, and thighs and marinate them in Mickey's soy sauce recipe. She took the recipe from the refrigerator magnet and dropped the chicken in the sink to rinse. That night she'd cook it on the grill.

Reid had somehow managed to fit their two cereal bowls and mugs in the dishwasher, which was already full because she'd forgotten to run it the night before. She had poured in the powder but now it was damp and sticky, like cake batter, in the little plastic dispenser. He closed the door and pushed Start. He didn't have a class until afternoon. Now he had a toothpick and was digging out the grease that collected in the crevices where the stove top met the red Formica.

He was still doing everything he could to help. But it felt as if he was hovering, leaning into her, as though any minute she could drop what she was holding and he'd be close enough to catch it before it hit the floor.

She washed the chicken pieces, one by one, and laid them on paper towels on the counter to dry. When he finished with the toothpick, he reached around her for the sponge, turning on the faucet full force, letting it run until the water was steaming. She wasn't finished at the sink but he was crowding her with the side of his body. He held the sponge under the water, squeezed it, then started wiping down the counters. Usually, when he finished the counters, he'd take the dish towel and buff everything dry. This time, though, he kept going over the same spot with the sponge, bearing down so hard with the heel of his hand, his fingers turned white. He kept scrubbing, scrubbing, like someone disturbing a sore that needed to be left alone to heal.

"Reid, stop it!" she cried. "If you don't stop rubbing that same stupid spot, you're going to put a hole in the counter!"

But he wouldn't stop. He acted as though he hadn't even heard her. Was he deaf? He was going to scrub that counter for the next fifty years. She had to make him stop. She looked at the chicken, the water soaking the paper towels, pooling on the counter, dripping over the lip onto the floor, the sound like a clock ticking.

"Stop it!" she screamed and grabbed a wet drumstick and threw it clear across the room. It smacked the window overlooking the backyard, making a sound like the squirrel that had tried to leap from a limb through the kitchen window the week before, its body a pitiful ramming.

The drumstick left stringy threads of skin all over the glass.

"The baby!" she heard herself cry. The baby? Where was this coming from? "If it weren't for you, we'd have a baby!" She was sobbing. Everything felt wet, her face, her hands, the whole room. "But no-o-o," she screamed. "Couldn't stand to raise somebody else's child. It wouldn't *feel* right to you—isn't that what you said? It wouldn't *feel* right to you? Great! Just great!" She picked up a plump chicken breast and threw it. As hard as she could. It hit the wall with a blunt slap, just above the light switch, a little to the right, leaving a pinkish blotch. "So, here we are. Just the way you wanted. No children! No parents! No sister! *No nothing*! Are you satisfied? Are you *satisfied*?" Why was she saying this?

"Thea, what are you doing?" His voice sounded hoarse. She shot him a glance. He looked stricken.

"What am I *doing*? What am I *doing*? I'll tell you what *I'm doing*! This is for all your bullshit reasons not to adopt a baby!" She reached behind, like someone feeling for a gun. Her fingernails dug into a slimy thigh—her entire arm was shaking—and she hurled it at the brass light fixture over the table. "*This* is what I'm doing!" Missed. The abstract painting hanging on the wall caught it. A dull *thumpf*. Soppy smear across the canvas.

"Are you crazy?" The muscles in his jaw were knotted.

"Yeah, I'm crazy! How do you like it? I'm crazy! Crazy! Crazy!"

"Thea! What, what are you talking about?"

She was crying big heaving cries and slinging. Every time she reached behind, she found another breast, leg, thigh, wing. Enough chicken to feed an army. Each piece she threw harder than the one before, aiming at a different place in the room—slap after watery slap—hitting a cabinet, a chair, the picture again, a vacant place on the wall, skidding across the bare floor. She had to keep letting the pieces fly until nothing, absolutely nothing, was left.

In the end, raw flesh lay all over the kitchen. Body parts everywhere.

She looked at her hands, the yellow gunk stuck under her fingernails. She looked at Reid, standing beside her, his arms loose at his sides. His features were flung in disarray, like an amateur's version of Picasso, eyes here, nose there, nothing where it was supposed to be. She blinked to put everything back in order, but his face was fixed, as if it might stay that way the rest of his life. Without drying her hands or putting on a coat, without saying a word, she grabbed her keys and ran out the door.

. . .

End of the day. Back home. Reid still at school. She was relieved to have the house to herself. The kitchen had been scrubbed clean of all the blood and flesh. Three boneless chicken breasts—he must've gotten rid of the other pieces and gone out and bought new—were marinating in a Pyrex dish in the refrigerator. She should have called him during the day to apologize. She wished she had. All he'd done was try to make things easy for her, show her in every possible way that he cared. And how had she responded? By getting mad at him for wiping off the counters and then she'd said the cruelest things she could think of. The minute he walked in the door, she'd tell him how sorry she was.

There was time for a nap before he got home. First,

though, check the answering machine. Only one message. Good. She hadn't been returning calls anyway.

"Thea." Evelyn. "Mama's been . . . in the hospital. Spent one . . . night there. She's fine now." It sounded as though she was sighing between words. "They thought she might be having . . . a heart attack. But she wasn't. She's really okay. Just needs to . . . rest. She's home now. She just called, in fact, and wants me to pick up a pizza. We have a new place . . . with really good cesarean pizza . . . oh, for crying out loud, I meant Sicilian! . . . listen, I'm going to hang up now. You don't need to call me back. She's fine."

Thea played the message again. "She's fine." Evelyn said that. Clearly. She's fine.

She has to be.

Check the mail. Probably more sympathy cards to put off answering. She'd been letting them collect in a pile on the table in the porch, spilling over onto the floor.

In the basket, catalogs. Drugstore coupons. A letter from Charleston, the rabbi at Mickey's synagogue. A letter from Belle. She and Ann were doing better—this letter sounded almost everydayish. Thea was trying to be a part of their lives, calling them when she could. It all just took so much energy.

She reached in the basket again and pulled out a letter with Helen Feinman's familiar handwriting. The wedding letter!

It was almost as if something lifted from her chest. As though light were coming into the screened porch in a different way, the sun rising a second time that day. She felt as if she could be at the beginning of something instead of at the end. Each breath she took was like a reprise.

The wedding letter.

Finally.

The possibilities. The endless possiblities.

But why wasn't Mickey here to share this with her? Would she even have wanted to share it? Thank goodness, Florence was okay. Thea would be able to read it to her. They'd talk about it. They'd go over everything together.

Helen must not have known Thea's sister died. She didn't mention it in the note she'd paper-clipped to the translation: "The first half of the wedding letter is complete . . . with many extra asides that make Bella's letters so dear. How satisfying it must be for you to know of the fine details of your parents' wedding day. I apologize that this portion of your grandmother's letter has taken me so long to translate. My husband and I took a lengthy vacation and when we returned, our daughter became ill. The months passed. She is well again. I promise to send the last part soon. Best wishes, Helen."

January 6, 1938

Loving, devoted sister Celia leben, also your loving husband and children,

Celianke, you must be anxious to know about Mollie's wedding, and I with my greatest pleasure, dear sister, will tell you all.

Everything was in best order, just as we hoped. Everything turned out good and lovely and orderly. Many guests came to see the shayner bride. And the reception ran from 2:30 until after 6 o'clock.

We left the guests still at Rabbi Kline's house and we drove to Abe Bogen's house to set the tables for the great supper that we prepared. Many of the guests who traveled had to return the same evening. There were three married sisters from Mike's father and mother and a girl the same age as Mike from a twin. Also a cousin. Such a nice family my Mollie married into.

We were well prepared for the meal. We set the tables twice for supper for our family, such a large crowd.

Many telegrams were received. Also your telegram was very nice, a long one. Dear sister, you were missed greatly, by me and by everyone. When the telegrams were read aloud, everyone clapped and drank wine and schnapps. A few non-Jewish neighbors from town came to see a Jewish wedding. They know Mollie well. They drank heavily. Enough said, especially since no rabbis were at the dinner. So they drank.

All of Columbia's Jewish families were to the chuppah at Rabbi Kline's house and to the reception at Abe Bogen's house. So many people at both, such hugging and kissing.

Everything was beautiful. The dining room table was very lovely. Bedecked over the table, a large, white bell. On the table, in the middle, a silver basket with white carnations. Further, everything was in silver dishes, all the good cakes. Four candlesticks with white candles burned, adorned with white tulle. Over the wedding everything shined. Mollie and Mike shined. May the beautiful bride's mazel glow always, her life long. Amen.

I am writing to you in detail, just as if you were present. And I ask you to send this letter to Cousin Yetta. Because after such a letter, for me to write another is not possible. I feel exhausted with everything. I must lie abed a few days to rest, then I will again be all right.

Now I will tell you about all of the delicious desserts that we had. I baked my special mandel bread, no more than that. Florence made honey tayglach, plenty, and she made ginger cakes good. Mrs. Rubin is an expert of honey cake. At the Jewish baker I had baked a large sponge cake and 7 dozen fancy cookies, white icing with green little flowers in the middle. It cost a lot but it looked very nice on the table, in silver dishes. And a very large babkeh that took over half the table. That was for the supper sliced. All the guests enjoyed the supper.

Now comes the meats:

2 geese
2 containers chopped liver with eggs
1 duck
2 roasted tongues
3 stuffed kishkas

Potato salad, cranberry sauce. Appetizer, marinated herring. Dessert, fruit salad from Jell-O with all sorts of fruits mixed and frozen in my icebox. Everyone enjoyed it, I am sure, because nothing was left from it all.

Believe me, dear sister, that I did not taste one thing because I was too busy attending the guests but that made me feel nourished. I had my cook with me, also Mrs. Rubin's. Everyone worked well together. Also we hired a Negro man to carry around drinks and cookies. We had enough punch. Two girls served this good punch. Everybody had their hands full.

We brought everything ready-made to make it all easier for me. Everything was done with a full hand. We should all live to my Florence's wedding. It could not be better.

Mina Sutker was there with her family, Cousin Sam Bogen with his shiksa wife, and more of our relatives who you do not know, Southern friends, some families from our side.

Was visited this morning at home by two non-Jewish customers we know from the store who came to ask about the wedding. Very nice. One of the women carries on her person a small raw potato to absorb the rheumatism she suffers from. Have you heard of this?

Helen wrote at the bottom of the last page: "to be continued."

The wedding sounded wonderful. Nothing about Thea's mother's illness. Nothing about her having to get out of bed for the ceremony. Nothing about her refusing at the last minute to let the photographer come because of hives and swelling. Had Thea dreamed it all up? Had her mother dreamed it up? Here in Thea's own house—late afternoon winter sun turning the rough brick wall of the porch to China silk—holding this letter, reading about the silver dishes, the geese and duck and roasted tongue, she could pretend that all her life she'd had a normal mother. A mother who had a perfectly beautiful, perfectly normal wedding.

. . .

The letter back in the envelope and on Reid's pillow for him to see as soon as they made up, the chicken basted and cooking on the gas grill outside, salad made, potatoes in the oven, she sat down in the den to wait for Reid, eager to tell him how much better she was feeling. She reached for a gardening magazine on the trunk, opened it to the Annual Round-up of Proven Performers, and started reading about a perennial that flourishes in sun or light shade, good soil or clay, in zones 2 to 8—she was too light-headed to read. She closed the magazine and tossed it on the floor. She'd just sit there, do nothing till he arrived. Nights were cool; she heard the furnace come on. It sounded like the house was bracing itself.

Five minutes, maybe ten minutes later, the back door opened. Slow footsteps in the kitchen. Keys on the hook. Book bag on the floor. No hello.

"Reid?"

"Yeah." Flat voice.

"Reid, I'm sorry." She stood up to go to him, but he walked right past her, flicking on the TV and pulling his chair close. "I don't know why I acted the way I did this morning. But I'm sorry. Really."

"It's all right," he said in that way that clearly implied nothing was all right. He was flipping channels, his eyes fixed on the screen. Six o'clock news. *I Love Lucy* rerun. "Just forget it. I want to see if the game's on. I turned the chicken on my way in. You go ahead and eat when it's ready. I'm not hungry."

Not what she had in mind. No discussion, no back and forth hashing out until they both felt okay again.

She had to admit, though, part of her was relieved *not* to have to go over what she'd done that morning. She was embarrassed about it; how in the world could she explain her behavior? At the same time, barely touching on it bothered her, too. Like an old family pattern. Ignoring things. Pretending they didn't happen. Not a good way to resolve problems in a marriage.

She had more than a few theories about marriage. Mainly, she believed in an "equalness," that each person should feel he or she was the lucky one to have gotten the other. If only one person felt that way, there'd be trouble.

Her father, she'd bet, felt lucky to have gotten her mother. Even through all the hard times. But Thea knew her mother did not feel the same way about him. When her parents first met, according to the story her mother once told, they each felt lucky *not* to be paired with the other. Her mother was queen of the Key Club dance, and her father showed up drunk with a carful of buddies, the evening half over. She was dancing with her boyfriend and he broke in on her. She took one look at his rumpled suit, the necktie pulled loose from his collar, and said scornfully, "You're just the type of man I don't like. Showing up late. Rough and tough. A bottle under the table."

He looked at her peachy skin, her frizzed hair, her smile bright as the Hollywood lights around the bandstand, and said, with equal scorn, "Well, isn't that a coincidence! *You* happen to be just the type of woman I don't like. Everybody's sweetheart. Miss Queen of the Dance."

And then, oddly enough, they were weekend guests at a mutual friend's house in Columbia and started dating. This was about a year after the disastrous first meeting. When they ended up together, people were shocked. Thea's sorority sister's father—a man who'd grown up near Denmark, who'd dated Mollie when they were young—said that Thea's father may have been attractive and, of course, a football player, but everyone thought he was a "dark horse," as far as Mollie was concerned. Mollie, he said, was so beautiful, so vivacious, so popular, she was clearly out of Mike's league. Thea had seen the clippings in her mother's scrapbook, her being crowned Miss Denmark and first runner-up to Miss South Carolina.

While her mother's feelings toward her father always were in question, her mother did care how their marriage appeared to other people. Once she told Thea she had a plan for when they turned into an old married couple sitting in a restaurant with nothing to say to one another. She would look at him lovingly across the table and whisper, "a . . . b . . . c . . ." Then he'd whisper back, "d . . . e . . . f . . . g . . ." She'd raise an eyebrow and ask, "h . . . i . . . j?" and on and on, so anyone nearby would think they were deep in intimate conversation.

What caused two people to eat together in silence? How

could Thea begin to know the answer if she didn't even know why she'd treated her own husband so badly that morning?

Had her mother ever been in love with her father? If so, what happened to change that? In some of the letters, her grandmother described two people Thea hardly knew—Mollkeleh and Mike—newlyweds so in love, shining, their glow apparent to everyone around them. Could this version of the story ever be told in a tongue other than the concocted language of Yiddish?

. . .

"Evelyn called today and said they took Aunt Florence to the hospital," Thea was saying to Reid's back. "She had chest pains and they thought she was having a heart attack. They don't know when she's going home." Sometimes you have to stretch the truth a little to get the reaction you want.

"What?" he mumbled, still not turning around, the patter between two nattily-dressed sportscasters on the screen drowning them both out.

During the time since Mickey died, Thea *had* been hard to live with. She hadn't been able to think of anything or anyone but her sister. All she'd wanted to do was save up things during the day to tell Mickey—the young couple with the adorable baby moving in across the street, the caller whose daughter had an imaginary friend, and now, the first part of the wedding letter from their grandmother.

Of course, she'd been sleeping a lot, drifting off early, as deep as memory went, dreaming dreams that took place in the rooms of their childhood—she and Mickey doing this, she and Mickey doing that. When she woke, it was a fresh shock—every morning—to remember that her sister was gone.

But she'd pushed Reid's patience too far. She'd begin getting back on track. He'd see.

By the time she got to the chicken, it was burnt all the way through. The potatoes had exploded in the oven.

. . .

Later that night, they were lying in bed reading. He'd kept his distance all evening, ending up with a bowl of corn flakes in front of the television while she had a bowl of Cheerios in the kitchen. She'd put her grandmother's letter in the drawer for him to see another time. Now he was reading a collection of poetry by Al, the guy out at the university. He was completely engrossed. She was starting a new book, *How to Break Free of the Habits That Defeat You,* which was pretty boring. Nothing new. Same old stuff. But she believed that if you started a book, you should finish it.

The phone rang. The house had been so stone-quiet it felt as if it were the middle of the night. Even with no children to worry about, Thea and Reid had been trained, after years of emergencies with her mother, to react to a late-night phone call with dread. Reid quickly picked it up.

"Hello? Joel! How're you doing, buddy?"

Joel? She couldn't think of a single time he'd ever called.

"Glad to hear it. Sure. She's right here. No, no, it's not too late." He handed over the phone, keeping his eyes on his book.

She laid her book face up on her chest. It closed by itself with a weak clap. "Joel?"

"Thea, I've got something to tell you." He sounded rushed. "I should've told you weeks ago, and I don't have any reason why I didn't. I guess something about this made me sort of upset . . . Hell, Thea, I'll just go ahead and say it.

It made me feel like you meant more to Mickey than I did. Anyway, I'm calling to tell you so I can clear my conscience. It has really been bothering me."

"What in the world, Joel?" She pictured his narrow face, the same face his two daughters had, earnest and intent. People were always telling Belle and Ann to smile. They hated that.

"Well, it's about that last day. Remember right before she died? The whole day she didn't move? When she was in the coma? And you went down to the cafeteria to get a sandwich?"

"Of course I do. I remember every single second of that day." Why had she left the room and missed her sister's dying? Why wasn't she with her at the very end?

"Well, something happened that I didn't tell you about."

He stopped there. She didn't say anything. She moved the phone a little away from her ear, as if that might take the pressure off, as if she were going to do things differently from the time she'd frightened Florence away. She would not make the same mistake again, whatever that mistake was.

Joel cleared his throat.

"I was there by her bed," he said, "reading the paper and she was just lying there. You know, the doctor had said she might stay that way for days. She looked so peaceful, like she was just sleeping. It was easy to forget she was in a coma, so I was trying to be really quiet. Anyway, all of a sudden, she sat straight up and opened her eyes. She looked around the room, but when she looked at me, it was like she didn't see me. She looked right through me and . . . well, she was looking for you. In a perfectly normal voice and with a big smile on her face, she said, 'Thea!' It was like she'd just gotten up from a nap and you'd gone in the next room for a minute and she suddenly remembered something she wanted to tell you. Then she pulled her hands out from under the covers and started feeling all over the bed as if she'd lost something and was frantic to find it. She was picking at the blanket. Plucking. Nervous little gestures. Going over and over the same place, in a circle. It's hard to describe what she was doing."

Thea could picture it, though. She'd read about how the dying sometimes reach for something only they can apprehend.

"I jumped up and put my hands on her shoulders to calm her, but she fell limp. I let her down slowly, and then she was lying there at a slant, sideways across the bed. I was afraid to try to move her. Her eyes were closed and she looked like she was back in the coma. The next few minutes, her breathing got slower. There were longer and longer spaces between each breath. Until she just didn't take the next breath. I waited for it, but it didn't come. And that was the end. The only thing she'd said was your name."

Now there were long spaces between Thea's breaths.

Whatever all that had been about, she felt sad to have missed it. She pictured her sister's fingers picking at the fibers of the blanket—as if she could trace the shape of something, their relationship maybe, their years together, the ridges and dips of the bed linens setting everything in bas-relief.

But then, maybe it was only some kind of release before the end. Purely physical. The way a jet, after landing and taxiing toward the airport gate, revs its engines one last time before shutting down. Like the lines from that poem Reid had read in a literary journal and copied for her:

> . . . How the horse, finally free
> Of the saddle, danced for a moment.

Now Thea was out of breath. But it didn't matter; Joel said good-bye, she said good-bye, they hung up. It would not have added anything to the conversation for her to tell him she now knew that the person she'd wanted most, wanted her.

Chapter 15

Thea ended up telling Reid that Aunt Florence was fine, and she apologized again for the chicken episode, saying she was sorry, that she'd been totally unaware of how much she'd been holding in—for twenty-seven years—about the baby. He said he knew how hard it had been for her since Mickey's funeral and that maybe her death is what opened up the subject of the baby all over again. They talked and talked, back and forth: all the things that went on so long ago—she'd felt this way, he'd felt that way, she'd wanted to adopt, he had not. Too late to change those old decisions, tears, hugs, sadness grinding down to acceptance, acceptance thickening into a love they both knew would keep going, no matter what.

A week after that conversation, they were in the den after dinner. He'd bought a CD of old baseball music and they were listening to "Take Me Out to the Ball Game" played on a bluesy piano. He was sitting in the wing chair across the room, grading exams, tapping his foot as though he were hitting a piano pedal. She was lying on her back on the love seat, her head propped on one of the arms. She held the morning paper, but was not paying any attention to what was in front of her. Instead, she was singing along with the music.

The song reminded her of the early years of their marriage, around the time they were trying to get pregnant, when going to the Charlotte Knights' games at the old stadium was a good way to get their minds off what was not happening. He loved baseball; she loved the roasted peanuts and the lights, which made the field look as if it were painted—the early summer green, players running around the bases, the numbers on their shirts almost silver, the pitcher's hard mound of dirt the center of it all.

. . .

The rude ring of the phone.

She hopped up to answer it. "Hello?"

"Mrs. McKee, how're you this evening?"

"Fine," she answered. Her level voice. It was obviously someone who would say they'd be in her neighborhood next week steam-cleaning carpets or sweeping chimneys.

"Mrs. McKee, this is Mrs. Hixson and I want to know if you've accepted Jesus Christ as your savior."

Before Thea could answer, the woman was off and running. "Have you been saved? Our Lord Jesus Christ wants you to be cleansed of your sins and take Him into your life—"

"Wait a minute. I find this call very offensive. How did you get my name in the first place?" Thea said, trying to interrupt, but the woman kept going, even over Thea's voice.

By this time, Reid had put down his papers and was looking at her with a wrinkled forehead. She glowered back an answer, circling an index finger next to her head.

The woman had not stopped talking. "Jesus Christ loves you, Mrs. McKee, and wants you in His flock. He wants you to accept Him as your savior . . ."

"Wait just a minute!"

But the woman hung up.

Before Thea could tell Reid what had happened, the phone rang.

"Hello." Her level voice again.

"Mrs. McKee, this is Mrs. Hixson and I want to know if you've accepted Jesus Christ as your savior."

The woman hadn't realized she'd made a mistake and dialed the same number.

"Now wait, Mrs. Hixson. You just called a minute ago and hung up on me. Don't hang up this time, and *don't start talking yet!*"

But she could feel the woman gathering momentum. Thea heard herself pleading, "Don't hang up. I've got something I want to say to *you*."

Immediately, the woman launched into a rush of words, all her Jesuses like a train slamming through the house, the saviors in her sentences like steam filling the rooms. "Jesus loves you and He wants you to accept Him as your savior. You can be saved if you commit your life to Him and, through His blessed love, find eternal life. Jesus Christ our Lord and—"

Thea tried to make herself heard over the woman. "It seems to me someone who loves Jesus as much as you would be a better listener—"

But the woman had hung up on her again. Thea slammed the phone down.

"What the hell was that?" Reid asked.

She started explaining, but he burst out laughing. "I can't believe you actually tried to engage that person in a conversation. You're almost as crazy as she is!"

"Yeah, but it just galled me that she—" Now she was laughing, too. He left his papers in the chair, crossed the room and bent over her, burying his face in that tender, meaty place where the neck meets the shoulder, a place they used to call the filet when they were first married. She was trying to stop laughing so she could ask why people who loved Jesus so much were never very lovable themselves, but he was kissing her on her neck, cheek, moving to her lips, and she could smell the lemony sweetness of his face.

"Ah-hm convi-enced," he was saying, in his old-time tent revivalist voice, "thay-re are a mu-ultitude of people out thay-re who have not heard that Je-esus is on their si-i-ide. And even though yew have not ac-cey-epted Him as yoh-ur sav-yuh, ah still lo-ove yew. But it is not too late for yew to be saved . . ."

He slid in next to her on the love seat. They folded and refolded their arms and legs, eliminating the sharp angles of elbows and knees so they could curl into each other, as though they *were* settling into something that could save them. He took off her glasses and dropped them over his shoulder on the rug. The newspaper was crushed somewhere beneath them. She eased her fingers inside the waistband of his jeans. The skin over his pelvic bone was smooth. He unbuttoned her blouse and easily unhooked her bra, slipping his hand in, the heat like a balm on her breast.

It was the first time they'd made love since before Mickey died, maybe even longer than that. Thea closed her eyes and let him carry her away from wherever she had been, as though the entire length of her body were balancing on an open hand.

. . .

The next day, the second part of the final letter from her grandmother arrived. This was the end of the letters. Her last chance to know. If she were Mickey, she'd be twirling her hair. If she were her mother, she'd be puffing away on a cigarette, narrowing her eyes when thin sheets of smoke began to cut. But she was not either of those people—though they were very much a part of her—so she just held the letter with both hands, her face tight, and read the last words she'd ever see of her grandmother's.

> *It has disturbed me to read in your recent letter that your dear Meyer does not feel well, suffers from a gastric stomach. What can that be for Meyer to suffer with his stomach? He used to eat at bedtime a piece of herring, well salted, a good sour pickle, and he also found in the icebox a little sour borscht from beets. Everything seemed to agree with him. Cold potatoes, a little burnt, was also not bad for Meyer. This happened the last time when I was with you, the day when I left after dessert. Well, God should help him, he should be well with the fullest, best appetite.*
>
> *And you, Celia, have to wear glasses at this same time. I use my glasses only to write. I am sorry to know.*
>
> *Let me know at once how Meyer is. When I will come, both of you will be healthy, that is how I want it, no other way.*

I chose for myself a dress, black, trimmed with a light collar, very stylish. And I purchased a hat, also, in black, with a light buckle as trimming. Black kid gloves. That is what I wore to the wedding. Oh yes, a pink corsage of roses, on my shoulder. Mike bought this for me, and one for his mother and for Mollkeleh and for all of the men who were in the wedding. The four men wore white roses in their coats.

I am sending you a piece from my flowers. Mollie's is from white roses, white ribbons with tulle, it was exceptional. She was dressed in a white dress, not long to the floor but to cover the legs, with covered buttons down the front, very good high-heeled shoes, also a little piece of veil to pull over her face, silk stockings, kid gloves in white. The dress had a scalloped neckline trimmed in fur, also white.

Florence, a dress with a jacket, the color of wine. Everyone shined of course as from such a lovely family. Everything was lovely and fine. Sorry that you and Meyer did not see this, then I would not have to write so much. It is, perhaps, to laugh about my writing but it is because you want to know from everything in detail. It gives me much pleasure to create happiness for you. I will do everything to be able to please you. You know that for a long time.

Surely you have received my postal card. When I wrote it, it was in a busy moment. We were ready to leave, everything had already been taken out to the car. Still, I wanted to let you know that your present arrives. My best, heartiest thanks from me and from Mollkeleh. She will surely write to you when she comes home from her honeymoon.

Yes, a letter from both of them from their honeymoon, from hotel. Everything like a dream . . . Mollie already married and to a nice boy from a nice Jewish family.

If I did not have Easy in the house I would be very sad. But he is always in the store. They are taking stock today.

The weather is rainy, cold, not appealing to go to the store. I rest but not now. I am writing but am very tired. I started writing this letter right after the noon dinner and now must prepare evening supper, already six o'clock.

Giving you regards from my entire family.

Yours always,
your sister Bella

P.S. In a second letter I will surely write more. Perhaps I have some things forgotten. Please, this time, forgive me.

Be healthy and do good business.

P.S. I do not remember what I last told you in my letter from November, if I told you anything at all. Please forgive me, some things I cannot remember. Until we are again together in person I will tell you that everything is all right. Do not ask questions. Everything I will explain. Do not mention to anyone. As I say, the last word you keep to yourself. There was another man. God willing, Mollie will not know from him and she will have happiness with her loving Mike.

Before Thea had a chance to think, before she had a chance to reread the letter, to concentrate on each word so she could try to read *through* the paragraph at the end and understand what her grandmother was talking about, she had a phone call from Evelyn.

"I took Mama to the emergency room last night." Evelyn was breathless with crisis. "They think she might have had a stroke. We were talking on the telephone and all of a sudden, I couldn't understand a word she was saying. She probably thought she was talking but she wasn't making any sense at all. I got in my car and drove over there as fast as I could . . . unh, that drive was awful! Can you imagine? I had no idea what I'd find when I got there. She was able to make it to the door to let me in, but she was dragging one leg behind her, like a wagon. Between her speech being garbled and her leg, I'm telling you, it was a double-headed sword."

"Can she have company? Can I see her?" Thea could not lose her. Not before she had a chance to talk to her, to try again.

"I think it would mean a lot to her to see you. She's in Intensive Care but they let you in for a few minutes every hour. You can tell she knows what's going on. She *looks good*. You'd never know anything was wrong to look at her. It's just that she can't make any sense when she talks. I have a feeling she's foaming at the bit to talk and be understood."

"I'll get in my car right now and be there in an hour and a half."

She got directions to the hospital from Evelyn. Then she called Reid's office and left a message with the department secretary that her aunt was sick and she was on her way to Columbia. She'd call him later.

She packed an overnight bag and double-locked the door behind her.

. . .

How long had it been since Reid called at the station and she'd driven home in the rain, when he called to say Mickey's cancer had come back? At least today it wasn't raining. In fact, the sky hadn't seen a cloud in days. There was the sweet possibility of spring in the air, the tease, the promise that something better was on its way.

She would ask Florence. She had to. As soon as Florence was able to talk. But would she ever be able to talk again? Why did the women in her family stop talking? What was it that was so terrible no one could say the words? *There was another man. God willing, Mollie will not know from him and she will have happiness with her loving Mike. There was another man. God willing, Mollie will not know from him and she will have happiness with her loving Mike.* Maybe if she said it over and over, she could strip it down to the bare root.

If you tell me, Aunt Florence, you won't be betraying Mother, at least not any more than you do when you tell me those memories of yours. Each story is a small betrayal. Every time you tell me my mother was selfish. Every time you tell me my mother took more than she deserved. Every time you tell me my mother was too pretty. Too popular. Too much your mother's favorite. Every time you try to correct the balance in your family, to tip the scale a bit, to even the score.

Hold on, Aunt Florence. I'm coming. Don't be like your mother and keep the last word to yourself. Please God, don't let her keep the last word to herself.

. . .

Florence looked small in the high hospital bed. Without makeup, her face was sweet and natural, the way it had been when Thea was growing up. She loved the tiny wrinkles that spread out from the corners of her aunt's eyes when she smiled. Thea leaned down and kissed her cheek. She wasn't sure which side had been affected so she put her hand over the hand that didn't have an I.V. and patted it lightly rather than trying to hold it. A curtain, the washed-out green color of hospital cotton, separated her aunt from the next patient. Machines next to the bed were whispering.

"Aunt Florence, how are you feeling?"

She opened her eyes, nodded, and freed her forefinger from under Thea's hand to tap Thea's fingers. Could she speak at all now? The noise from the machines was rhythmical—*Shhh*-sh, *shhh*-sh, *shhh*-sh.

"I'm so sorry you're going through this," Thea said, suddenly aware that she hadn't thought to bring a gift. Her mother had always turned illness into an event, with elaborately wrapped gifts and flowers from the yard in a vase on the bedside table. She loved her daughters when they were sick—especially Thea and her headaches. She'd bring up meals on a white wicker bed tray and use the special china—a small plate and cup and saucer, pale blue and white with pearly pink roses—because, she said, a regular-sized dinner plate was too big for a sick person's appetite.

Evelyn was standing beside Thea, edging her over. No one would be able to observe what was happening, but Thea was having to baby-step sideways to keep from being thrown off-balance, as if some invisible force were moving her away from Florence. Finally, Thea stood firm, anchoring herself. Evelyn stopped pushing.

"Mama, don't try to talk. Just enjoy Thea's visit. You rest and take it easy and let Thea do the talking. Like that commercial, let your fingers do the talking!" Evelyn laughed a slightly artificial laugh and Florence smiled again, tapping Thea's hand as if she were speaking to her in code.

A nurse, whose hair was the same flesh color as her skin, came in and said softly, "It's time for our patient to rest now. We can come back in a little while." Thea thought she heard the nurse's teeth click when she talked.

Thea and Evelyn followed her out. When she'd disappeared down the hall, Evelyn told Thea the doctor had spoken with her that morning, and yes, it looked like her mother had had a stroke, but he believed there was a good chance for complete recovery. It was a very small stroke, he said, and she was in reasonable health, otherwise, for a woman her age.

"Oh, Evelyn, thank goodness. That's wonderful news. I'm so relieved," Thea cried.

. . .

When it was time to see Florence again, Evelyn had gone back to her mother's to pick up a nightgown in case they moved her out of Intensive Care. Thea went in alone.

"Aunt Florence, hi. How're you feeling now?"

Her aunt opened her mouth, ready to speak.

But instead of moving her lips, her mouth locked in that open position. Then, abruptly, she closed her eyes and was apparently asleep. Thea stood there, watching the monitors with their jagged neon lines, listening to the machines, wishing it were her aunt who was doing the whispering.

After a few minutes, Florence opened her eyes again and looked as if she was surprised to see her niece standing by the bed.

"Hello again," Thea said, touching her aunt's cheek, lifting one stray gray hair back, away from her face.

"I want to—"

"Yes, Aunt Florence . . . ?" Thea's voice went up at the end of her sentence and she raised her eyebrows as if to pull more words from her.

But she closed her eyes. It looked as if saying those three words had exhausted her, as if *I want to* were three huge stones she'd had to lift alone.

Thea waited. Her aunt's mouth dropped open, and she was breathing harder. She was asleep again.

The nurse came in and touched Thea's arm. Time to leave.

"She spoke to me with perfect clarity," Thea said when

they were out of the room. "Has she been able to talk at all before this?"

"No, she hasn't, dear. But I'm glad she spoke to you."

She could tell the nurse didn't believe her.

. . .

When Thea drove home from Columbia that night, she rolled down the windows, letting the air wash the hospital smell from her skin. The days were getting longer, and the late afternoon light turned everything in the car golden, almost buttery. She was glad she'd decided not to stay over.

The next day she was at the station, waiting for her first caller. Through the glass, Tim gave her the cue, ready to go. The mug of coffee he held spilled over his fingers. He bent down to lick his knuckles and the coffee sloshed again. No matter what he was doing, he was awkward. The Ichabod Crane of radio.

. . .

"Hello, Ken. This is Thea McKee. You're on the air."

"Can you hear me?"

"Yes, go right ahead."

"Thanks for taking my call."

"Sure."

"So, Mrs. McKee. How're you doing?"

"I'm fine. What's up?"

"Well, first I want to tell you that I listen to your program every chance I get and I enjoy it. I really do, I'm not kidding."

"Thank you, Ken. I appreciate that. Now what is your question?" There ought to be a law against callers taking up time like this.

"Well, what I want to talk about is, I've been married for

eight years and last year I found out my wife had an affair. I won't go into how I found out, but let's just say I did. By the time I said something to her about it, the whole thing was over. She told me it only went on for two months. She says it was a bad mistake on her part and she swears it'll never happen again. I believe her, you know? I can tell she's telling the truth. But don't you think I have a right to hear the whole story? I would feel a lot better, you know, if she would just tell me everything that happened, but she says she doesn't want to talk about it. She says it's over and done with and it didn't mean anything and let's forget it. What do you think, Mrs. McKee? Don't you think I have some rights?"

"I'm curious, Ken. Why do you want to know?"

"What?"

"Why do you want to know?"

"Well. I think it's important to be honest with each other. You get what I mean?"

"I wonder if it's honesty you're after, or whether you want to punish your wife—or maybe even yourself—a little. It might be helpful for you to understand why you feel it's important to go back over all this, when your wife is assuring you it was meaningless. What would it take for you to let it go?"

"You don't understand," he said, his voice turning hard and bitter. "I'm just asking her to tell me the *truth*. All that time they were messing around and I couldn't even tell. I *deserve* to know. What if it happens again? I want to know what to look for."

"Ken, what will it take for you to believe your wife?"

Tim was cueing her to wrap this one up and go to the next caller. He was also holding up three skinny fingers to let her know all the phone lines were busy. There were plenty of problems out there. The more callers she had, the happier Tim was, as if they were selling lawn mowers and customers were lined up around the block.

"She's got to tell me a helluva lot more than she has so far—"

"You might want to consider talking with a therapist or your minister. You sound as though you're still very hurt," she said, trying to soothe him.

"You're *damn right* I'm—"

"Your wife may not be the one who can make you feel better. I think you need to speak with someone other than her to help you put this to rest. Thank you for calling, Ken. I hope you can find some peace so you and your wife can move on."

. . .

"Hello, Carol, welcome to the program. What would you like to talk about today?"

"I'm a little, uh, nervous."

"Oh, you don't have to be!"

"Well, I was listening to your last caller, and going along with him, I want to talk about, uh, jealousy. See, my husband is real nice most of the time, but sometimes he gets on a kick of thinking I'm, like, flirting with every guy I talk to. And the truth is, I don't care about anybody but him, and I haven't cared about anybody but him since the day I met him. I love my husband. But we have, uh, lots of fights about this. Last night, we had a big one. We'd been at a cookout at our next-door neighbor's house and he thought I was, like, flirting with one of his buddies. All I was doing was talking. My husband got so mad we had to leave early. When we got home, he was yelling at me and saying all kinds of crazy things. I wish you could've heard him! He said he didn't believe he's our son's daddy. He says he knows that the guy I went with before him is our son's daddy. We've been married almost a year, and he comes up with something like this! He's so jealous he'll say anything, even if it's the furtherest thing from the truth. One thing, he would never, uh, hit me or anything like that. It's just, like, he has a real bad temper and he yells like all get-out."

"Do you and your husband ever talk about this when you're not in the middle of an argument? Do you ever have a calm, unemotional conversation about his jealousy?"

"Uh, no. One of us'll leave the house mad, and then, like, time'll pass and we'll cool off and it'll be like nothing ever happened. The only time it comes up is when he thinks I'm flirting and he gets mad."

Perfect chance to bring in the article she'd just read. She should've mentioned it with the last caller.

"Interestingly, Carol, there's a new study out on jealousy. It seems that men expect and demand sexual faithfulness from their wives, but they want sexual variety for themselves. Women, on the other hand, want emotional faithfulness from their husbands. Men get extremely angry when their wives stray sexually. Women forgive their men when they stray *sexually*, but not when they stray *emotionally*—in other words, when they form *emotional* attachments with other women. The reason for this difference between men and women is that men face a particular problem—paternity uncertainty. Everyone knows who the mother is. She's the one who's been pregnant for nine months! Did you ever see the movie *Stalag 17*?" She didn't wait for an answer. "You know, when the POW who hasn't seen his wife for over a year receives a letter from her saying she's pregnant and he's the father? And the poor guy keeps saying to himself, 'I believe it, I believe it.' Anyway, Carol, back to the study, I can't remember the exact numbers, but a large percentage of children have fathers who they think are their genetic fathers but aren't. Isn't that astounding? A *large* percentage! The chances are, I believe, one in ten—one in ten!—for a child's genetic father to actually be a different man from who the child believes to be the father. Sadly, the child is often the last to know. Have you ever heard the expression, 'Mama's baby, papa's maybe'?" Again, she didn't wait for an answer. "But regardless of what the studies may or may not show, you two need to learn how to communicate honestly and with sensitivity. It sounds as if there are layers of misunderstanding between you. Please, talk with your husband about the two of you going to see a good marriage counselor. And I wish you luck. Let me know how you are."

"Uh, thank you, I will."

How in the world had she come up with "Mama's baby, papa's maybe"? As soon as the words were out of her mouth, she could see Tim out of the corner of her eye waving his hands, doing everything he could to get her attention. She brought the program to a close, with a little bumbling, and in two seconds he was in the room standing beside her chair. She looked up his long legs to his face.

"Listen, Thea, you've got to rein it in. Way too long on that last caller. We've had complaints."

"Complaints? About this last call?"

"No. In general. Somebody on our board said something. At the last meeting."

"About what?"

"About you, well, coming unglued on the air." He was backing away. "You just can't go off like that." He opened the door. "And telling people to go to a marriage counselor is not the best advice you can give. They've come to *you.* That's like a lawyer telling clients they need to see a lawyer." One leg out the door. "Not to mention all the callers we're not getting to. If this problem continues . . ." Gone.

Through the glass she saw him trot down the hall toward his office, still working his mouth.

Chapter 16

Florence was better. Her speech had returned, Evelyn said on the phone, and there was only a slight weakness on one side, which the doctors thought would improve with physical therapy and time. The day after Florence came home from the hospital, Thea drove to Columbia to see her.

Florence looked so dressed up in her red and white flowered bathrobe she could've been at a party. Once when she'd visited Thea in Charlotte they'd gone robe-shopping. It had amazed Thea how she drew up a list of requirements in her mind first, then set out to find the perfect robe: Long, so she could wear it over any length nightgown. A print that wouldn't show "every little spot." Buttons, not a zipper, down the front. Two pockets to hold Kleenex and eyeglasses. Fabric thick enough for her gown not to show through.

"I'm so sorry Evelyn's not here to see you," Florence said. Evelyn had been staying there until her mother was well enough to be alone. "She was waiting all morning, thinking you'd get here earlier, but when the cleaning lady came about an hour ago, she took advantage of somebody being here and left to run errands. She'll be sorry she missed you."

"I'm sorry to miss *her*." What luck! But when should she bring it up? And how?

Florence let herself down gently onto the unyielding Victorian love seat. She folded her robe over her legs. "Just look at these thin legs! You know what they used to say about them? 'You ought to be able to sing real good because you've got mockingbird legs!' No wonder I was so shy when I was growing up. I couldn't even walk across a room that was filled with people. Now your mother was outgoing and loved parties. But not me, honey. Not me."

Florence was her old self.

"Your mother was like Papa in that way. After Mama died, Papa moved to Florida, but he would come to Columbia to stay with me and your uncle Jack during the summer months. He was fun-loving, always with the jokes. Great company. He'd have this little black book filled with all the names of his lady friends in Florida and then he'd sit down and write them all letters."

Florence was gathering steam as she went along. Thea sat in the small, carved mahogany chair, close to her, satisfied—for now—to let her tell whatever she wanted to tell. Thea settled into that voice, so much like her mother's, the low, early morning timbre that was there all day.

"Even after Papa got married again, he and his new wife

would come and stay with me, like he always did in the summertime. She was a short, buxom woman. Every morning he'd get up and tell me something else she wasn't doing right. She'd still be in the bed sleeping. In those days we didn't have the fitted sheets, and she didn't tuck the bottom sheet under tight enough to suit him. He'd say, 'Florence, teach her how to make up the bed.' Papa was used to being pampered by Mama, see. One time it got cold in the middle of the night, and Papa woke up his new wife and told her to get up and find an extra blanket to put on the bed. He told me she got so mad at him for waking her up that she got the blanket and stood at the foot of the bed and *threw* it over him, and he actually caught a cold from the breeze! Of course, he said it in Jewish and it sounds better that way: '*Ashka volfin* the blanket!' Actually threw the blanket! Speaking of sleeping with people, did I ever tell you about the time when I was little and Papa's mother—you know, my grandmother—came to visit, and I had to sleep with her? Of course, they didn't make your mother sleep with her, just me. But you know me, I'm not one to complain."

Welcome back, Aunt Florence.

"See, some women of that generation wore *sheitels* and some even shaved their heads and wore a wig all the time. Papa's mother had a red-headed one for the sabbath and a black-headed one for every day. Well, when it was time for her to go to bed, she took the *sheitel* off and there were these little wisps of gray hair. Then she took out her false teeth. And I had to sleep with this lady who was missing all those body parts! Scared me to death! I had nightmares all night. When she came to our house, she'd say, '*De bubbe a du! De bubbe a du!*' The grandmother is here! The grandmother is here!"

Oh, the hum of her stories. It felt like she was holding Thea in her lap and rocking her.

"You know, my mind wanders in the past an awful lot lately. You don't mind if I tell you these things, do you?"

Thea started to shake her head, but realized the question didn't call for an answer.

"You do know our name was originally Katzenellenbogen, don't you? Some of the members of the family took Katz, some took Katzen, and Papa chose Bogen. One time we read a story in school about somebody named Katzenellenbogen and there was a footnote saying it meant 'cat's elbow,' and I was so excited I told my classmates that was my name originally. They looked at me like I was some kind of freak!"

"Is it true Grandpa Bogen shortened his name because it was too long to fit on the front window of his store?" Thea asked.

"No, no, that's just a *meise*, a story that was told. But there was something else I wanted to tell you. What was it? Oh, I remember. You know, when your father met your mother, they didn't like each other. But then when they met again later, they struck up a friendship. Nobody realized they were courting."

Thea felt someone tapping her on the shoulder. Go on, she heard a voice say, this is your chance. She twisted her neck to one side, then the other, freeing it from the kinks that had set in. She stretched her arms out in front and turned her palms under and away, like someone getting ready to stand up and leave.

"I don't know why I think of these things when I'm with you," Florence began again, before Thea had a chance to speak, "but you know what just popped in my head? When Papa would go to New York on buying trips for the store, he'd bring back a great big stick of salami because we couldn't get that in Denmark. No matter what time he'd get in, we'd eat that salami, even if it was the middle of the night. Right now, if I think about it—"

Before Florence could become nostalgic over the salami memory, her hands fluttered to her chest like little birds. She delicately patted her chest.

"—it makes you burp?" Thea finished her sentence for her and laughed.

"I haven't thought about what it would do to me now!" Florence hardly took a breath before starting a new story. "Did your mother ever tell you that when Mama was giving birth to her, Tante Celia was the one who stayed with her—with Mama—during the entire labor? And Tante Celia was pregnant herself? And do you know that Tante Celia worked so hard with Mama, pushing with her, helping Mama push that baby out and all—the birth of *your* mother, Thea, I'm talking about—that Tante Celia had a miscarriage? Tante Celia told me that herself."

Thea swallowed hard. Florence kept going.

"But being a young wife with two little girls, Mama was so harried with everything, doing the housework, cooking the meals, keeping the house quiet while Papa took his afternoon naps, helping him in the store . . . until when she'd come in at night . . . and one time Tante Celia came to visit us and Mama was so upset and aggravated and I was such a crybaby and so bad . . ."

Thea wondered if it was okay for Florence to become this agitated. She didn't want anything to happen to her. Not now. Face-to-face, Evelyn gone, this could be Thea's best chance.

". . . Mama was at the end of her rope and she took me and

made like she was going to throw me out the window! She was holding me under my arms and had me *out in the air* . . . and as little as I was then! I still remember how frightened I was! If I wiggled the least bit, she could've dropped me! Tante Celia screamed, '*Bella! Bella!* You know what you're *doing*?' Tante Celia grabbed me back in, and I always felt she saved my life. And when I'd tell that to Tante Celia years later, she remembered it."

Florence got up and left the room, her walk favoring one side.

She came back holding a snapshot. It was cracked but Thea could recognize Tante Celia, in a striped hammock, her legs over the side, a little girl in her lap, no more than four years old. The two faces reflected the sun. Tante Celia looked as though she was in her twenties. The child's head was tucked under Tante Celia's chin, the two of them a fit.

"Here, you hold it." Florence pressed the picture into Thea's hand. "Tante Celia loved her little niece. Your mother was so shocked. She thought *she* was Tante Celia's favorite. But she wasn't. *I* was the main one." She pointed to the child, whose face was shaped like a valentine, hair tossed about. "That's me. Why'd they say I was such an ugly child?" She went back to the love seat.

"You were cute!" Thea said.

"I think so, too!" She patted her bosom and chuckled. "There goes that salami again!"

"Who said you were ugly? You were the only one who said it! Nobody else did. You were adorable!" They were never going to get back to Thea's parents. How was she going to work it into the conversation? "Aunt Florence, I want to ask you—" Thea laid the snapshot on the table between them.

"Oh dear, I can't believe how rude I've been," Florence

said. "Here I've been babbling on with all these *bubbemeise* and I haven't even asked if you'd like a cold drink . . . a glass of milk or a Coca-Cola . . . and a piece of apple cake. It's very good. Jewish apple cake. My non-Jewish neighbor makes it!"

"No, thank you. I'm really not hungry or thirsty. But I want to ask you something. I feel bad bringing this up again, especially after you've been sick. Well, the easiest way to do this is to show you the last letter from your mother."

"Oh, I forgot there was another part to the wedding letter. I remember reading the first part right before I went into the hospital. I had the stroke, in fact, the very day I got the letter, after I read it, I think. Now this is the second part, right?"

"Right." Of course, the day Florence got the letter about the wedding she had a stroke and stopped talking. That made sense. In this family.

Thea watched her carefully pick a piece of lint off the love seat, peel it from her finger and drop it on the coffee table. She took her glasses from the pocket of her robe and put them on. Thea got up, handed her the second part of the letter and went back to the chair, keeping an eye on her. Would another letter mean another stroke?

. . .

"Hmm," Florence said as she finished. "This is my copy to keep?"

Thea nodded, and her aunt folded it and put it in her pocket. Then she took off her glasses and put them in the other pocket. She rubbed her eyes, small grinding motions with her knuckles.

"Please, Aunt Florence, please, please tell me what that last thing means."

She didn't answer. Thea looked at her face, still heart-shaped, and tried to determine if she was okay. It was hard to tell what she was thinking.

Finally, Florence spoke. "How can I do that? You know I promised your mother I would never tell you or your sister. Think about what you're asking me to do. I would never want to betray anyone. If anybody should tell you, it should've been your mother. She was the one who should've told you. Not me. Evelyn was just saying last night—"

"But, Aunt Florence, with Mother gone, it's no longer *her* secret. It's a piece of *my* story. A crucial piece. And maybe it'll help me learn where I belong in the world. With Mother gone, and you—well, I hope you'll live to be a hundred and twenty—but you *are* getting older and you won't be here forever. So it's up to you. I really believe in my heart that Mother would say it's all right for you to tell me now. *Now* she would. Please, Aunt Florence."

"Let me get a drink of water."

Her black velvet slippers made soft little sweeps on the hardwood floor. Since she walked leaning to one side, the sound of her footsteps was like a heartbeat, two sounds—one, the accent, the other an echo. She returned from the kitchen, taking her time, sipping as she took each slow step. She sat back down on the love seat, pulling her robe over her legs, smoothing out the wrinkles in the fabric. Then she tapped next to where she was sitting, once, with her index finger, meaning Thea should come there. Thea squeezed in beside her. Her aunt finished her water, then centered the glass meticulously on a burled wood coaster next to where the picture of the Key Club dance had been when Thea was there before. The picture was gone. A cloisonné vase of silk flowers was there now.

"You know, dear, I'm going to tell you something. When you came to see me in the hospital, I made a decision then that I would tell you. Lying there for so long, not being able to talk, I had plenty of time to think, and I decided for myself that if the good Lord ever let me speak again, I'd tell you the story. I made that promise to myself."

Thea's heart was beating so hard she had to hold herself still to keep it from jerking her whole body around.

"Then keep that promise you made to yourself," she begged. "Be true to *you*."

Isn't that what Florence had been doing all this time, since Thea's mother died, with the stories she'd been telling? Wasn't she just trying to be true to herself, take care of herself? Maybe it was the healthiest thing she could do—to say out loud how overlooked she'd felt her whole life, to say out loud that her sister was the reason she'd been overlooked. Telling me, Thea thought, was the closest she could come to telling Mother.

Florence screwed her mouth to one side, giving her face the appearance of being pressed in a vise. Thea took her hand and it was cold, so she sandwiched it between hers. Her aunt's face began to soften and relax into a little smile. The creases in the outer corners of her eyes deepened. She looked like the Aunt Florence Thea had grown up with, the one who'd taken care of all of them.

"Thea, darling, that day in the hospital when you put your hand on my hand, that's when I made the promise that if I ever got better, I'd tell you. I am going to tell you. I just hope to God I'm doing the right thing."

"You are." Thea wished Mickey were with her. How she wished it were the two of them.

"It's okay. I really do think it's okay," Florence said.

Thea felt like she was sliding, like butter heating on a griddle. Smooth. There was not a trace of dread. No fear of what she'd hear. It was time. The hard edge that had always felt like a boundary would melt away.

"Well, let me start at the beginning. Your mother was still living at home, in Denmark. She was working at South Carolina Power and Light, and she was going with a nice boy, a *goyisher* boy, a Gentile, from Sweden, a few miles down the road. He was not too tall, very slim and very handsome. Like a Robert Redford type. Blond hair. Wavy hair. White, white skin and light blue eyes, the color of that teacup over there on the table. A courteous boy, quiet-natured, smart as could be. You know the picture I had out on the table when you came that time? The one of the Key Club dance?"

Thea nodded.

"It was a picture of your mother and that boy. I was in the back row. I was going to tell you that day and that's why I took the picture out, but Evelyn didn't think it was wise. I forgot to put it away before you got here. Evelyn took it home with her, but I'll ask her to send it to you."

Again, Evelyn, keeper of the secret.

"Anyway, your mother and that boy were courting every night," Florence was saying. "They'd sit out in the swing on the porch until late, long after Papa and Mama and I would go to bed. Well, Mama was real upset about this. She didn't say anything to Mollie, but she told me. And I know she and Papa discussed it privately. See, back then, Jews and Gentiles didn't go together and they certainly didn't get married. I know it's a more accepted thing now. Look at you and Reid.

He's darling and you two have a nice marriage. Back then, it was different. Mama couldn't even read English. She and Papa talked Jewish a lot of the time in the house. Around then, your mother and your father met again. You know they'd met the first time at that dance when they didn't like each other. But one weekend Mollie went to Columbia to see Rose Kline, Rabbi Kline's daughter, who was a friend of hers, and Mike was visiting the Klines that same weekend. Mike liked her right away this time. He'd just moved to Newberry from Atlanta. Remember, your father had been doing some kind of coaching at a boys' school in Atlanta, but he lost that job. Oh, times were hard then and nobody had money. But what kind of job is that for a Jewish man? Coaching! Well, he moved to Newberry because he knew a Mr. Vigodsky there, who gave him a job in his shoe store. That was a good job back then. And sure enough, it wasn't long before Mike was able to open his own store with shoes *and* dresses. Well, your mother and father met for the second time, and he began writing to her. I know Mollie only thought of him as a good friend. She told me that. She was still going with that other boy, but she would write Mike back. So, she was writing these long letters to Mike but seeing that boy almost every night. Oh, what was his name? Carter something. I can't remember whether Carter was his first name or his last name. Mama had a bad bout with her stomach then and she had to go in the hospital. They ended up operating—exploratory, they called it, and they had already taken one of her kidneys years before, which they never should've done. Oh, she was so sick and weak. And that's what I was talking about on the phone to you that time. When I came close to telling you."

Carter! That name! We're so close—don't let anything stop her. Please, God. Let her tell the whole thing.

"Your mother and I were in Mama's hospital room. Mama was sleeping and your mother and I were just sitting there, waiting for her to wake up. She'd had the operation a few days before and was in a lot of pain. She opened her eyes. I can remember it like it happened yesterday. I can still see that room. Anyway, Mama motioned with her finger, like this, for us to come nearer. Mollie and I moved together, right over next to her, the two of us like we were Siamese twins. Mama looked straight at Mollie and said, in her broken English, 'Mollkeleh, that *goyisher* boy is no good for you. His family is not right for our family. They're a nice family, but they're not the same as us. You can love Mike just as easy as you can love that other boy. I'm telling you what's the best for you.' "

Florence was running her hands over her arms. "And your mother started crying right then and there. She knew Mama was telling her the truth, but I believe, in her heart, she truly loved that boy. Carter something. But the main point is, none of us knew the situation your mother was in at that time. At least I didn't. I don't know about Mama. I always assumed she didn't know anything. Mollie cried and cried. She put her head down on the side of Mama's bed and wept bitterly. I remember Mama was combing Mollie's hair with her fingers and saying in Jewish, 'Such a white scalp.' Which is what she used to say when we were little and she would take a comb and part our hair."

Chapter 17

Afternoon sun through the window was turning Florence's gray hair silver. Thea knew it would soon be that in-between time, the hour of change, when mid-afternoon glare would collapse into late afternoon, and the sky, for that short period before dark, would be very tender.

"So your mother did exactly what Mama told her to do," Florence was saying. "She stopped courting that boy and started courting Mike. They were a good-looking couple, Mollie and Mike. People would stop and stare when they passed on the street, that's how stunning they were together. The football player and the beauty queen. And, after a little bit of time, oh, I'd say it was less than a month, Mike gave

Mollie an engagement ring. And they got married. And that was only a few weeks later. It all happened very fast. And that's the next part I'm going to tell you. Now, you know your mother didn't want her picture taken at her wedding. She didn't want any pictures at all. And you know she got out of a sick bed to go to the ceremony. Well, here's the truth about that. Your mother always told everybody she had hives and that's why she looked so swollen, and that was true—she did come down with hives—but that wasn't the whole story. She was sick and she was swollen because she had hives and—"

Thea knew what was coming next. Maybe she'd always known it. But when her aunt said the next three words, Thea found herself mouthing them along with her.

"—she was pregnant."

Thea pictured Rabbi Kline standing under the *chuppah* with her parents, pronouncing them husband and wife. Her father would stomp the glass wrapped in the pure white handkerchief, and that small sack of dreams would shatter into a million fragments. *Mazel tov*, everyone at the wedding would breathe out. *Mazel tov*.

"Thea, your mother was pregnant with you. And your real father was that Carter person."

She felt like she was being ripped down the middle and was jagged on both sides. She could taste metal.

"How did you find out about this?" Thea gasped. "When did Mother tell you?"

"Honey. It shouldn't be me telling you this. I didn't want to be the one. I swear, on my own life, I have never told a soul before now. I sent you Mama's letters, thinking there might be things in them and you could get a general idea about some of this. Not that I wanted to betray your mother."

"When did Mother tell you?" *Why didn't she tell me?* is what Thea was really asking. *Did Mickey know? Is that why she didn't want to have the letters translated? Who told her? Daddy?*

"Well, your mother didn't tell me right away," Florence was saying. "You know the way she would just stop talking, and go to bed, and stay there. Well, after Mama said that to her in the hospital, Mollie went to bed, like she was sick. We thought it was because she was so tired, with working and Mama being in the hospital and all. Your mother always did take things harder than anybody else. But you see, we didn't know about things like that back then. About depression and all. But I did something terrible. When all of a sudden your mother started feeling better and seemed to be lighthearted again and out courting Mike, I went in her room—I don't know why I was snooping or what I expected to find—but I looked through her dresser until I found her diary. And that's how I discovered the truth. May God strike me dead! I'm ashamed to tell you. I hoped I would never have to tell a soul that I went prying into someone else's business. But I did. And in that diary, your mother said how much she loved that Carter boy. I remember her words: *Diary,* she said, *he is the love of my life*. See, your mother loved well, but not wisely. He wanted to marry your mother, but she would not dare disobey Mama. Your mother also wrote that she told Mike she was pregnant with someone else's baby—I don't think she told him whose it was. Back then, people didn't ask questions. Maybe Mike knew it was Carter, or maybe he didn't and he didn't have to know those details. But in the diary, she said that Mike told her he still adored her and wanted to marry her. And she said, too, that he told her they would never tell a soul he was not the baby's father. I think, from that minute on, your mother decided that if someone loved her that much—if he could accept the baby, if he could accept *her*—she could learn to love him back."

If someone loved her that much, she could learn to love him back. What Thea herself had thought when she'd almost married Richard. Unlike her, her mother had gone through with the wedding.

"And in the diary, your mother wrote about her depressions and how she'd always had low times, even when she was young. But she specifically said she started getting worse right after Mama was in the hospital. If you ask me, *I* think it was when Mama told her she couldn't marry that Carter boy. From then on, your mother had a very hard time.

"And you know, your mother never told Mama about the baby. It would've killed Mama if she'd known. Although when you think about it, it *was* around that same time—was it before or after you were born?—that Mama died. I wonder. I wonder if it's possible Mama *did* know. You think about some of the things Mama wrote to Tante Celia in these letters. Hmm. I never put two and two together. Mama dying, the baby being born."

Florence had forgotten that Thea's grandmother died the day after she was born. Was Florence saying she blamed Thea's mother for Thea's grandmother's death?

"How did Mother find out you knew?" *Did you ever tell her you read her diary?*

"One night everybody was sleeping. The house was very quiet. Your mother and I slept in the same room then, in Mama and Papa's house. For some reason, I woke up and saw your mother's bed was empty. Then I heard sounds coming from the bathroom. I listened. She was vomiting, she was so sick. Naturally, I got out of bed and went down the hall and cracked the door to the bathroom. She was sitting on that cold floor, leaning over the toilet, sick as a dog. I grabbed a washcloth and got it as cold as I could under the faucet and sat down beside her on the floor and held that washcloth to her forehead while she heaved and heaved. That's the way Mama used to do with us when we were sick, hold a wet washcloth to our foreheads. When your mother finally settled down and was over being sick, I gave her a little Coke and got her back in the bed, and we just lay there, she in her bed, me in mine, in the dark, neither one of us saying a thing. And then she told me. Everything. And that's when she made me promise never to tell a soul. And she said she wasn't going to tell the baby—of course, that was you—and she wasn't going to tell anybody ever."

Florence had not told Thea's mother about reading the diary.

"Mollie was very self-conscious, but really, she hardly showed with you until she was in her last months, so no one had any idea she was pregnant when she got married. She wore a wedding dress. Cream-colored. Trimmed in fur! Very expensive. And when you were born, you were so little—like a wren—you could have been premature. And everybody just assumed you were. In fact, you were very sick when you were born. What was it? You couldn't breathe? Or swallow? Anyway, you know how they rushed you to Columbia in an ambulance and your mother held you on a little satin pillow in her lap in the back of that ambulance? She fought with those ambulance people to let her hold you. That was strictly against the rules, but oh boy, she fought them. She was *not* going to let go of you. Not for anything. Then the doctors at that hospital saved your life. Now. I'm going to tell you something else, because you may as well know the whole story."

Thea held her breath.

"Did you ever wonder why your mother had you and Mickey so close together? Well, I was staying with her and your father in Newberry and one night I heard them talking. They didn't know I could hear them through the wall. But in that little place they had, you could hear everything. You were two months old. Mollie was so overwrought, with Mama dying and all, she could hardly take care of you. I was married and living in Columbia at the time, but I went to her, to try to help and get up with you during the night and take care of the cooking. I didn't mind. You know me, I never like to complain. Anyway, you were doing all right but you were still so little. You were sleeping in a bassinet in the living room, where I was sleeping. In fact, I gave them that bassinet when you were born. It was a very nice one, lined with cotton batting, not so fancy-schmancy, but a good one that would hold up. Anyway, I heard your mother crying, saying she didn't want to get pregnant again, that she wasn't ready. Your father was saying he wanted a baby he could call his own, he didn't want to wait, what if they had trouble, what if she couldn't get pregnant . . ."

Those last three words, Thea knew so well.

"To tell the truth, I believe that night he sort of snapped. And I can understand. It must've been hard on him. The baby and all. He took such good care of your mother, always giving in. This one time, he wanted his way. So—"

So.

"I don't know how to say this, but . . . well, there were sounds. The bed making noises. And the shushing, like your mother didn't want me to hear what was going on. And maybe I shouldn't be saying this part, but it sounded like . . . and I heard her saying, please, please . . . I kept hearing that.

I just think he snapped . . . something got to him. Anyhow, the whole time they were making love, please, please, she kept saying . . . on and on it went . . . I couldn't help but listen. And then . . . your sister was born nine months later."

All Thea had ever heard about Mickey's birth was how excited her father had been the night she was born. He'd taken champagne to the hospital and even gotten a little drunk. He'd gone up and down the halls handing paper cups to all the nurses and doctors, filling their cups to the brim. "My cuppeth runneth over! My cuppeth runneth over!" he kept saying, tears rolling down. It was a story Mickey loved, a very different story from the one told about Thea's birth, when a screaming ambulance took her mother and her away from him.

. . .

Florence had not wanted Thea to drive home right away—she was worried about her—but Thea didn't want to be there when Evelyn returned. She was desperate to get back to her own house.

Now here she was, an hour later, still trying to find the road out of Columbia. First, she'd ended up going the wrong way on a one-way street, and now she was on Bull Street, which everyone in South Carolina knew was where the state mental hospital was. When they were young, Mickey's direst threat was that Thea would end up on Bull Street if she didn't "start acting right."

The high brick walls surrounding the hospital rose right from the street. She wondered if the Hillberry Clinic, where her mother had been, looked like this. She thought of the one letter from there she'd read and the locked doors and how her mother had felt like a prisoner. This place did look like a prison. Thea even heard the kind of siren you might hear at a prison—maybe someone was trying to escape—but then the sound broke apart into a car horn. In the rearview mirror she saw the crabbed face of the driver behind her. He was pounding on his wheel and following her as close as he could, as if he wanted to shove her out of the way. He was probably going to use an obscene gesture next. The sound of his horn congealed into other horns blowing all around her. She needed to pay attention if she was ever going to get out of Columbia. Where to turn? The names of the streets here were so exotic—Gervais, Trenholm, Divine. Different from Main Street and Cherry Road in Rock Hill, Queens Road and Kings Drive in Charlotte.

Now she found herself in a neighborhood—WELCOME TO GROVE PARK. NEW HOMES FROM $80,000 TO $110,000. There were freshly-planted, scraggy pine trees along one side of the street. They looked lost.

A left turn. Busy street up ahead.

Finally. A sign to I-77.

Down the ramp. Click on the turn signal. Ease into the lane. Press the gas to pick up speed. Stay over to the right. Let everyone else pass. Easier to drive on the interstate. No decisions to make, time to think.

She'd start from the beginning, from when she first asked her aunt. Plenty of time to go back over everything that was said. Time to go back farther. To the afternoon her mother told her she'd paid for only half the ice cream cone. Yes, Thea *was* the half in this family.

She'd go back, dream all those memories up again—but for now, relax, just keep the car on the road.

In the brassy light of oncoming cars, the highway was washing out. Exit signs for Ridgeway, Great Falls, Richburg floated up like tiny messages in the magic eight ball she'd had as a teenager. She would close her eyes and ask a question, turn the eight ball over, hold it steady, and an answer would miraculously appear in the murky liquid—*maybe, for sure, absolutely, never*. If she didn't like the answer, she'd shake the globe and wait for something better. She believed in those messages the way she once believed in Rose Black, the way her classmates at school believed in the Bible, the way Mickey and her father believed in the Torah, the way her mother believed in luck.

Sentences from an article in a psychology journal floated up, how there really are no secrets in families—only subjects people secretly decide not to talk about. On some level, everybody knows everything that's going on.

So now she knew what she had always known.

Everyone knew everything. Her grandmother knew. Mickey knew.

She pictured her father, the way he'd looked in photographs before she was born—his jaw set, his wide forehead smooth and unwrinkled, a monogrammed handkerchief folded just so in his pocket. What he took on when he married. How he said yes to fathering a baby that was not his. How he said yes to things a young man should never have to accept. Over and over, he'd said yes. That one night, he wanted a yes in return. He didn't know he would spend the rest of his life paying for it.

Thea tried to picture the man in the photograph in Florence's living room. She could see his hand holding her mother's hand, imagine how he was caught in her dazzle. But he kept slipping away. She could not remember his face. He was only a word her mother had kept to herself. Carter. Thea didn't even know if it was a first name or last. It was a name that had come to her through time and chance.

A secret bridge had been constructed and she was now on the other side. Like a traveler, leaving behind the haphazard rummage of a life and arriving into light and order and extraordinary detail.

It wasn't going to take a very large gesture to set things right. She did not have to track down her real father, make contact, push for an invitation into his life. A small veer of her mind would be enough. A quiet insight, a sudden knowing that, all along, she'd had too narrow a definition of what love is. The man she'd known as her father had done the most loving thing a person could do. He'd taken another man's baby, if not into his heart, into his home. And he'd loved and cared for her mother, even during times anyone else in the world might have found impossible, even though she did not return his love. This was the father Thea belonged to. Belonged to. Belonged. The word was a porcelain bell.

Gratitude washed over her, thick and slow and luxurious, smooth as the spice-scented hand lotion her mother kept with the lipsticks, rouge, loose powder, and glass-topped bottles of perfume on the mirrored tray on her dressing table.

Thea wanted to take her mother's beautiful face in both her hands and say thank you. She wanted to say thank you to her father. And thank you, Carter.

All three had given her her life.

Just concentrate on driving. There'd be plenty of time to understand all she'd absorbed from her mother in the womb, the ambivalences she'd come into the world with, the anxieties already in place, the anxieties that became the questions she asked, the answers she looked for every time her mother spoke, every time her mother stopped speaking.

Plenty of time to think about how she and Mickey were joined—different, it turns out, from the ways she'd always believed. They each had a piece missing. And those absences went as far back as they could go: A father who was not there when Thea was conceived. A mother who was not there when Mickey was conceived. More of a parity between her sister and her than she'd ever imagined.

Plenty of time to think about Reid and the baby they did not have, how they were part of a circle that had begun to widen before they'd even met.

Exit for Charlotte up ahead. Turn off the interstate, take the slow way back. Let the darkness of the silky fields beside the road reach in and hold her like arms. Reframe, rearrange, revise the memories that float up:

Sunday night . . . driving home . . . after spending the day in Columbia with Aunt Florence, Uncle Jack, and Evelyn . . . Thea's parents in the front seat . . . shadows flying in from the road like pigeons, making the outline of their heads wavy as they talk . . . her mother turning to her father, her father nodding yes to her mother . . . but all Thea can hear is the elegaic hum of the motor. Her mother is smoking, the fingers of her left hand moving to her lips, then to the upholstered curve behind his shoulders. When she takes a long drag, the tip of her cigarette reddens like the light on the dashboard.

Thea and Mickey are young enough to both lie across the backseat, the soles of their shoes touching at the imaginary line they've drawn down the middle. Their bodies fit that small space if they curl on their sides. When Thea stretches out in the direction of Mickey—like a cat, before turning over—Mickey has to pull in tighter. When Mickey stretches out, Thea pulls in. One stretches, the other pulls in, stretch, pull in: their old, familiar rhythm.

Their heads are propped against the windows, tweed wool coats balled up for pillows, turned inside out so the slick lining is a whisper against their cheeks. The heater in the car keeps them warm, though they can feel the outside chill through the glass.

Their father reaches up to adjust the rearview mirror and Thea sees him check on the two of them in the back. She wonders if Mickey is sleeping. She isn't trying to hear the conversation in the front seat like Thea is.

Soon she lets herself drift off, knowing that when the tires spin gravel and the Oldsmobile comes to a stop in the driveway, she'll know without opening her eyes they're home. Her father will turn off the motor and come around to the back to lift Mickey and carry her in. Her mother will stay in the car until he returns for Thea.

Then he'll carry her in and place her gently in the twin bed next to her sister's. He'll sit on the side of Thea's bed, and for a few seconds, he'll lean down close enough to touch her face with his lips and listen to her breathe. Then he'll fold the sheet back over the parrot-colored quilt and smooth the hem flat with the palm of his hand. He'll think she's sleeping. But she'll surprise him by opening her eyes and pulling her hand out from under the covers to find his hand. He'll slowly trace her fingers, trailing his finger around and around her hand, as though he is claiming it.

She'll begin to recite the first prayer she ever learned in synagogue. He'll sit there listening.

Shema Yisrael Adonoi Eloheynu Adonoi Echod.
Hear, O Israel, the Lord our God, the Lord is One. Amen.

The words will roll around in her mouth like hard candy, tart at first, growing sweeter and sweeter, apricots, limes, cherries ripening, finally ripening.

LARCHMONT PUBLIC LIBRARY
3 1014 15067807 0